The Ghosts
of Midgard Manor

by
Roger Thomas

Published by JCK
Fort Gratiot MI

ISBN 978-1-7330809-3-4

This entire work is a tribute to
C.S. Lewis, to whom I owe so much
of my thought, my imagination,
my personality, and even my life.
I hope someday to thank him in person.

Table of Contents

I would be a fool and an ingrate not to acknowledge my immense debt to C.S. Lewis for my education in Christian thought and the formation of my moral imagination. Those familiar with his work should be able to see many parallels between this story and themes in Lewis, particularly classics like The Great Divorce. *I hope those intimately familiar with his thought will be able to see that the story as an imaginative rumination on one of his cleverest analogies.*

The Ghosts of Midgard Manor

Midgard Manor was full of ghosts. There were ghosts wherever you turned – in the hallway, up and down the stairways, and in almost all the rooms. There was plenty of space for them, for Midgard Manor was vast, with many rooms and wings.

None of the ghosts knew why they were there. Some said they'd always been there and always would be, and that's all there was. But others spoke in dark whispers of a great catastrophe in the distant past which had imprisoned them in the Manor. But whatever the reason, Midgard Manor was thronging with ghosts.

In some ways, ghostly existence wasn't bad. If a ghost wanted a new set of ghostly clothes, he had only to wish for them, and they would appear. If he wanted ghostly food, he could just wish for it, and anything he wanted would appear – from ghostly crackers to an entire ghostly banquet. If ghosts wanted ghostly chairs or beds, they could wish them into existence. But they rarely did that, because they had no need to sit or lie down. Gravity didn't affect them, so it was easy for the ghosts to float in midair.

But the Manor was also full of things that were not ghostly, but substantial. There were real tables and chairs in the rooms, real clothes in the closets, and real pots and utensils in the kitchens. Mostly the ghosts ignored these substantial things, sweeping right past or through them, but occasionally they would try to pick them up or move them. This was extremely difficult, but if a ghost concentrated very hard, he might be able to move a substantial candlestick a little, or nudge a substantial chair, or push open a substantial door just a bit more.

This made some ghosts wonder about being substantial. They would sit in the substantial chairs around the substantial tables and discuss being substantial. Some theorized that they had all once been substantial until something had happened to make them insubstantial. Others thought that the things in Midgard Manor were substantial, but the occupants were not, and that's how it would be forever. Nobody really knew.

Sometimes a ghost might exert immense effort to put on a substantial hat or shirt, in order to show how substantial he was becoming. Some ghosts, putting in weeks of struggle with the help of many friends, managed to put on entire suits of substantial clothes – shirt, trousers, socks, shoes, and everything. It took tremendous concentration, and they could never maintain it for long, but some took it as proof that ghosts could become more substantial if they tried hard enough.

Most of the ghosts didn't wonder a bit about being substantial, and even those who did wonder usually gave it up after a while. It was too easy to just ignore the substantial items and treat them just as they did the walls and floors. After all, what sense did it make to worry about wearing substantial clothes when you could have all the insubstantial clothes you desired just by wishing for them?

There were some substantial things that all the ghosts knew of but rarely thought or spoke about. One was the exterior walls of the Manor, through which they could not pass. The interior walls were substantial, and any ghost could pass through them as they could other substantial things. But the exterior walls were impenetrable, and no one knew what lay beyond them. The only way through them was by the other impenetrable thing: the main door, which was large and made of thick wood. It was so substantial that it could not be penetrated, and no ghost could move it no matter how hard he tried. Occasionally a very determined ghost would put forth tremendous effort to try to turn the great brass doorknob, but to no avail – it would not budge an inch.

A few suggested that over time, the ghosts became increasingly insubstantial. This was hard to confirm, because any change was barely noticeable, happening in such small increments that many ghosts denied that it took place at all. But others maintained that over time the ghosts became more vaporous, their voices fading until they became barely audible whispers. They would lose the ability to move even the smallest of substantial things, and would be able to hold their positions only with the greatest effort, since they tended to float upward through the ceiling. Some whispered that the more one performed insubstantial acts such as drifting through walls or squeezing through keyholes the more quickly this fading would occur. But no one was certain, and the ghosts did not discuss it readily, for it was a terrifying mystery. Dark rumors hinted that the attic was packed with the wispy, chattering remnants of every ghost who had ever dwelt in Midgard Manor, and that the same insubstantial fate awaited them all. But nobody knew, for not even the bravest ghosts would venture to the upper floors of the Manor.

One day a new ghost appeared at Midgard Manor. Nobody knew where he had come from, but this was true of all new ghosts. He looked like most of the other ghosts, though even from the first there was discussion as to whether he looked a bit more substantial than most. But nobody denied that he behaved differently from the outset. Only a few would learn just how differently.

It was a ghost named Andy who found him first. Andy was roaming about a smaller wing of the Manor and drifted into a dining room. He was quite startled when a firm, friendly voice spoke.

"Good morning," the voice said, causing Andy to nearly jump through the ceiling. Andy was surprised to see that the ghost was seated at the table. Most ghosts would have been drifting around the room or floating above the chairs.

"G-g-good m-m-morning," stammered Andy. "I'm sorry, I wasn't expecting to find anyone here."

"I'm sorry if I startled you," the ghost replied.

"Are...are you a new ghost?" Andy asked, drifting closer.

"Let's just say that I'm new to these parts," answered the ghost. "My name's Manuel."

"P-pleased to meet you. I'm Andy."

"Well, Andy, why don't you bring your friend, and we can talk?"

Again, Andy was startled – how had Manuel known that he was just thinking about fetching his buddy Pete? "Um – sure – I'll be right back."

Andy zipped off to find Pete and tell him about the new arrival. On their way back they bumped into Nate and Phil, who came along to see what all the excitement was about. They were soon back in the dining room, drifting around Manuel and chattering about what they could show him of Midgard Manor.

Remaining seated at the table, Manuel allowed the pleasantries to continue for a while before gathering the ghosts around him. Once they were assembled, he asked a question that stunned them to silence.

"Would you like to become substantial?"

The ghosts gaped at him. It was Pete who finally spoke.

"Can – can you do that?"

"Yes," Manuel answered.

"How?" Phil asked.

"It will take time," Manuel explained. "There is much you must learn, and many things you must unlearn. If you wish, I will teach you how to live substantially, and eventually I will make you so. But know this: if you desire to be substantial, you must choose it completely. Ultimately, you cannot be both substantial and insubstantial."

The ghosts drew back, muttering among themselves. If true, this was the most amazing thing that had ever been heard in Midgard Manor! Presently they returned to Manuel with their decision.

"Sir," Pete said, speaking for them all, "we would like to become substantial."

The ghostly friends began to follow Manuel, and learn from him the ways of living substantially. First, they learned that they had to behave as if they were substantial. No more drifting through walls – if they wanted to enter a room, they had to open the door and go through it. If they wanted to get to another floor, there was no more jumping off a landing and drifting down, or gliding up through the floor. They had to find steps and use them.

This was difficult at first. Though most ghosts could manage to crack a door or open a window just a little, some of them found it nearly impossible, and none of them had done it very much. It seemed so bothersome to have to open and close doors, and walk around furniture and down hallways. Walking especially seemed silly at first, for their ghostly feet barely touched the floor.

"Don't worry about that," Manuel assured them. "The sensations will come in time. The important thing is to live as if you were substantial."

So they learned to help each other open doors and walk down stairways. In time other ghosts joined them, until there were several dozen following Manuel to learn about being substantial. They walked with him all through Midgard Manor, and noticed that he always behaved as if he was substantial. He opened doors without thinking about it (it never seemed difficult for him), and always used hallways to get between rooms. The ghosts noticed something else odd – when they were with him, doing these things came more naturally to them. It seemed easier to open the doors, and they could almost feel the hardness of the floor beneath their feet.

"Will doing all this make us more substantial?" Nate asked one day.

Manuel smiled. "No. If it could, I would not have needed to come. You will obtain the substantial life by other means. But you cannot walk the ways of both substance and insubstance at the same time. Once you have substantial life, you can hinder, damage, or destroy it by walking the ways of insubstance."

"You mean," asked Pete. "Once we have the substantial life, we could lose it?"

"You cannot lose it by misplacing it," Manuel said. "But you can walk away from it. The more you learn and practice the ways of substance, the less likely you will be to walk away from the substantial life."

One thing that made the whole process more difficult was the teasing of the other ghosts. Most of them thought this pretending to be substantial was so much playacting and putting on airs. The Followers (as they'd come to call themselves) were taunted mercilessly. The other ghosts would pop up through stairways just as they were trying to descend, or would try to shove them through doors they were trying to open, or would stretch substantial twine across hallways in an attempt to trip them. And wherever they went, they were teased and mocked for even thinking about becoming substantial.

This teasing proved too much for some of the ghosts, who gave up even trying to follow Manuel and went back to being normal ghosts. Some of these joined in the taunting, and turned into some of the worst teasers of all. But Followers took the abuse in stride, redoubling their determination to become substantial.

"Being substantial isn't always easy," Manuel explained. "Taking the long route upstairs is only the beginning. The more substantial you become, the more you will feel the pull of gravity, which will tire you. You will begin to feel true hunger and thirst that no ghostly food will satisfy. You will actually breathe, which means that you won't be able to go into tight spaces where there is no air. All these things are difficult at first, but in time you will grow accustomed to them – you must."

"Why is that, sir?" asked Phil.

"Because over time you either become more substantial, or less," Manuel replied.

The ghosts gasped. "You mean – it's true?" said Nate. "That we fade over time, and eventually end up..." He didn't even complete the question, but gestured toward the attic.

"Yes," Manuel assured them. "None of you can remain ghosts forever. In the end, if you do not become substantial, you will become completely insubstantial. But don't be afraid – I have come to make you substantial, and to show you how to help others do the same."

It was hard to keep such startling statements quiet, and whispers quickly carried Manuel's words throughout the Manor. By now many ghosts were gathering wherever Manuel spoke, but some of the Followers began to notice that not all the ghosts came to listen. Some of them scoffed openly at what Manuel said, and muttered to those around them, and asked questions that were veiled challenges. Most of the ghosts still heeded Manuel, but there was an undeniable tone of hostility from some quarters.

About this time Manuel changed his style of teaching. Though he still welcomed and talked to whichever ghosts wanted to come, he would often take his oldest Followers like Pete, Nate, and the others away by themselves to teach them. He spoke at length about what it meant to be substantial, and how important it was to follow the ways of substance. The ghosts could not understand some of what he said, but tried to pay attention.

Then one day he did something so startling that it amazed even the ghosts who were growing accustomed to his unusual ways. He took just a few of them – Pete and a couple others – into a secluded room. They were expecting more lessons or obscure statements; what they got frightened them half out of their wits. Manuel said nothing but simply stood beside a table and suddenly, right before them, turned completely solid. He no longer looked like a translucent ghost – he looked like a true man, with living flesh on his bones and real blood pumping through his veins.

The ghosts gasped and shrieked at this abrupt change, but Pete could see that even though his form was real flesh, it was the same familiar Manuel.

"Then – then you are substantial?" asked Pete.

"I am," Manuel answered. "I have taken ghostly form in order to walk among you, but by nature I am substantial.

"How?" asked one of the others. "How can you be both substantial and insubstantial at the same time?"

Manuel smiled. "You would have to learn far more than you know – or that your minds could currently hold – to understand the answer to that."

"Who – who are you, sir?" Pete stammered the question that was in all their minds.

"I am the Lord of Midgard Manor," Manuel announced calmly. "I built this entire hall, and filled it with substantial furniture and hung it with substantial clothes and intended it to be the home of substantial beings. But since the Catastrophe, it has been the abode of the insubstantial. I have come to rectify that, and to offer substantial existence to all who wish it."

The ghosts gaped at one another. They had all heard the rumors of an ancient Catastrophe that had deprived them all of what they needed. Some had heard even less common tales of the Lord of the Manor, but most regarded these as mere fancy.

"How, sir?" Pete asked again. "How will you make us substantial?"

"That you will learn soon," Manuel explained. "I will give you substantial food, and show you how to give it to others. Then I will be assaulted and accused and cast out of my own Manor. You must remember what I have taught you about being substantial, and pass it along to others. Do you understand this?"

"We – we think so, sir," Pete answered, and the others nodded, though none of them were at all sure they did.

Manuel smiled, as if he knew full well how little they grasped. "It will become more clear in time." With that his substantial shape faded back to the familiar ghostly form. "Come, let us be going. But one thing – speak to no one of what you have seen here until after I have come back through the main door." Having said this, he passed out of the room, leaving the Followers gaping at one another in bewilderment. Come back through the main door? What could he possibly have meant by that?

By now the Followers could see that some of the ghosts were becoming increasingly hostile, and would gather in large groups to roam the hallways, seeking out Followers. Those they found alone or in small groups were surrounded and abused. At times they would whip at the Followers with cords or leather straps, which was about all the substance the ghosts could lift. But the lashes stung, and the Followers fled, pursued by taunts and jeers.

One evening the word went around: Manuel was summoning his Followers to the room where they had first met him. They came furtively, two or three at a time, to find the table set with a ghostly banquet. Manuel was seated at the center of the table where all could see him easily.

"Welcome," Manuel said when they had all assembled. "Welcome to this banquet, for which you have all been waiting, at which much will be made clear."

The Followers looked at each other, puzzled. What did he mean? They hadn't been waiting for a banquet – had they? But Manuel continued.

"I have been waiting anxiously for this last night with you, not least to ask you a question." He looked around at them all. "Ghosts, what is it you are lacking?"

Again, they looked at one another, mystified. Every ghost knew the answer to that question – why would Manuel even need to ask?

"Ah –" Pete finally stammered, "breath and blood, sir."

"Indeed," answered Manuel. "Those two things you have lacked since the Catastrophe. The lack of them is what prevents you from being substantial, from being truly alive. I have come to give you both, that you may give them to others."

With that Manuel took a loaf of bread that lay before him on the table, spoke a particular blessing over it, and passed it around to them.

"Eat this," he said, "It is substantial food that will nourish the substantial life within you."

As the bread came around, Nate took a piece and looked at it.

"'Substantial food'?" he whispered to Pete. "Looks like ordinary bread to me."

Pete looked at his piece and thought the same thing, but then remembered how Manuel had shown himself to be substantial even though he'd always appeared insubstantial. They both ate, and wondered.

Then Manuel picked up a goblet of ghostly wine, again said the particular blessing, and passed it around to them all. "Drink your new life," he said.

To the ghosts it looked just like common wine, but they drank anyway. Phil asked what they all wondered:

"Sir – what is this?"

"It is blood," Manuel answered. "My blood, which I give to you that you may have life – my life, which is now yours as well. This blood you will give to all who come seeking life."

"Ah – this blood, sir?" asked Andy, who was holding the near-empty goblet.

Manuel smiled. "Once my blood is spilled within the walls of Midgard Manor, it will be with you forever. It will always be here for those who seek substantial life. Come, I will instruct you in this."

The ghosts never forgot that meal. Manuel taught them the words by which ghostly bread would become substantial food, and common drink would become lifeblood. He reminded them by word and action of what he had taught them about living substantial lives. He comforted and reassured them, for they were saddened but knew not why.

The meal lasted late into the night, until finally Manuel had them all follow him. Without effort he threw open the doors and strode purposefully out of the room toward the front of the Manor.

"Where are we going?" Nate asked Andy, who just shrugged. They followed Manuel, not knowing what to expect but wary of hostile ghosts.

As they were passing through a great archway they were suddenly surrounded by a crowd of angry, howling ghosts. The

10

mob had been lying in ambush, and now they swarmed all around Manuel. Each was carrying some small substantial item – a lamp cord, or length of coarse twine, or a leather strap with a buckle – whatever the ghost could manage to lift. They plied these on Manuel cruelly, lashing him about his head and body while they shrieked at him.

The Followers were stunned and dismayed. Taken totally aback by the sudden violence of the ghostly rabble, they gaped in horror at the spectacle. But before they could compose themselves, some of the crowd turned toward them, snarling and brandishing their whips. This proved too much for the Followers, who scattered in all directions. Only a couple, Pete and Young Jack, halted before going far and dared to turn back, timidly following from a safe distance.

The mob was now leading Manuel away. Some of the ghosts had bound his wrists with cords and were dragging him along while others continued to circle him, jeering and lashing him. "Fear monger!" they cried in their fury. "Liar! Rabble rouser! False teacher!" They didn't seem to notice that the cords seemed to be actually biting into his wrists, rather than passing right through. Pete, following far behind, noticed what the mob did not: that dark red liquid was seeping from the cord cuts, leaving a trail of droplets on the Manor floor.

The furor attracted more ghosts, who thronged to the spectacle. Some of these joined in the abuse. It soon became clear where they were taking Manuel: to the great foyer and the main door. Pete and Young Jack watched from one of the upper floors, peering timidly around the edge of an archway at the angry ghosts churning around Manuel. He seemed to be at the center of the tumult, his back against the thick and immoveable main door. The crowd swirled around him, howling abuse and lashing him with their cords.

Finally, two ghosts managed to silence the mob and approached Manuel, floating above where he stood before the door.

"Well, liar," one of them boomed. "Do you wonder why you have been brought here?"

"I know why I am here," Manuel replied.

"You have been sowing fear, spreading dangerous lies about how we lose substance. You have put yourself forward as one who teaches the way of substance. You have taught that we must follow you or ultimately fade away."

To this Manuel made no reply, which seemed to infuriate the ghosts all the more.

"So," continued the ghost, "We have brought you here to prove yourself – or be proven a liar. Behind you is the main door. Since the building of Midgard Manor, it has never been opened. Here is your opportunity: if you are as substantial as you claim, you should be able to open that door and walk through it. If you do not, all will know you for the liar you are."

The ghosts below roared at this challenge while Pete and Young Jack stared at each other in horror. How fiendishly clever this trap was! If Manuel did not do it, then he would be disgraced and hounded forever. But if he did, he would be lost to them, for none could open the main door to let him back in. Indeed, was it even possible, even for their beloved master? He had proven himself capable of many things, but the door had never been opened by anyone. They had great respect for his abilities, but could even he open the door?

Down in the foyer, the mob was now taunting Manuel with cries of, "Do it! Do it!" Manuel did not reply, but stood watching them all while the leader ghosts looked at him expectantly. Finally, the two ghosts again quieted the crowd.

"Well, fraud," one asked, "What will you do?"

"This will I do," Manuel answered in a ringing voice that carried to the corners of the foyer. "Not because you can force me or out of any dread of you, but that you – even you – may know the path to substantial life. For this is why I have been sent." With that he lifted his bound wrists above his head and twisted them. The cords binding them fell away, not by passing through his arms but by snapping into fragments and falling to the floor. Then he turned, seized the great knob, turned it, and pulled the door open. Without a word or backward glance, he strode through the doorway into the blackness beyond. The door swung shut behind him with a crash that echoed through the hallways and rattled the windows throughout the Manor.

For a moment all was deathly still in the aftermath of that great crash. Then many of the ghosts around the door began to whoop and cheer in triumph. They soared and swooped and saluted each other as if they had opened the door themselves and thrust Manuel out. Some of them even took the cords they were holding and tied them tightly between the door knob and door frame, as if to more tightly close the door that nobody could open.

But not all the ghosts were so exuberant. Some of them were subdued and quiet, as if the crash of the door had awakened them to what they had done. These ghosts started drifting away while the others were still loudly congratulating themselves. Slowly the crowd began to dwindle, until the last few ghosts made their way off.

Only then did Pete and Young Jack descend to the foyer. Crushed with grief and shock, they approached the door to see another couple of Followers coming through a doorway. Before long they were joined by a few others, and presently all of Manuel's scattered followers were huddled together before the main door. Though they had scattered in different directions, they had all heard the roof-rattling crash and sensed that it had had something to do with Manuel.

But nothing they had imagined was as dire as the story told them by Pete and Young Jack. They were almost too stunned to grieve. A couple of them sobbed quietly, but most of them wandered aimlessly around the foyer, sometimes stopping to stare at the immense door. There was no escaping their failure. They had thought themselves the great students, the devoted Followers making true progress toward being substantial. But at the moment of crisis, their determination and courage had proved less substantial than smoke. Raw fear – the fear for which

Manuel had so often chided them – had scattered them, leaving their friend and master to face his enemies alone.

Now they had nothing left. Instinctively they looked to the senior Followers, like Pete or Andy, for what to do next. But these were just staring around with empty eyes, as adrift as any of them. A heavy silence fell on the foyer as the darkness in the ghosts' hearts overwhelmed them.

Then the doorknob began to turn.

Young Jack gasped and pointed, and the rest barely had time to turn before the great door flew open. The feeble ties which the ghosts had laced across the door frame were shredded like cobwebs as the door swung open as if it were made of balsa, smashing into the wall behind with another shuddering crash.

Standing in the doorway, bright against the darkness with light streaming from his substantial body, stood Manuel.

The Followers could not believe their eyes. "Is…is it really you?" one of them stammered.

Manuel smiled as he strode through the door. "Yes, friends, it is me. Here – give me your hand." He reached out and took Nate's hand in a firm, familiar grip. To Nate's amazement, he felt as if his own hand was gripping back.

"But we saw you thrust out – right through that door!" Pete exclaimed.

"So you did. And I'm back. Do you think a door I installed myself could keep me out of my own Manor? Come with me – I have work to finish with you so you can begin yours." He led them to the room where they had shared the meal with him so few hours ago, the room where they had first met him.

As they crowded around him, Pete felt obligated to speak. "Sir, we're sorry we abandoned you. It – they – everything happened so suddenly, and…" His voice trailed away, for the look in Manuel's eyes told him that excuses were futile.

"Think not on that now," Manuel said. "But remember it when you are tempted to judge another harshly for his failure. But here – I have one more gift to bestow before I go."

"You're not – going again, are you, sir?" asked Andy. "You just got back!"

Manuel smiled. "I am going, in one sense, but in another I am now with you more closely than I have ever been. My blood has been spilled within the walls of Midgard Manor; now it will ever be yours. This is my blood you must drink in order to live. But one more thing you need." With that he went around and kissed each of them, breathing full in their faces as he did so.

The ghosts were startled by this, and even more startled by what the breath did to them. It entered into them and filled their ghostly chests with life. They could feel it inflating lungs they'd never known they had. The breath didn't just pass through them like a breeze might – it stayed inside them. They could feel the first rudiments of a heartbeat in their chests.

"That is my very breath," said Manuel. "I give it to you that you may give it to others. Never forget that you share the same breath and the same blood. That makes you my brothers, and brothers to one another, and brothers of all who live by my blood. Come, let us be going."

Manuel led them out, giving them further instructions as they went, until they came to a tall and narrow staircase that was rarely used. He gave them all one last embrace then began to swiftly ascend the stairs in the direction of the attic. It all happened so fast that he was gone almost before they knew it. Their heads were still spinning with amazement and joy and wonder that some of them thought it might have all been a dream. But there was one fact they could not deny:

"Andy," Nate cried in astonishment. "We're breathing!"

And so they were – with shallow, tentative breaths, to be certain, but clearly breaths. Young Jack inhaled deeply, bent over the stair railing, and blew the dust off it with nothing more than his newfound breath. The ghosts stared at one another with wide, shining eyes and then burst into the loudest clamor they had ever made. The laughed, they chattered, they whistled, they called and whooped and hollered their way through the halls. They hammered on walls with surprisingly substantial hands and jumped for joy, landing again with satisfying thumps. Ghosts who heard the ruckus drifted through walls and floated out of doorways to see what the excitement was.

The Followers paraded noisily and joyfully through Midgard Manor, celebrating the substantial life they had been given. Pete realized that they were coming near to the drawing room, where the more self-important ghosts tended to gather and discuss their latest schemes. He got an idea, and turned down the hall that took them to the room. Pausing briefly before the double doors, he drew a deep breath, seized both doorknobs, and hurled the doors open with an echoing crash. The clusters of ghosts in the room – some of whom had led Manuel to the main door – jumped at the sudden noise, and gaped at the crowd of ghosts flooding into the room. Out in front were the Followers, led by Pete, striding confidently across the floor. He went to the center of the room, raised his arms, and called in a loud, clear voice:

"Ghosts of Midgard Manor! Through the years you have hungered and thirsted, and discussed and theorized, and schemed and plotted about how to gain life substantial. I stand here today to tell you how to obtain it. There is only one place to get it, and only one way to go about it, but it is a free gift for all who wish to live substantially."

So it was that what the Followers had feared was an ending turned out to be only the beginning. Ghosts flocked to hear of this new path to substantial life. Even that day many accepted the Kiss of New Life, ate the Substantial Bread, and drank the Blood of Life. In the halls of Midgard Manor, the ghostly whisperings, mutterings, and moanings were soon augmented by the cries, calls, and songs of those who breathed. The Followers, and those who followed them, grew slowly but steadily more substantial with each Substantial Meal, and soon breathing was coming as naturally as moaning had before.

As Manuel had warned, not all the ghosts who answered the call were able to walk the path. It was difficult for ghosts accustomed to passing through walls to have to learn to use doors and stairs. Some were frightened by the manifestations of substance – the steady increase of the pull of gravity, and the solidity of their own flesh. Some ghosts ceased following and returned to ghostly ways, often with deeper scorn for the Followers than before.

Scorn there was, and worse than scorn – something else Manuel had predicted. As more ghosts joined the Followers, those self-important ghosts who'd had followings of their own began to be envious, and then hostile. The Followers were harassed in hallways and rooms, and some were summoned before ghostly tribunals to give account of their beliefs and actions. The Followers answered fearlessly and in loud voices, so that all who listened could tell who it was who had true breath. This infuriated the self-important ghosts so much that eventually they began dragging the followers to the main door and hurling them through it, to share their master's fate.

For the main door which had been hurled back when Manuel returned had remained wide open – there was no ghost substantial enough to close it again. Nobody knew what lay beyond, for only thick darkness could be seen through the vast doorway. To the ghosts this was ominous and terrifying, but the Followers saw it as a great mystery and a sign of hope. Their master had come through there, opening a door that could never be closed again. It was true that those who were thrust out vanished into the darkness, but it was told that someday Manuel would again return with all his Followers, this time to take up residence in his Manor, forever surrounded by living, breathing, flesh-and-blood residents.

But that time was not yet, so for now the Followers in the Manor had to deal with the day-to-day struggles of what it meant to be ghosts who were becoming substantial, and the nature of the new life growing within them, and how to remember Manuel's instructions, and a hundred other concerns. Not least of these was the constant requests from ghosts desperate for substantial life. Typical of this was what happened one day to Phil.

Phil was in an out-of-the-way room, trying to get a quiet hour to himself, when his reverie was interrupted by the barest of whispers. At first, he thought it was just a breeze, but when it persisted, he began to attend more closely.

"Is someone there?" Phil asked, listening carefully.

"I am," came a whisper that was barely audible. It was off to Phil's left, so he peered in that direction. After much squinting, he saw what appeared to be the outline of the least substantial ghost he had ever seen.

"Is that you over there?" Phil asked the outline.

"It is," the whisper replied. "Can you help me?"

"Yes," Phil replied, "but please come closer – I can barely hear you."

The ghost drifted right up to Phil. "My name is Simon, and it has taken me much effort to make it down here. Word has reached even the upper levels that you can give substantial life."

"We can only give what we have been given," Phil explained. "But that we give freely."

"As you can see, I have almost completely faded. Can you help even one as insubstantial as I?"

"The substantial life is for all," Phil explained. "In your case it may take a little longer for you to firm up, but –"

Just then the door creaked open a little and into the room drifted another ghost. The newcomer looked much more substantial than Simon, but was clearly in distress. He seemed to be holding something – with great difficulty – in his hands.

"They – they say you can help me," the newcomer gasped.

"I don't know," Phil said. "What do you need help with?"

"My name is Luke," the ghost explained. "And I…your master…oh, I might as well come right out with it. I was one of those who helped cast Manuel through the door. In fact," he threw onto the table a clump of what looked like stiff, dark twine. "It was my twine that they used to bind him and drag him through the halls."

Phil just looked at him and motioned for him to continue.

"I never meant for that to happen. I never thought it would go that far," Luke continued. "But when he – I mean, when it was over, there was my cord lying on the floor in pieces. I picked it up, and that's when I got this."

Luke held out his arm, and Phil could see on his wrist a dark red smear. It took him a moment to grasp the point.

"Ahhh," Phil said at last. "Manuel's blood."

"Yes," Luke confirmed. "And I can't get it off, and furthermore..."

"It gets heavier and heavier every day, and you can't bear the weight anymore," Phil completed for him. Luke stared in wonder.

"How did you know?"

"It's the nature of the blood," Phil replied. "It is the most substantial thing in the Manor, and no ghost can bear the weight for long."

"Is there anything you can do?" Luke asked.

"Me? No," Phil responded. "I can no more prevent Manuel's blood from being substantial than I can push over Midgard Manor." Seeing Luke's ghostly face fall, he continued. "However, there is something you can do."

"What is that?" Luke asked eagerly.

"You can become more substantial yourself," Phil said. "That's the only option I can see for you. Either you become more substantial so you can bear the weight of that stain, or you remain as you are until you are crushed beneath its weight."

"Can you help me do that?"

"I can teach you the way of substantial life," Phil assured him. "I can pass along True Breath, and give you the Substantial Food and Real Blood, but only you can choose to become more substantial."

Luke looked discomfited. "Is there no other way?"

"None that I know of," Phil replied.

"You'd do that even though I – I helped push him out?"

"And I abandoned him," Phil shrugged. "Yet he still gave me breath and blood. None of us stands higher than another in this matter. We're all insubstantial, we all need to become substantial, and there's only one way to go about it. Luke, meet Simon. He's somewhere over here."

"Hello," whispered Simon.

"Simon, you've just heard Luke's story. Luke, as you can see, Simon is almost completely insubstantial. He's traveled from the upper storeys of the Manor, hoping something can be done before he fades to a wisp. You two have different problems, but they have the same solution. Are you willing to hear it?"

Both ghosts assented, so Phil spent the next hours explaining the basics of the substantial way – what it required, what they could expect to happen, and so forth. When he asked if they were willing to make the commitment, they both said yes, so he gave them the Kiss of New Life. Then he prepared the elements, said the blessing, and served them their first Substantial Meal.

"It looks just like ghostly bread," Simon commented when he held the substantial food.

"It does," Phil said. "It is the substantial hidden within the insubstantial. Otherwise you wouldn't be able to pick it up, any more than Luke here is able to bear the weight of that blood."

"I don't feel any different," Luke said after drinking the Blood.

"You don't always feel anything – at least not right away," Phil explained, though he thought Simon looked a bit more substantial already. "And what you do feel isn't always what you expect. You have a new substantial nature now, growing within you – but it's growing right alongside your old, insubstantial nature. Sometimes your old nature will fight fiercely, and that's never fun. You've set your feet on a long path. With perseverance you'll grow steadily more substantial. One day you'll stand before Manuel himself, completely substantial. That's what he wants for you, and if you cooperate, he'll do it."

Sometimes we're so busy living our everyday lives that we don't see the bigger picture.

The Rock

Hardly anyone lived on the Rock any more. But Roland did, because he couldn't imagine living anywhere else. Roland had been born on the Rock, and during his childhood many people still lived there. His father had told him of days when the streets of town bustled with carriages and all the homesteads were occupied. It was during Roland's lifetime that so many had decided to move down to the plain.

The Rock was only very rocky toward the top, where bare stone and craggy outcroppings made tilling impossible. But there was plenty of arable land on the broad shoulders of the mountain, which sloped gently down to the valley floor. It was here that most people had lived, keeping their fields and orchards and tending their flocks. The mountainsides were washed by gentle rains which watered the fields and fed the streams which splashed down to where the great river wrapped around the base of The Rock and meandered away to the west.

It was on these slopes that the first settlers had built when they'd first arrived generations ago. Most had staked out farmsteads, but some had built their homes close together, forming the little village they'd prosaically named Rockville. The settlers had raised their crops and their flocks and their families on the slopes of the Rock, and had come to town for meetings and wares and elections. In time the town grew prosperous enough to build a village hall, and an opera house, and a school, and even a small library. Rockville had been the center of life on the Rock.

Even when the first Settlers children had grown and married and had families of their own, there was still plenty of room on the Rock. Farmsteads were divided for new homes, or new claims were staked out. One thing that people didn't do was move away to settle in other spots – like the valley floor.

At least, that's how it was for the longest time. But as the years wore on, things started to change, though nobody could quite figure why. Some said that folk got tired of living meager lives on the mountain slopes while looking down on all that rich land in the valley. Others said that a time of new thinking arrived, with new ideas floating in the air like pollen in springtime, causing people to question things they'd never questioned before. Still others said that the march of progress demanded change. Whatever the reason, there came a point when some began thinking and talking about moving off the Rock. After enough thinking and talking, some up and did it, packing their things and heading down to the valley.

Many were scandalized that anyone would think of living anywhere but on the Rock, and those who first went to the valley were of like mind. They protested that they were just working, not settling. The big draw of the valley was the river, from which folk could send off their crops and livestock to settlements downstream. At first folk set up wharves and seawalls at which barges could tie up to be loaded. They built sheds and barns and silos, but no houses. They'd go down for a spell, just to load the barges, and then return to their homesteads on the Rock.

Again, that's how it was at first. But once folk were living off the Rock, even temporarily, that got others thinking. First, people spent longer and longer times down in the valley, and soon businesses were opening up branches down there. Those who sent their goods away on the barges came back to the Rock with lots of real money, and word that there was more to be made. Folk told tales they'd heard from the bargemen about how life was in other places, and the variety of goods that money could buy.

Nobody knew who first outright moved from the Rock down to the valley, but it didn't matter. Once living off the Rock was no longer scandalous, moving became more common. Most settled along the river, close by the silos and warehouses. They set up shops, and inns, and stables. Soon the settlement had a grand sounding name: Riveropolis.

Once founded, Riveropolis expanded quickly. Barges floated away down the river full of grain and cattle and returned full of fine cloth, rich foods, strong drink, and other exotic items. Other settlers also came, settlers who had never lived on the Rock, and they set up shops and restaurants and salons. Riveropolis grew larger, and its lights could be seen from miles away for most of the night.

Up on the mountain, one could see the valley clearly from Lookout Rock, which wasn't far from Rockville. The folk there did a lot of talking about the doings down in the valley: the money to be made in Riveropolis, and the fine things you could buy with that money, and how you could work in a shop or a bakery and go home at the end of the day and relax. More and more folk began looking at their plain homes on the Rock, and their fields and their flocks and their simple clothes and simple means, and the neighbors and kin with whom they'd grown up. To some it began to seem bland and boring, especially compared to the fabulous goods and gourmet foods and nonstop thrills they heard could be had down in Riveropolis. Over time, more and more people decided to leave their houses in Rockville or their farms on the mountainside to move to where the excitement was. Those who could find buyers sold, but increasingly folk just shuttered their houses and walked away. Eventually the streets of Rockville were punctuated by vacant homes, and derelict homesteads dotted the sides of the Rock.

Most of this had happened while Roland was growing up, though it had started not very long before. Roland lived on the family farm with his parents and his older brother Jay. The farm had belonged to Roland's grandparents, and it had been in their time that Riveropolis had been founded. The grandparents had stayed on the Rock, and they were now buried in the Rockville cemetery while Roland's parents raised their family on the old farm.

Roland loved living on the Rock, and along with Jay learned from their father the ways of soil and weather. He loved learning how to coax a crop from a field or chivvy a herd into a corral. He loved the simple farm fare, the long days of hard work, and the satisfaction of a job well done. He loved the quiet evenings around the fireplace, with his mother knitting and chatting while he mended or whittled. He loved the chores and the animals and the gentle rhythm of life on the Rock.

As much as Roland loved his family and the farm, he also loved to wander alone around the Rock, especially up toward the rocky peak. He loved how being that high on the Rock caught the first light of each new day, and held the last rays of sunlight when the valley below was shrouded in shadow. He loved how far he could see – the hills and valleys and forests and rivers stretching off to the majesty of the mountain ranges far in the distance. He could see Riveropolis down in the valley, so small in comparison to the vastness of everything around it. The city's shiny lights and noisy bustle didn't interest him. He'd far rather watch the storm clouds sweep across the ranges, with lightning flickering and the deep rumble of thunder following, or watch the flocks of birds swoop around the Rock, or smell the wildflowers that grew along every pathway.

Roland also liked to spend time at the Rockville library. The librarian, Mrs. Spenser, was good at finding him books that were interesting and helpful. She had plenty of time for him, for the library was seldom used any more. Often the only sound heard among the shelves was the click of her heels and the swish of her feather duster.

It was in a back room at the library one day that Roland found the big book of Settlers Laws. Of course, he'd known of them, as had every other family on the Rock. They were very old. Most families had a copy of the Laws, usually in a big decorative volume that sat on a shelf or end table and was rarely opened. Roland couldn't remember where his family's volume was – it had once been in their parlor but he couldn't remember having seen it for some time.

The library's volume of the Settlers Laws lay on a great stand, and Roland decided to try reading it. He followed it for a while, but the language was old and there were many references to events he knew nothing about. He was about to give it up, but decided to ask Mrs. Spenser for help. She found him many books that explained the history of the Laws, and things about the people who wrote it, and even helped with the archaic language. She even found him a smaller volume of the laws that he could take home.

With all these resources, Roland was soon understanding the Settlers Laws. The Laws had been the basis for the entire settlement on the Rock. The laws he'd grown up learning regarding property rights, criminal prosecution, inheritance, and other matters seemed to have been drawn directly from the Settlers Laws.

One distressing thing Roland noticed was how often the Laws warned against building in valleys and lowlands. They sternly cautioned that settlements should be built on high ground that had plenty of solid rock. This answered Roland's longstanding question as to why the settlers had built on the mountainsides instead of the more appealing valley floor, but it also made him wonder why the ancient injunction was being ignored now.

Besides the study of the Settlers Laws and other works, there was something else that kept drawing Roland back to the library. Every once in a while, he'd catch sight of a young lady perusing the shelves. It was rare enough to find another patron in the library; to find a young woman was almost unheard of. She wasn't a dramatic beauty, but to Roland's eyes she was pretty enough. She had curly brown hair that didn't seem to want to behave and a shy smile that he only saw once or twice. Every time he came, he'd look for her, but the few times she was there he couldn't muster the courage to walk over and start talking. Once or twice he thought he saw her shooting sideways glances in his direction, and imagined himself casually strolling over and striking up a conversation with her. But shyness always overwhelmed him and he'd stare down at his book, and the next time he'd look up, she'd be gone.

One day he was out rambling along the trails that laced the top of the Rock when he saw another hiker ahead. Since Roland occasionally enjoyed company on his walks, he quickened his pace to catch up. When he got within earshot, he hailed the hiker, who turned at his call. It was the girl from the library.

It was hard to tell who was more surprised. Roland stammered and, recollecting himself, pulled his hat off. The girl's eyes went wide and her lips made an 'O' of surprise. Roland feared for a moment that she would simply run away, but he couldn't seem to do anything to prevent it – he just stood there wringing his hat in his hands and grasping for words.

Fortunately, the girl recovered more quickly. Her lips widened into the shy smile and her eyes twinkled. "Good morning, sir," she said in a rich soprano. "At last we meet under circumstances more conducive to conversation."

"Uh – right. Certainly," Roland bumbled, still not knowing what to say. The girl smiled sympathetically.

"My name's Jill," she offered, holding out her hand.

"Roland. I'm Roland," he replied, taking her hand. "Pleased to meet you." Though her grip was firm her skin was soft, and its touch thrilled him. He had a slight impulse to lift her hand to his lips, but thought it would be too forward.

"A pleasure, Roland," Jill answered. "Perhaps we can find somewhere to sit and get started on some of those conversations we've had to forego?"

Roland's heart was hammering – Jill actually wanted to talk to him? He couldn't believe his good fortune. "Ah – just a bit up the trail there's a hollow under a tree, with a stream flowing by. We – we could be in the shade, and maybe cool our feet, if we wished."

So began the first of many delightful meetings along the trails of the Rock. Jill lived on a farm not far away – Roland knew the family name – but hadn't gotten out much because her mother had been an invalid for years. As the eldest, Jill had taken the brunt of the burden of her mother's care, as well as all the chores mother would have done had she been well. But early that spring Jill's mother had died, and after burying and mourning for her, Jill had started getting out to all the places she'd always wanted to visit – like the library at Rockville, or the flower-lined trails about the Rock.

Roland and Jill spent the rest of that morning chatting beside the mountain pool. They agreed to meet there a couple of days later, and so enjoyed that meeting that they arranged to meet again, and soon they were meeting regularly to walk the trails or visit the library or gather flowers from the meadow. Roland had never considered himself much of a talker, but with Jill it seemed like he could talk about anything and enjoy it. But one topic he felt anxious broaching was that of their relationship – what it meant, and where it was going. However, the topic could not be ignored, and they both understood the significance when one day he suggested that they meet each other's families.

The following week Roland rode over to Jill's home to meet her father and siblings. The farm was small but well-tended, and the house was clean, if a little sparse. Jill's family welcomed Roland with good cheer. He sipped tea with the sisters and talked livestock with the brothers and made sure to accompany her father to the barns at chore time. There he asked permission to court Jill, which her father gave.

Roland's family embraced Jill with enthusiasm and delight. Roland assumed his mother would accept Jill as the daughter she'd never had, but he was delighted to see how readily his father took to her. So did his brother Jay and Jay's steady girl, Roxanne – something that surprised Roland, who thought Roxanne a bit flighty and doubted she'd take easily to Jill's personality. But it didn't seem to matter – within five minutes of meeting, the women were all chatting in the kitchen like magpies.

With all intentions clear and permissions granted, Roland began courting Jill in earnest. Father loaned him the buckboard to go calling, and he took Jill to Rockville for visits to the library or recitals or the rare dance. Once, wondering if Jill was wearying of the slim social offerings of Rockville, Roland offered to take her down to Riveropolis. She rejected the suggestion so firmly that he never made it again. Instead, they kept to their beloved trails and meadows, wandering and discussing the profound and the trivial.

One clear summer day, when the warm breeze was caressing the leaves and the sun was glinting in Jill's curls, Roland felt he could wait no longer. They were holding hands while walking through the glade where they'd had their first conversation when Roland suddenly stopped, tugging on Jill's hand to turn her toward him. There by the stream he knelt on the path and asked her to be his bride.

"This wasn't how I'd intended," he explained. "I'd meant to ask your father, right and proper, but I'm guessing he understands."

Jill said yes, and her father did understand, shaking Roland's hand emphatically and grinning all over when he was told. Roland's father and mother were equally excited, and Mother and Jill quickly bustled off to start planning the wedding. This was fine by Roland, who had a few requests to make of his father. That very evening Roland was out in the supply barn sorting materials and loading the heavy wagon for his project.

Word traveled fast around the Rock, and soon everyone – Mrs. Spenser in particular – was congratulating the new couple. To Roland's surprise – but not Jill's – a week after their engagement, Jay announced that Roxanne had accepted his proposal. Since neither girl objected, the brothers agreed to a double wedding to be held at the meeting hall in town, which would be the only place large enough to accommodate all the guests.

Much as Roland relished the hours with his fiancée, they became fewer. Haying time was upon them, with harvest not long after that, so days became busier at both farms. Roland's secret project also occupied many of his scarce spare hours, but he and Jill still found the occasional afternoon for each other.

Jill and Roxanne decided a Christmas wedding would be romantic, which gave Roland just enough time after harvest to make satisfactory progress. Circumstances worked in his favor: his family thought his long hours away were spent with Jill, and

Jill thought he was discharging his family responsibilities. Since both parties approved of what they thought he was doing, he was able to work in relative peace.

Finally, the week before Christmas, nearly all the town and many of the farm families gathered at the hall in Rockville for the wedding. The walls were hung with garlands of holly and pine, and most guests came clad in festive reds and greens. Jill's dress was simple lace, while Roxanne's was much more glamorous, set about with satin and pearl-like beads. Roland didn't pay much mind - in fact, he barely noticed his family or the minister. He had eyes only for his Jill. In a daze he recited the words they'd practiced, the vows that bound them for life.

Roland barely remembered the wedding dinner, with the music and dancing and all the toasts. He endured with good cheer the congratulations and good wishes, but wanted nothing more than to get away with his bride. They took their leave as soon as they could do so graciously. Father had given them the second buckboard as a wedding gift, and with the back full of bedding and pans and hams and other gifts, they headed off on their first journey as man and wife.

Jill seemed subdued, which Roland hoped wasn't out of fear or disappointment. When he turned the team toward his family farm, she asked, "Where are we going?"

"You'll see," Roland answered. They rode past the farmhouse, following the trail until, about half a mile further along, it curved into a small hollow.

"There," Roland pointed. "My wedding gift to you."

Jill gave a quiet gasp as she looked with wide eyes on the small white house perched on a shoulder of rock. It was near by the stream that chattered down the hollow, but not too close, and comfortably higher than the stream bed. She gazed for some time without saying a word, until Roland began to worry.

"I know it's not much, yet," he ventured. "Little more than a cottage, really, and the inside's not quite finished. But I built it so we can add on easily. Don't worry about heat – I put the fireplace central to the house, and the chimney draws well, and..."

"Roland," interrupted Jill, tears streaming down her cheeks. "It's beautiful."

So Roland and Jill began their life together in the little house on the shoulder of the Rock. Roland had sited it well, driving thick steel pins deep into the bedrock. To these he had anchored strong hardwood beams according to the methods his uncles had taught him. As a result, the little house stood as solid as the rock upon which it was built. Jill didn't mind that most of the lath was still unplastered or that her kitchen cupboards were nothing more than bare boards. Working together to finish the inside was one of the delightful chores of their newlywed days. But before winter was gone, Jill told Roland he'd have to move quickly to finish the second bedroom so their newest family member would have a place to sleep.

So their first year passed in peace and bliss. Since their house was on their parent's land, Roland helped about his family farm. Jay and Roxanne lived in the farmhouse with Mother and Father, for there was ample room. Every other weekend they rode over to Jill's family farm, where Roland helped with the plowing and haying and harvest. Mother fussed over Jill's pregnancy, and the happy couple spent time planning the expansions to their little house, for in time even more room would surely be needed.

The birth of their firstborn came right at the end of harvest. It distressed Roland to see Jill in labor, but the midwife said she "carried well" – whatever that meant – and soon he was ushered to her side where she presented him with his first son. That sobered Roland considerably.

The little family was joyful together, but just after the turn of the year a shadow fell on their happiness. Mother and Father announced that when spring came, they meant to move down to Riveropolis. They said they'd been pondering the move for some time, and had been setting funds aside. Mother claimed that Father's rheumatism had been getting worse, and now that both boys were settled into families of their own, it was the time to make the move. They'd deed the homestead over to Jay and Roland so they could continue to work the farm, but they felt it was time for them to retire.

Roland was stunned. He had never expected this. He'd envisioned them all spending the rest of their lives together on the Rock as a great, growing, loving family. He couldn't imagine life without Father and Mother living in the old farmhouse. Jill shared his disappointment, though she didn't successfully conceal her opinion that the decision had been hastened by Mother having to share a kitchen with Roxanne.

Strangely, the prospect of having ownership and sole occupancy of the farmhouse didn't seem to excite Jay and Roxanne – indeed, the idea seemed to distress them. The day that the lawyer came with the legal paperwork to transfer the farm, Roland signed with a heavy heart, but Jay seemed agitated, as if he didn't want to sign. But he signed in the end, and not long afterward they moved Father and Mother's things out.

To Roland, the long ride down the mountainside seemed like a funeral procession. Father and Mother had found a small bungalow a couple blocks off River Street, which was the main street of Riveropolis. Father called the lawn "trim and tidy," but to Roland it looked pathetically small compared to the meadows around the mountain homestead. Mother pointed out how conveniently close they were to stores and banks, but all Roland noticed was the heat and the dust and the smell of so many people living so close together. Father commented on how many neighbors they had, and how close they were, but to Roland none of them seemed very neighborly. To be sure, the streets were full of people, but they bustled about without even a how d'ye do. None of them were interested in stopping to chat about the weather and crop prospects – they had business, and meant to be about it.

But Father and Mother seemed excited about moving here, so Jay and Roland unloaded their things. Mother wanted to take them to dinner at a nearby place, not a saloon but a genuine restaurant with waiters. Jay wanted to go, but Roland pointed out that he needed to get the team and wagon back so he could return to Jill and the baby. So, they bid farewell to Father and Mother amid the promises of many visits between the farm and the new house in the city.

"After all," Mother assured him, "It's only a short ride down the mountain. It isn't as though we've moved a world away." But for Roland, it was a long and lonely ride home. He feared many of the promised visits would never happen.

Nor did they. With spring came plowing and planting, and a hundred little tasks about the farm that Father had let go over the years. It was Roland who took the lead in the work, for Jay still seemed distracted. Through the summer they got brief and cheery letters from Mother about how well they were settling down in the city, but they never seemed to have time to hitch up and go visit. Before long haying and harvest were upon them, and his son's first birthday was approaching.

When harvest was nearly finished, Jay shocked Roland with the news that he and Roxanne also wanted to move down to Riveropolis. They'd talked it over and thought they'd have a fuller life down there. They would lease Jay's portion of the farm to Roland on generous terms and live down near Father and Mother. Jill and Roland would be able to move into the farmhouse, which had plenty of room for their expanding family. It was a perfect solution!

Jill was disappointed, and clearly thought that Roxanne was a major factor behind the decision. Roland was crushed – his dream of life in the midst of a great family circle was dissolving. He and Jill firmly rejected the idea of moving into the old farmhouse. They'd grown to love their snug little house on the Rock, and Jill was hinting that it might not be long before they needed to add another room.

For Roland it was another sad day when they loaded the wagons and moved Jay and Roxanne down to Riveropolis. Jill came, though it was a long ride for the baby, because they wanted to visit Father and Mother. Of course, the parents were glad to see everyone, and Mother doted on the baby and chatted with Jill while the men took the furniture to Jay and Roxanne's new home. It was a few streets away from Father and Mother's house, in a less well-kept section of the city. It was unpainted and had a small yard that was mostly mud. But the way Roxanne went on about it, you'd think it was a palace just because it was located in Riveropolis. Roland said nothing as he unloaded the wagon, but wondered what madness would cause Jay to give up the farmhouse and fields to live in an unpainted shack on a postage-stamp lot.

On the ride back, Jill chattered about how good it had been to see the parents. Roland didn't say much and tried not to brood. Nobody felt very talkative when they rode past the farmhouse, empty now for the first time in generations. The next day Roland returned to board up the place, sealing the chimney and nailing the windows.

Now the years began to fly by. Jill's suspicions were correct, and the next summer they welcomed a lovely baby girl to their home. By working with neighbors and cousins, Roland was able to keep most of the farm's acreage under the plow. Jill's younger brothers were getting old enough to be useful, and with their help Roland was able to keep both his and Jill's family farms reasonably productive. His smithing skills were coming into more demand now that the blacksmith in Rockville was putting on the years. To Roland's delight, his cousin Stephen proved adept at livestock management and breeding. Wise use of the stock among the farms produced a fine lot of calves and colts each spring.

There were some comings and goings with the relations down valley – mostly goings, in Jill and Roland's case. They took the new baby down when everyone was old enough to travel, and tried to schedule trips for major holidays. Father and Mother made noises about coming up to visit, but nothing ever came of it. Mother had functions in town, or Father's rheumatism was acting up, or something. Jay was constantly busy with some business or other, though Roland was never clear exactly what it was.

One time, Jay did make the trip up to the old homestead. Jill was expecting their third, Roland was already planning the next addition onto their house, and the farm was in its late summer lull. Unannounced, Jay came trotting up in a light carriage. He visited with the family for a bit, but seemed anxious to talk to Roland alone. They took a walk around the farm.

"Sure looks different, standing there quiet and empty," Jay commented as they gazed at the boarded up farmhouse.

"What's on your mind, Jay?" Roland asked.

"Yes – ah, well, I have a bit of a business proposition for you," Jay explained.

"A business proposition?"

"Yes," Jay said. "I've found my niche in Riveropolis as a builder. Building homes is a surefire business in the city because everyone wants to move there. Whatever I put into a house in supplies and labor, I get back twice as much when I sell it. It's like finding money in the street!"

"I'm glad for you, Jay," Roland said. "But what does this have to do with me?"

"I'd like you to consider coming to work for me," Jay explained. "Not full time – I know I can't pry you away from the old place that easily – but maybe during the winter months, after harvest, you could come down. Earn as much in a few months as you do in a whole year on this land, and be back in time for plowing!"

"I don't know, Jay," Roland replied.

"You have to understand, Roland, building down in the valley isn't like how it is up here. Up here on the mountain, you have to contend with bedrock. You have to drive in pins, and hammer away what you want level, and build your house around the outcroppings."

"That's true," Roland admitted. He'd had to do all those things to build his house.

"The soil down in the valley is much more accommodating than this rock," Jay went on. "It's sandy soil, not even heavy clay. Wherever you want to build, you just mark out your corners, dig down a couple feet, sink some footings, and there's your foundation. Then you lay your joists, throw up your frame, roof it in, side and shingle, and you're done! The houses practically build themselves."

"Sounds efficient," Roland said.

"Oh, it is – and lucrative," Jay assured him. "There's always a ready market for the houses. Now, don't think I'd bring you in as a common laborer. A man of your knowledge and experience, I'd set you up as a foreman, in charge of several building sites. You'd have responsibility, and the pay to go with it."

"Why not make some of your workers foremen?" Roland asked.

Jay made a sour face. "Honestly? I've tried, but it just doesn't work out. Labor in the valley isn't like what we're used to up here. For one thing, men seem to be weaker, not able to lift as much or pound as hard. The work ethic is weaker, too. I've tried everything. When I pay them by the product, they rush to throw up as many houses as they can, but they're shoddy houses. When I pay them by the hour, they sit around smoking and jawboning to stretch out their time. I tried a fellow who I thought would work out. He was a good worker, well-liked by his fellows – but when I made him foreman, he turned into a right little tyrant. At least, that's what the workers said as they left. I lost most of my men to other builders and fell behind on all my projects and eventually had to let the foreman go. But I know you wouldn't be like that."

"Well, I don't know, Jay," Roland said again.

"I don't expect an answer right off," Jay assured him. "Sleep on it. I know it won't be easy to pry you away from the old place – sentiment is a powerful thing – but think of the advantages: a whole year's pay for a season's work! Think what that would mean to your growing family. And you could come home on weekends, so you'd hardly be away at all. Think about it and get back to me. Talk it over with Jill – I'm sure she'll see the advantages."

Roland smiled at the thought. That Jay would make such a statement only betrayed how little he understood Jill. But he promised to consider the offer, and he did mention it to Jill after supper. Her scornful glance was all the answer he needed, and he sent a polite refusal note by the next mail.

The years that followed were full of laughter, tears, hard work, and delightful play for the little family. Roland and Jill were blessed with more children, and their house in the hollow kept growing until it spread all over the rock ledge.

But more and more neighbors died or moved down to the valley, which meant more work for those who remained on the Rock. Many of the shops in Rockville closed, and those that remained didn't keep the hours they once did. Mrs. Spenser finally retired from the library, which meant it had to be kept open by volunteers. Jill and the children often took a spell. There was a certain camaraderie among those who "stayed behind" (as most put it), and folk who once would have had little cause to do business now greeted each other as old neighbors.

The scarce visits to Roland's family had become even scarcer through the years, chiefly due to the difficulty of moving all the children as well as finding help to mind the farm in their absence. What visits happened usually involved just that part of the family who could get loose. They found Father and Mother older and weaker every time. Mother spoke of her new friends, and the exciting activities in the city. But when it came time to leave, the parents were left just as they'd been found: sitting on the front porch rocking in their chairs, as if that was all they ever did.

One year, Roland received another unexpected visit. It was butchering time, and he had just finished cutting up a hog and teaching one of Jill's brothers how to cure and hang the meat. He looked a sight in his butchering apron, but he figured he'd finish evening chores before washing up. He was just heading for the barn when a smart two-horse chaise came trotting up to stop in front of the old house. A finely dressed man in a derby stepped out, and Roland was just walking over to ask the man his business when he recognized that it was his brother.

Jay was portlier than Roland remembered him being, but that was masked by the elegant cut of the tailored wool suit. He also wore tinted glasses, and behaved like the sunlight hurt his eyes. Roland greeted him joyfully, but didn't offer to shake hands since his own were covered in butchering grime. He did offer to rub down and stable the horses, but Jay declined, explaining that he couldn't stay long because of business back in the city.

"Business, eh?" Roland asked. "I must say, construction must be treating you well – that's the finest suit I've ever seen."

"You like it? I just ordered three more," Jay said, tugging at the lapels. "But construction? Bah – I sold that business years ago. Insurance is my thing now. It's like printing money."

"Really?" Roland asked. "I hadn't heard."

"Oh, yes," Jay assured him. "Smartest move I ever made. Realized a tidy profit on the construction business, and invested it all in insurance. People are anxious to protect what they have, and are willing to pay for it. It's all office work, too – I never have to get my hands dirty."

"Sounds great," said Roland.

"Oh, it is. I'm the biggest agent in town. Roxanne and I have moved three times since I started, and now we live in one of the grander homes along River Street. Roxanne just loves the view. We have servants now – four of them. She has a cook and a parlor maid, and I have a groundskeeper and a stable boy to take care of the horses."

"Wonderful, Jay," Roland said, looking over to where the team stood sweating and panting in the hot afternoon sun. "Speaking of which, are you sure I can't at least water your beasts?"

"Oh, they'll be all right," Jay said with a wave of his hand. "Like I was saying, we can afford to buy our own bread at the bakery and our vegetables at the greengrocer and our meat at the butcher. No slaughtering for us – Roxanne takes Cook to the market, looks at the cuts all laid out in a case under glass, and points out the ones she wants. The butcher hands them to Cook all wrapped up in paper, and the next we see of them they're on our plates at dinnertime."

"Sounds wonderful, Jay," Roland replied. "Just the life you and Roxanne have always wanted."

"It is, that," Jay said, though he looked troubled. "But it's not – not like the old times we had, you and me, here on the farm. Those were good days, weren't they?"

"The best."

"But," Jay stammered for a moment, as if trying to recover his equilibrium. "But life changes, and we have to change with it, don't we?"

"Life does change," Roland admitted.

"Which is why I'm here with a proposal for you," Jay continued.

"A proposal?" Roland asked skeptically. "Jay, don't tell me you want me to help with your insurance business."

"Insurance?" Jay replied with a hearty laugh. "No, nothing like that. Something more in your line – farming. I've learned of a venture to start a major farming effort down in the valley. Some investors I know – call it a consortium – will be buying up and cultivating land that hitherto has been undeveloped. Vast tracts managed by this consortium, employing hundreds to work the land."

"Don't you have farms down valley, Jay?" Roland asked.

"We do, but nothing big enough to supply the needs of our population. Even now we have to import nearly half our food from the mountain here, and if our population grows as we expect, it'll outstrip everyone's production. Anyway, I'm in on the ground level with this venture, and it's all very hush-hush – we don't want the land speculators to get wind of it.

"At a meeting this morning one of the investors began wondering where we'd find people to manage these farms, and what jumped into my mind was you. Managing farms is right up your alley! You've been doing it for decades – you'd be ideal!"

Roland was surprised – this wasn't what he'd been expecting. "I don't know, Jay. All I've ever managed has been the family plot here."

"Now, hear me out, hear me out, before you go jumping to conclusions," Jay cautioned. "This is a ground-level opportunity with lots of potential for growth. We need farming expertise, which you have. You'd be doing what you're doing now, just on a larger scale. You'd be supervising workers and have a budget like you can't dream of from this little place. We'd set you up with all the latest farming equipment – no more mending broken harrows – and all the plow horses you need. Plus, you'd be working the rich, fertile valley soil, not this rocky mountain ground."

Oddly, it was that last point that gave Roland a moment's pause. He'd been thinking recently about the yield from the aging soil. Jay must have spotted his hesitation, because he pressed in.

"Think of it, Roland – a management position with a salary. No more getting up in the night to tend sick cows, no more worrying about crop failure. You'd get paid regularly, and could go home to Jill and the kids every night. I'm sure I could talk the partners into adding a percentage of yield to your salary, as an incentive bonus."

"I don't know, Jay."

"You could move down near Mother and Father, and the kids could see their grandparents regularly. Also, the town has just erected a new school, so you kids could get the finest education. Roxanne and I would be right around the corner, and you and I would be working together again, just like we used to."

There was just enough pleading in that tone that Roland turned to look more closely, but the tinted glasses prevented him from seeing Jay's eyes. The arguments for the position carried weight, no denying. The job sounded a good sight easier and more predictable than the farming Roland was used to. But even more persuasive was the hint of desperation, of loneliness, in his brother's voice. Part of Roland wavered – perhaps he could persuade Jill...

But clear as crystal and hard as iron there came the recollection of the warning he'd read so often in the Settlers Laws, the admonition against building or living anywhere in the lowlands. He and Jill had taken that to heart since before their marriage. They would not ignore it now.

"No, Jay," Roland said simply. "Tempting as it sounds, we can't leave our life here."

Jay was silent for quite a while, gazing out over the fields. There must have been something in Roland's tone that told him further appeal was useless, for when he finally spoke it was without any appeal or attempt to cajole. "I figured you'd say something like that, but I had to try." He again fell silent for a long time, and when he spoke again it was with unusual weariness. "I miss you, Roland. It's been so long, so – long. I miss you terribly."

"I miss you, too, Jay," Roland said, realizing as he spoke just how true that was. Buried under years of work and family concerns, the bone-deep yearning was still there: just to sit with his brother and chat as they once had. On a whim, he decided to make an absurd suggestion, nearly certain that it would come to naught.

"You know, you could move back up here. The family home is still empty, and there's plenty of room for all."

Jay looked up sharply, gazing at Roland for a long time. But then he shook his head and smiled. "Move back? Up here? Roxanne – no, no, brother, you can't turn the clock back. If your life is here, mine is down there. Thanks for the offer, but it can't be. Can't be."

"I'm sorry to hear that, Jay," Roland said sincerely.

"Yes," Jay replied briskly, dusting off his hands. "Well, then, I've made my proposal and gotten my answer. Thanks for your time, and for hearing me out."

"Jill will have supper ready soon, and you're welcome..."

"No, no. Work calls, and I've got to be going. Thank you, though – another day, to be sure."

"Goodbye, Jay," Roland called as his brother rode away.

The farming consortium must have found someone to manage their operations, for that fall they began the massive effort of clearing the ground. Looking down from the mountain, Roland and his neighbors could see immense tracts of land being cleared, stumps pulled, and dozens of teams ripping up the sod. Jay hadn't been exaggerating about the latest farm equipment – even from the mountaintop the farmers could see that the teams weren't simple two-animal hitches. They were wide, multi-row harrows pulled by teams of a dozen horses driven by a man seated atop the plow. A few teams like that could plow up hundreds of acres in a week, which was precisely what they did. Gradually the scrub growth and scant trees in the lowlands west of Riveropolis were tamed, so when the first winter snows came, they fell on vast tilled fields where the rich soil awaited the spring planting.

It was an unusually snowy winter, with travel hindered by great drifts which piled up here and there around the mountain. Jill and Roland were snug and warm in their house, though Roland was glad for his crew of boys who helped him keep the roof clear. They saw some of their neighbors, either when one dropped by with some implement in need of mending or on one of their rare trips into Rockville. The mountain farmers were concerned about the impact of the vast new fields in the valley. Some of them made what living they could selling their extra crop at market in the city. If the valley could grow all its own food, the market for mountain grain might dry up.

When spring came, some of those worries appeared justified. Being lower, the valley floor was just enough warmer that they could plant several weeks earlier than farms on the Rock. Roland knew the valley soil still had to be saturated with snowmelt, but it was apparently dry enough to plant, for they could see teams working the fields. Soon thereafter the fields were covered with the light green haze that bespoke new growth.

By the time the farmers on the Rock were breaking their soil for planting, a foot of growth was waving in the fields in the valley. By the time the mountain fields were sprouting, the valley crop was forming heads, promising a rich harvest.

Then the storms began.

Early summer storms were common, but the first storm of the year was unexpectedly ferocious. A thick line of towering black thunderheads came sweeping upriver with lightning flashing and rain slashing. Roland barely had time to get the livestock under cover before the storm broke on the mountain. It was a deep storm line, trapping them in their house for nearly a full day while it roared overhead. With shutters bolted tight they huddled while the rain and hail hammered on the roof and the wind howled through the rocks.

When it finally cleared, Roland and his family went out to survey the damage. It wasn't too bad – mostly things blown about or knocked over which could be set right with a day of cleanup. But from Lookout Rock Roland could see that the city had been hit hard. The streets were rivers of mud, and debris was blown all about. Many houses had lost shingles or fencing. Worse, the new crops looked blown and flattened, though Roland's experienced eye guessed that most of the crop would recover. The storm had been severe, but not catastrophic.

The next one was worse.

This time Roland was more prepared. He watched the sky warily, and spent his days tightening down and boarding up. Thus, he was dismayed, but not surprised, when he saw another line forming off in the western sky. He and his sons quickly checked the extra fodder they'd set out for the livestock, nailed strips across the doors, and were safely inside before the storm's fury struck. The house shuddered under the onslaught of the wind, and noon was as dark as midnight. But the strong timbers stood firm on their rock foundation and the firmly nailed shingles held tight against the driving rain. It stormed all that day and well into the night, but by dawn the wind had died to a breeze and the family ventured forth.

The stream which ran near the house was nearly overflowing its banks, and Jill was careful to keep the young ones far from the rushing waters. There was less damage about the farm than there had been from the last storm, mostly due to Roland's precautions. Amazingly the crops hadn't been washed away – it seemed they had enough root to hold soil against the wind and rain. The old house had lost some shingles, so Roland set a couple of the boys to lay planking over the gaps until they could be mended properly.

Down in the valley things didn't look so good. There were trees down all over the city, and many of the houses had lost shingles or siding. Roland wondered how those houses that Jay had built – the ones with the shallow footings driven into the sandy soil – were faring. More ominously, the fields had taken another severe beating, and Roland could see standing water in places. Some of that crop might be salvaged if those fields got drained quickly; otherwise they were looking at substantial loss.

A few days later, as Roland was putting the livestock in for the evening, Jill came out to him.

"I was wondering," she asked, "whether we should run over to check on Pa. His land doesn't drain as well as ours, and I want to be sure he's all right."

"I think you're right," Roland answered, "and for more reason than just that. See those high, wispy clouds up there in the west? You normally don't see them this time of year. I've seen them twice already this summer – both times just before those storm lines formed. We need to check on your Pa and siblings to make sure they're all right, and be ready to bring them back here."

The next day Roland and some of his sons set out for his father-in-law's farm, which they found in slightly worse condition than their own. They did some picking up and tying down, but mostly they packed up Pa and the rest of the family to go. Roland explained how he expected another storm line to sweep through, and how they'd all be safer at Roland and Jill's. Pa readily agreed.

"It may be this is the pattern for this summer," Pa said. "At least the storms only sweep through here, rather than lingering like they do off east."

"Lingering?" Roland asked. "What do you mean?"

"These storm lines – they roll over us in a hurry, but then move off to the eastern range and hang there for days. They must catch some kind of southerly winds, because the whole pattern just sits and rains on the mountains."

"You've seen this?"

"You can still see it from the last storm front. Step over here," Pa led Roland up the field to where he could get a good view up the valley. The river shimmered off to its source in the eastern range, where dark clouds brooded over the slate-gray slopes and sheets of rain slanted down. "It's been raining steady like that since the last storm."

Roland gazed at the dark skies, pondering, when suddenly his eyes widened. "Good heavens," he gasped. "Jay, Father, and Mother!"

"Pardon?" Pa asked.

"No time," Roland gasped, starting to sprint for the wagon. "Boys! Pile up, time to get back! Go!"

They jammed onto the buckboard and set out. Roland pushed the horses, muttering under his breath the whole way home. When they arrived, he told his eldest to stable the horses and secure the barns. To the west the distressingly familiar line of dark clouds was forming, blotting out the afternoon sun.

"How did you know the storm was coming?" his father-in-law asked.

"I didn't," Roland said as he dashed for the door. "It isn't that. Caleb!" Caleb was his youngest, and the best rider in the family.

"What's wrong?" Jill was at the door, and could see the concern on his face.

"Not now, honey. Where's Caleb? Caleb!" Roland answered.

"Here, Father!" Caleb cried as he came dashing down the hall. Roland grabbed his son's shoulder and thrust a paper into his hand.

"Son, this is your Uncle Jay's address. Take Satin and ride as fast as you can down to Riveropolis. Tell him to take Aunt Roxanne, and Father and Mother, and get to high ground immediately. Tell him the river is going to rise – not *may* rise, but *is going to* rise – and they must get to high ground. It isn't safe where they are, and they must move. Do you have that?"

"Yes, Father," Caleb answered, wide-eyed at being entrusted with such a critical mission.

"Roland!" Jill shrieked from the doorway. "You can't send him out into this!"

Roland dashed to the door to see the sky darkening at an alarming rate. The wind was already gusting erratically, rustling the leaves as it rushed up the hollow. Even as he watched, the first flash of lightning arced across the clouds, and thunder boomed against the mountain.

Roland dropped his head. "No, no, I can't. Stay put until this blows over, Caleb."

The storm didn't seem to last as long as the first two, though it may have been that they were growing accustomed to them. They huddled together in the dark, listening to the rain pour down and the wind howl about the house. They ate biscuits and dried fruit, for they couldn't light a cook fire because of the draft down the chimney. Nobody got much sleep for the creaking of the house, but not a drop of rain got in.

By noon the next day the storm had passed over and they could emerge. Caleb was hastened on his mission while those that remaind busied themselves repairing the damage. Satin was not only fast but strong and sure-footed. If any horse could get Caleb down the rain-washed mountainside and through the chancy streets, it would be Satin.

Sure enough, shortly after supper Caleb came riding back, looking bedraggled but proud. Satin was spent, and Caleb was distressed to deliver his report.

"I told him, Father, just like you said. But Uncle Jay said to tell you that you needn't worry. He said that the river has been rising but has been contained by the new, strong flood walls the city engineers have erected. He thanked you for your concern, and will keep an eye on things, but is sure the walls will be able to handle any flooding."

"Flood walls?"

"Yes, Father, that's what he said," Caleb answered with some anxiety. "I hope I did what you wanted, Father. They asked me to stay for supper and spend the night, but I reckoned you'd want me back soonest."

"I did, son," Roland assured him. "You've done a heroic job. Thank you. Now, stable up Satin and get inside." As Caleb went off, Jill looked at Roland with concern, but he didn't seem to see her. He was gazing in the direction of the city, muttering to himself. "Dammit, Jay, no flood wall will contain what's coming. Get out of there, get everyone to safety."

"Do you think it'll be that bad?" Jill asked.

Roland looked at her with somber eyes. "Honey, your father showed me how those storms have been moving off east and drenching the range. The headwaters of the river are in those mountains. When all that rainfall works its way down, nothing will contain it. The entire city could be lost."

"When might that happen?" Jill asked.

"Hard to say – depends on the river flow and a number of other things," Roland replied. "The snowmelt will have saturated the soil across the valley. I'd guess three, maybe four weeks from when the rains began."

"It's been two weeks already," Jill observed.

Then next several days were a torment of anticipation for all of them. Roland especially was a bundle of nerves. He couldn't focus on any work, and kept riding up to Lookout Rock to watch for any sign of the river rising. He felt torn in several directions. He wanted to ride down and shake sense into Jay, though he knew it would do no good. He wanted to force Father and Mother to come with him, though he knew he couldn't. He wanted to go to where the river wound around the east face of the Rock and gather evidence of rising water to bring to the city, though he knew nobody would listen. He wanted to ride through the streets of Riveropolis urging everyone to make for higher ground, but he knew they wouldn't follow. The river had risen before, they'd say, and it would rise again. They wouldn't believe that this rising was going to be like nothing they'd ever seen.

Above all, Roland couldn't shake the sense of foreboding that grew with each day. By the time he noticed the wispy clouds forming high in the sky again, he was nearly frantic. In the few hours they had left before the next storm, he and Jill rode out to get one more look at the valley.

Riveropolis had tidied up again, and the rooftops were mottled here and there with either storm damage or new planking. From this distance, the city appeared to be recovering. But the three major storms had destroyed the fields in the valley. Jay's consortium had completely lost their first year's investment.

"Roland, look!" Jill gasped, clutching his arm and pointing. In the city's easternmost streets they could see brown water. It seemed to be rising even as they watched, lapping further up past the houses.

"Jill, it's starting!" cried Roland. "It's starting, and we can't do a thing!"

Indeed, they couldn't, for even as they watched the water rise, more dark clouds were forming overhead. From the roiling and churning front, they knew they had less than an hour to get everyone under cover. "The flooding is going to hit them in the middle of the storm!" Roland exclaimed.

In anguish they rode back to the farm, where the boys had already secured the property. They hastily gathered in the house to await the storm's onslaught. From the booming and crashing it sounded like the worst storm yet, and they cowered beneath its fury.

But the raging cacophony outside wasn't as great as the howling inside Roland's head as he imagined what must be going on down in the valley. Jill stayed beside him, sharing his anguish. He paced the floor, or stared at the shuttered windows, or just sat at the table with his head in his hands. Once or twice he even dashed to the door and flung it open, only to be rebuffed by the ferocity of the wind and rain. Jill sat at the table and watched him in the light of the one lantern they kept lit. In the end they both fell into a fitful sleep there at the table, their heads cradled on their arms.

It was still pitch dark when Roland awoke with a start. The night was still; the howling wind and drumming rain were silent. Outside was only the sound of water dripping from the eaves, the rushing of the nearby stream, and the after-storm ruffling of the breeze in the leaves.

"It's passed!" Roland exclaimed. "Boys! Get the lanterns! To the barns! Hitch up the wagons! Get moving!"

"Roland!" Jill said sharply. "It's still dark! You don't know what the storm has done – the road could be washed out or blocked! There may be trees down..."

"Honey," Roland interrupted, "I promise I won't do anything rash. We'll be as safe as we can. But think: if anyone escaped the flood, we need to find them, and quickly!"

Jill thought this over, then nodded. "All right, but you be careful!"

The boys were assembling in the kitchen with every lantern they could find. Within half an hour they were all on the road that led to the valley, with some in the wagons and some on horseback. They all carried lanterns and traveled slowly, watching their footing. They were so intent on the road that they hardly noticed the eastern sky growing lighter. When they were nearing the turn to the final descent, they stopped and looked out over the valley, now illuminated by gray predawn light.

"Oh, my heavens," whispered Roland.

Where Riveropolis had stood surged a vast lake. Dirty water spread as far as they could see. The only sign that there had ever been a city were the tops of a few of the taller buildings. There were a handful of rooftops, but many of these were being nudged along by the flowing water. Debris littered the surface, but it was being pushed along so quickly by the current that Roland guessed that much more had already been swept away. To their right, toward where the new fields had been, rippled an expanse of brown water. The entire valley had been drowned.

Roland was too stunned to feel anything. How could an entire city be totally destroyed in a matter of hours? How many people had died? He buried his head in his hands while his sons gazed in shock at the devastation.

"Father!" cried Caleb, pointing off to their right. "What's that?"

"What? I can't see anything," Roland replied, squinting into the twilight.

"It looks like something moving," one of his other sons said. "It might be people."

"Then go! See what it is!" Roland urged them. Those on horseback galloped off while the others followed with the wagons. As they drew closer, they could see a handful of people by the waterside, some moving about and some lying still. As the riders approached, the mobile ones heard their galloping and whooping, and began waving in response.

By the time the wagons caught up, the survivors were clustered around the horses. One detached himself from the group and stumbled toward Roland.

It was Jay. His clothes were soaked and stained and his face and hair were streaked with dirt. Roland jumped down and grabbed his brother, who was swaying as he clung to the wagon. He was amazed at how cold Jay was. Grabbing one of the blankets from the wagon, he stripped off Jay's shirt and wrapped him while calling to his boys.

"Fire, lads! And bring those others here! I've blankets in the back!" Jill had sent along every blanket they had. Some of the boys busied themselves wrapping the survivors while others tried to kindle a bonfire. Roland attended to Jay, who was shivering and coughing weakly.

"Some of them didn't make it," Jay explained, waving vaguely at some of the bodies that lay by the waterside. "We lost others in the flood. It was cold, Roland, biting cold, and it flowed so quickly."

"We'll have a fire going shortly," Roland reassured him, tucking another blanket around his brother. "The lads are gathering wood. Tell me what happened. Who are these people?" He scanned the faces and recognized none of them.

"Strangers," Jay explained. "I don't know them myself. All I could get to come with me. I should have listened to you, Roland. I should have listened to you, and to my gut." He fell silent for a minute then drew a deep breath and continued in a shaky voice.

"Even after I got your warning, I didn't think the danger was all that immediate. I knew the rains had been unusually strong, so I made a point of wandering down by the waterfront, where they'd erected the new flood walls. That's been a big project over the past year – huge timbers sunk deep into the riverbed, with massive beams nailed on. I saw the water rising, but I'd seen that before. It wasn't until I saw the beams buckling that I realized how much force the river was bringing to bear."

"When was that?" Roland asked.

"Yesterday afternoon, right before – right before the end," Jay replied. "I was actually watching when the timbers began to crack under the strain. Then I knew I'd best heed your warning, and I dashed back to the house to fetch Roxanne." He paused to draw another deep breath.

"She refused to go. She laughed at me and called me a worrywart. She said the river had risen before and would rise again, and we'd still be here. I tried to explain that this wasn't like other times, and that we needed to get out. She said we'd have plenty of warning if things got really dangerous. I insisted, but she put her foot down and refused to come.

"Then I thought about Mother and Father. I hitched up the wagon and went to get them, figuring I could return for Roxanne later. It was just about then that the storm broke, so I was fighting the wind and rain.

"Well, they wouldn't listen, either, any more than I listened to you. They couldn't see the urgency, they wanted to wait out the storm, their house was on high ground – any reason they could think of not to move. I nearly tore my hair out, and in the end I decided to go back for Roxanne.

"Outside it was raining and thundering madly. The wind was howling and it was nearly pitch dark. Just when I made it back to the wagon, I heard this great sound, something between a tear and a crack – as if a giant had snapped a huge plank – followed by a rushing roar. I knew it wasn't the storm, and figured the flood wall must have given way. I just panicked and began running north and east. I knew I couldn't get back to Roxanne, for River Street would be gone. Having built all over the city, I knew the eastern neighborhoods slope down to Laurel Street, which is the lowest point in that area. I knew if the water was rising, it would run along Laurel first."

"I think Jill and I saw that starting," Roland said, "Yesterday afternoon, right before the storm."

"Yes, well, it was much worse by the time I got there. I knew who I'd left behind, but I also knew that to turn back would be to run right into the rising water. I thought I heard that rushing behind me, and maybe some cries and shouts, but it was hard to be sure for the wind and thunder.

"There was hardly anyone out-of-doors because of the storm, but those I saw, I urged into the wagon. I must have looked like a madman, careening through that storm, shouting about the oncoming flood. Some clambered aboard, but most just ran away.

"When I got to Laurel Street, things were worse than my darkest fears. The street was already flooded, like a deep river with a powerful current. I could see houses along the street with their first floors submerged. I knew there would be no crossing it there, so I turned north and ran along the street, looking for a shallower spot. By now it was full night, black as pitch, and the storm was raging with full fury. We got to a spot where I thought we might ford the water, so I turned the horses into it. They didn't want to go, but I urged them.

"It was a mistake. It was still too deep, and the current too strong. The horses lost their footing, and then the current pushed them over. They got all tangled in the harnesses and were swept away. That tipped the wagon, too, dumping us all into the icy water. Some were lost then, carried away by the current. The water was already up to my neck, and the current pressed us terribly, but some of us managed to wade across. We crawled out on this side, hauled each other out of the water, and just dropped on the bank. But within the hour we had to move again, because the flood had risen that much. We spent the night huddled together in the rain, listening to the water rush by and trying to stay warm. Eventually the storm blew over, and then we saw your lanterns."

They were silent for a moment, wrapped in their grief. Then Roland spoke.

"I'm sorry about Roxanne."

Jay shook his head. "Roxanne and I – well, she died where she wanted to live. I tried to warn her, just as you tried to warn me, but she wouldn't leave her house." Jay chuckled grimly. "Kind of appropriate, come to think of it. Mother and Father, now – well, they were getting along in years, though I wouldn't have wished that end on them. They never were happy down in the city, you know. They moved for the convenience, and once they were settled in, they were – well, settled. Didn't want to put the trouble into moving again. But they never were happy, not like they'd been on the Rock."

They fell silent, gazing out over the expanse of brown water that had so recently been a bustling community.

"Well," Roland sighed, "now we know why the Settlers Law warned so sternly against building down on the lowlands."

"Did it, now?" Jay asked. "I never knew that. Never was much up on those old writings."

"At least you have a place to live, and I'm sure we can find places for these others," Roland said. "Heck, you have a whole house to live in – we've kept the old place up."

"Eh?" Jay said, as if he'd been thinking of other things. "Place to live? For a while, I suppose. Have to do something, that's for certain – I'm wearing the sum total of my worldly goods. I suppose it'll have to do for now." He drifted away into muttering.

Puzzled, Jay looked at him, catching bits of sentences like, "...some market, to be sure, but not enough..." and "...maybe further up or down..."

"Jay," Roland asked sharply, "what on earth are you mumbling about?"

"Pardon?" Jay responded, then shook his head. "Oh, just thinking out loud, that's all."

"About what?" Roland pressed.

"Why – the insurance business."

Roland was stunned. "Insurance?" He gestured toward the flood. "In the face of this, you're still thinking about insurance?"

"A setback, brother, that's all this is," Jay explained. "A big one, to be sure, but only a setback. Every man has to find his niche, that's the important thing. I found mine in insurance. That's where I truly excelled, where I made a difference. Sure, I've been knocked off my horse; now it's a question of getting back in the saddle. It may be sooner, it may be later, but I will get back in that saddle."

Roland just stared speechlessly at his brother.

This is intended as a refreshing story of friendship and coming of age. Any incidental commentary on current social conventions is almost certainly unintentional.

Rosalia

"You should marry Rosalia," Papa announced one day after dinner. "She's a nice girl, and she comes from a good family. You're getting of an age to think about marriage."

"Yes, Papa," I answered, making sure he didn't see me roll my eyes. Papa didn't like me to roll my eyes, especially at something he'd said.

But some things just call for rolling eyes.

Not that I mind Rosalia. We've practically been raised together. She's the daughter of Papa's good friend Señor Torres, and we're about the same age. Ever since we made our First Communion, people have been taking pictures of us together and nudging each other and suggesting what a fine couple we'd make some day.

Which hasn't prevented Rosalia from being a great friend. She's like a sister – well, more like a cousin. We live just a few blocks from each other, which makes it easy to hop over for working together on our studies or going lizard hunting (when we were younger) or whatever. I got the first dance at her *Quinceañera*. We enjoy each other's company, and the chance to commiserate about our problems.

Which was why, when Rosalia dropped over the next day to borrow some anchos, I told her of Papa's little hint.

"It's started," I announced.

"What's started?" she asked.

"Yesterday after dinner Papa told me that I should marry you."

To my immense satisfaction, she rolled her eyes. "Parents can be so pushy."

"I know!" I replied, grateful for her sympathy. "For years now I've heard about how Mama and Papa only met thrice before they were married, and how their parents arranged everything, and so on. Like I didn't know what they were hinting at!"

"The 'good old days'," Rosalia groaned.

"Exactly!" I said. "They don't understand that these are modern times, and things are done differently now. But I promise you this, Rosalia: whatever they say or do, I won't let it come between us."

"Why, thank you, sir."

"Our friendship is too important to be ruined by a bunch of presumptuous adults."

"Ramón," she said, patting my cheek, "you're a peach."

"Thanks," I replied. "Hey, are those anchos for your mother's molé?"

"Indeed, they are," she assured me.

"And we're just having tortillas and fruit tonight. Mama! I'm going to Rosalia's for dinner!"

"Fine, dear," Mama called back from the kitchen.

"This is one bright part," I grinned, grabbing the anchos and tucking Rosalia's arm in mine. "Now I can do anything I want with you and they'll agree, because they'll think I'm coming around."

Rosalia laughed out loud at this.

Shortly thereafter I first met Liana. I was doing some studying at the café on the square when a beautiful woman sat down at the next table. She was well dressed and very poised, but she seemed to be having trouble with the menu, and indeed the entire ordering process. Seeing my opportunity to be gallant, I leaned over and suggested she try the *café de olla* and some *pan dulce*, for which the café was famous. As I'd hoped, she was very grateful, and invited me to sit at her table and chat. It turned out that she was the daughter of one of the rancheros outside town, and had lived most of her life out there. But now that she was old enough, she'd insisted on being allowed to come live in town. Her parents had given her an allowance and found her an apartment, and now she was learning the way of street cafés and other aspects of town life.

I wish I could say I was a brilliant conversationalist, but I wasn't. I mostly just sat and gazed while Liana rattled on. She was the most beautiful woman I'd ever seen, with deep dark eyes, long black hair, and full red lips. Her every move was gracious and every smile was dazzling. In fact, I was so dazzled that I totally forgot to find out where she lived or how I could keep in touch with her. Suddenly she was standing up and thanking me and walking away. I would have run after her, but I had to stay behind and settle her check, which she'd either forgotten about or didn't know she had to pay.

I was disappointed, but determined to keep my eyes open. Our town was small enough that I guessed I'd see her sooner or later. As it turned out, I was right, but not in a manner I would have chosen.

One evening I was walking past one of the town's seedier cantinas when I heard a woman's cry from within. It was one of those hard-to-evaluate cries, somewhere between a laugh and a shriek. It seemed to me that whoever had cried like that didn't like what was happening. I had limited sympathy – any woman who went into that cantina should expect some coarse treatment – but Papa had raised me to be chivalrous. I wasn't keen on going in, but I stiffened my spine and walked through the door, hoping the appearance of a strange face would encourage the regulars to tone down the rough stuff.

It turned out that the entertainment of the evening was Liana herself. She was dressed in a showy, expensive outfit that looked far out of place, but her head was bare and her hair was disheveled. Some of the patrons, of the farm and field hand variety, had snatched something from her and were passing it among themselves, making her run about grabbing at it. My throat tightened when all those surly faces turned toward me, but I decided to bluff my way through.

"Liana!" I called, holding out my hand. "You went to the wrong cantina. I've been waiting for you for nearly an hour."

"Oh!" she cried, running over and clutching my arm. "Those mean men took my hat and won't give it back!"

"No matter. Come on, let's go," I urged. I wasn't far inside the door, and began backing toward it while watching the patrons. They looked none too pleased to be losing their evening's amusement, but the bartender was watching so they didn't try to stop me.

"But – my hat!" Liana cried, pointing to the bedraggled item clutched in a worker's hand.

"I'll get you another one," I whispered fiercely. "Let's go." Nodding and smiling at the glares, I reached the door and pulled Liana out into the street. My heart was hammering and I was never so glad to leave a place, but Liana was spitting mad.

"Those brutes! Filthy animals!" she snarled, and proceeded to call them many names I'd heard before but never from the lips of a lady.

"Just be glad you got out of there safely," I said. "Liana, there are many cantinas in this town, but some you just don't go to. That was one of them."

"How was I supposed to know that?" she asked.

"I – uh," That was hard to answer – I'd just grown up knowing. I suppose Papa must have told me over the years.

"You must show me this," Liana demanded imperiously. "Tomorrow night you come to get me, and take me to the proper cantinas."

My head swam. I walked her to her apartment and fairly floated home.

So began my time with Liana. I couldn't believe my good fortune. I got to call on the most beautiful woman in town and escort her out! She called me her pet, and her little village boy, and gave me a reward kiss when I fetched her a drink or did her some other favor. We visited all the suitable cantinas and cafés, and if there was some public dance or fiesta in the area, I took her. I saw Liana nearly every day.

However, my family hardly saw me at all. I'd drag myself out of bed, rush through my studies, gobble supper (if I had supper at all), and dash off to squire Liana to the evening's festivities. I'd spend the evening drunk with her beauty and grace and joy of life. We'd dance and laugh and drink toasts far into the night. I began to dream of a life of bliss with the beautiful Liana by my side.

One afternoon, when Mama was pouring me some coffee while I studied, she said ever so softly, "You know, Rosalia is a pretty girl, too."

"I know, Mama," I snapped. "And I'll thank you to stop pestering me about Rosalia." Mama said nothing, but walked quietly away, leaving me feeling terrible about being sharp with her. My head was pounding, it had been my fifth night in a row with only a few hours of sleep, and I'd slept through both breakfast and my morning class. My grades were starting to suffer, and I was quickly burning through my meager savings just keeping Liana entertained. She had an allowance, but preferred to spend that on new clothes and decorations for her apartment, letting her escort pay for meals and entertainment. I didn't know how much longer I could keep this up, but I'd figure something out.

I gathered my books and headed off to class, comforting myself with thoughts of the evening. It was long-planned – I'd take Liana to her favorite restaurant, then we'd go to a dance party at a friend's house on the edge of town. I had no commitments the next day, so I could spend a carefree evening with Liana.

When I arrived at Liana's apartment, the sight of her beauty enabled me to put aside all my worries. She was a vision in a flowing, richly embroidered dress. All through dinner I couldn't take my eyes off her. At the dance she outshone all the other girls, and I knew every man was jealous of my place at her side.

The night was heavenly – warm, with cool breezes coming off the river. Our host's estate was right along the water, and he maintained beautiful gardens along the bank. At a break in the dancing I took Liana for a walk among the trees. I thought I was in paradise – a full moon floated in the sky, stars adorned the heavens, fragrant breezes whispered through the leaves, and a vision of loveliness walked by my side. (I'd also had a few glasses of sangria.) My heart felt full enough to burst.

In a whirl of passion, I pulled Liana to me and kissed her fervently. Then I fell to my knees and asked for her hand. I promised always to be with her, to make her happy, to give her anything she asked, if only she would marry me.

My heart beat for a long minute in the quiet night as she looked down at me. Then she threw back her head and gave a loud, long laugh.

"Marry you?" she asked. "Marry you?" She gave another loud laugh. "Silly little village boy, whatever made you think I would marry you? When I marry, it's not going to be to a cheap, clingy schoolboy who hangs around like a sick puppy. I'm looking for more of a man than that!"

I felt the blood hammering in my ears. I was having trouble breathing. What was she saying? My Liana, my own – what was she saying?

She gave another laugh. "You know, Ramón, I've been getting tired of you. You want to monopolize my time and won't take hints that I'd like to see other people. Well, then, here is plain speech: go away. Find some nice village girl to marry, but leave me alone."

"But...but...," I stammered, "I thought we were –"

She laughed again – one of those laughs that but an hour ago I had thought was music from heaven. But when she spoke, her voice had a steely edge.

"Didn't you hear me? Go away. You've had your fun. I've let you take me places. I've sat and listened to you meander on for hours about your drab little life. I've given up evenings for you. But I see now that I've been too kind. I should have said this weeks ago. You bore me. Go away." With that she turned and strode back into the hacienda, leaving me on my knees in the garden.

I don't remember much of the rest of that night. I recall stumbling along the river, and even contemplating throwing myself in. I wandered the streets of town aimlessly, berating myself. How could I have been such a fool? Recalling my times with Liana, those hours I'd so prized and sacrificed so much to obtain, I saw now that the laughter and jokes had been on me, not with me. She'd been glad enough for my protection and companionship when threatened in a bar, but when she was done with me, she'd thrown me away like an empty bottle. I think I went through every cliché there was during that long and bitter walk, but the most galling thing was realizing that I was the cliché.

I don't know when I made it home, and I don't remember collapsing into my bed. Between the anguish and the sangria, I was numb. I didn't care if I ever woke up. At some point I thought I heard Mama knock, but I didn't stir. I heard bits of household bustle outside my room, but paid no heed. I would have willingly died there of a broken heart, but (annoyingly) the most trivial things forced me up: a splitting headache, a raging thirst, and the call of nature. Grumbling at a body that had no sympathy for the agony of my soul, I stumbled out to take care of what I could. I heard voices in the kitchen, but thankfully nobody came to look in on me.

As I made my way back to the quiet darkness of my room, I saw a tray on the floor outside my door. It had a pitcher of fresh juice – which suddenly looked very appealing – a mug of cocoa, and some warm tortillas wrapped around brown sugar and cinnamon. Comfort from my youth – it had to be Mama. I took the tray inside and drained the juice right off. Then I sat on my bedside, gobbling the tortillas, sipping the cocoa, and drowning myself in self-pity. I wept shamelessly, grieving my loss and folly.

In the weeks that followed my family was far more gracious to me than I deserved after how I'd treated them. They never asked what had happened and I never told them, but I was moping about the house sighing, and wasn't seeing or talking about Liana any more. They could add things up. Rosalia dropped by from time to time, and she, too, had the grace to pretend that nothing had happened. We did school work, and it was certainly due to her help that I passed any classes that semester. She even got me to smile once or twice.

But I didn't want to smile. I had been jilted, betrayed. Now I knew firsthand what the poets and songwriters had written of.

One day I got out my guitar and began to play some mournful chords. The music seemed to express my pain and loss in a way mere words couldn't. I started taking long walks by myself, bringing my guitar so I could sit in groves or on lonely rocks and play sad tunes. I even tried coming up with some lyrics, but even in my blindest folly I never imagined myself a songwriter, so I mostly kept to music – all slow and morose melodies.

One day I was sitting by a fountain in the park, plucking at my guitar and relishing my loneliness, when I heard a flute behind me. I tried to ignore it and focus on my playing, but it continued. In fact, as I listened, it seemed that the flute music was following what I was playing on my guitar. Curious, I stopped playing – and shortly thereafter the flute stopped. I started again, and the flute soon began. The flutist was following me but not mimicking – the strains wove around my music, complementing and highlighting it. Amazed, I tried some more intricate chords. The flute followed effortlessly.

Driven by curiosity, I stopped abruptly and jumped to my feet. I walked around the fountain, determined to find this musician who could improvise so beautifully.

And that's how I met Julieta.

Julieta was not a towering beauty like Liana. Neither was she plain. She dressed simply and wore no makeup. What struck me most were her eyes – they were large and deep and soulful. When you spoke with her, she gazed at you with those eyes in a way that penetrated your depths, laying bare your deepest feelings and joining you to her in utter, unguarded honesty.

At least, that's what it felt like.

Julieta was a poetess and a musician, like her mother. Being about my age, I was surprised that I had never seen her in school. She explained that her mother disdained formal education, maintaining that it stifled the soul. She encouraged Julieta to learn from the wind and the birds and the flowers, to pour her heart out into the world so it could return to her laden with wisdom.

Julieta talked like that, but for some reason it didn't sound so odd when she was fixing you with that probing gaze.

Julieta had thought my chording "important," which was why she had played along. She thought she'd heard my heart singing, and had wanted me to know that it needn't sing alone. Amazed by her perception, I explained that I'd recently suffered a loss (even then I was reluctant to impart specifics), and that I was playing to assuage my grief. She put her hand on mine, gazed deeply into my eyes, and solemnly assured me that I would someday love again. Then she offered to play with me again if it would lighten my burden, for what was life if not an opportunity to help one another with our burdens?

So we played together all afternoon, which did help lift my mood. Julieta was very good on the flute, but also knew the guitar and oboe. She helped me rediscover my love of music, which had been buried for several years. By suppertime we were talking like old friends, and I walked her back to her mother's cottage. I returned home with a lighter heart than I'd had for weeks, which Mama and Papa appreciated.

I began to meet with Julieta regularly. We'd play our instruments, and sometimes she would sing, or read poetry she'd written. We talked about all manner of things – the nature of life, the meaning of love, the burden of pain, and whether people could ever truly know one another. Sometimes I had trouble following what she said, and I occasionally wondered if she wasn't making an awful lot of fuss out of nothing. But when she fixed me with those dark, soulful eyes and made some profound statement, it was hard not to take her seriously.

I can't deny that Julieta helped me get over Liana's rejection. After we'd been meeting for a while, I opened up to her about that painful incident. Julieta didn't laugh or scoff or lecture, but simply listened and nodded. The next day she read me a poem that she'd written, something about paying the tolls on the road to love. It was very meaningful.

Back home, it didn't take long for my parents to notice that I was once again away from home a fair amount. One day Papa saw me slipping out with my guitar, and asked where I was headed. I was reluctant to tell him, for my times with Julieta seemed intimate and sacrosanct. But then I realized that if I behaved like I was hiding something, my parents might get the wrong impression. So I told him about Julieta, how we met to play music and talk things over.

"Hmm," Papa said. "Sounds like a quieter girl than the last one."

"She is," I assured him.

"You know, Rosalia is a talented girl, too."

"Yes, Papa," I smiled.

"Any friend of yours is welcome here, of course," said Papa, ever gracious. "You should bring your friend around for dinner sometime, so we can get to know her."

"I'll ask her," I said, though the thought of Julieta at the family dinner table seemed – incongruous.

I'm not sure exactly when I realized I loved Julieta. It grew on me during the deep discussions and duets. I had come to understand that my passion for Liana had been no more than an adolescent infatuation, an obsession with superficial beauty and glamor. What I shared with Julieta was a profound fusion of two kindred souls, a union of hearts that beat together. She understood me as no one ever had or could. This was true love. This was what the poets had written of, as now I could truly understand.

It was hard to discuss it with her, because (as I was learning) discussing everything deeply makes it hard to isolate the truly deep topics. But, I reasoned, perhaps we didn't need to discuss anything. Part of being kindred souls that moved in harmony was that you just understood things about each other. So one day, as she lay with her head in my lap gazing up at the clouds, I leaned over and kissed her. She didn't seem surprised or offended, but just sighed deeply and stroked my arm. Words were unnecessary – we understood one other.

Our love was a melancholy affair, conducted in a twilight of purple and sepia and set to music in a minor key. We knew the world was full of pain and struggle, and life was probably hopeless, but at least we had one another. We took long walks and spent a lot of time sitting together gazing at sunsets or fields or the river. We'd sit at a café table for hours, sipping espresso and discussing philosophy. Sometimes we'd play our instruments, and always we'd meditate on solemn, serious things. At times I wondered if maybe a little more social activity might be enjoyable – certainly not the frantic pace that Liana had demanded, but perhaps an occasional dance – but then I reminded myself that our relationship was deep and serious, untinged by frivolity.

What we had was beautiful and precious, and the thought of admitting anyone else into the intimacy we shared seemed like the profanation of something sacred. But, steeped in antiquated social mores as I was, I couldn't help but consider proprieties from time to time. So, one evening when I remembered Papa's invitation, I hesitantly broached the possibility of her coming to dinner to meet my family.

Julieta looked puzzled. "Meet your family? Why?"

I was taken aback – I thought she understood why. "Well – when we're married, you'll have to meet them sooner or later."

"Married?" she asked, gazing at me with those deep eyes.

"Well, yes," I replied, confused. "I thought you'd – understood."

Julieta said nothing, but leaned her head back against my shoulder. Shortly thereafter I walked her home and thought no more of the incident.

It was a couple of days before we met again. I wanted to play for her some tunes I'd worked out, but she pulled out a poem she wanted to read me. It was about butterflies, or a butterfly, and how they were like the flowers of the air, rootless and free. There was a bit about how to capture one was to wound it and to keep it was to kill it. I knew that much – I remember trying to catch a big monarch for Mama, only to mutilate the poor thing in the process. When Julieta finished the poem, she fixed me with those sorrowful eyes.

"Now do you see?" she asked.

I was confused – was there something I was supposed to see? Maybe I needed to hear the poem again. "It was beautiful," I encouraged her.

For the first time I saw her eyes narrow and her lips tighten in what had to be frustration. "No, no! Me! That was about me!"

I was totally lost – Julieta was a butterfly? "Why don't you read it again?" I suggested.

"No!" she exclaimed, stuffing the poem back into her pack. "I won't read it again. I could read it a dozen times and you'd still be too dense to understand it!"

I was stunned. Anger and insults from my Julieta? But she continued. "I thought what we had was special! I thought I'd found someone who truly understood me! But no – it turns out you just want to pin me to a card and keep me under glass as a trophy to show your family!"

Now I was utterly bewildered. "My family? What does that – what are you talking about?"

"We were doing so well, and then you had to go ruin everything with your talk of marriage!"

"But – I thought girls always wanted to talk about marriage!"

Wrong thing to say.

Ten minutes of vehement tirade later, it was clear that not all girls wanted to talk about marriage – especially Julieta and her mother. It was also clear that Julieta had no intention of being any man's property, that I was betraying how petty and patriarchal I was by even thinking along those lines, and that she was very disappointed in me.

Another thing that was clear was that whatever relationship Julieta and I had had was in irretrievable tatters. After trying a few halting responses, I gave up and let her rant until she ran herself out. Then I nodded to her, slung my guitar on my back, and walked away.

This was becoming distressingly familiar.

As I walked home, I kept expecting to get hit by a shock like the one which I'd felt when Liana jilted me. I was a bit surprised when it didn't come. Sure, it stung, and I shed a few tears, but I didn't fall into blackness. Perhaps because shadow and melancholy were where Julieta and I had dwelt, having her cast me away was to be cast out of those twilight moods as well. I thought that since I'd just been rejected (again), I should be feeling something extreme, so I tried rage, indignation, and hurt, but none of them were genuine – it was like play acting. When I relaxed, what I felt was a sense of freedom and release. Perhaps the gloomy atmosphere in which Julieta dwelt hadn't been good for me.

When I got home, I affected an air of nonchalance, and if Mama was surprised to see me home so soon, she said nothing. I set my guitar in the corner of my bedroom and plunged into my schoolwork.

Mama and Papa were glad to see me around the house again, and made no comments about who I wasn't going off to see, though I'm sure they discussed it between themselves. For my part, I was glad to be rid of feminine entanglements. It felt like normal life was resuming again. I attended classes, helped Papa around the shop, and started seeing my old friends again, including Rosalia. It was odd, because when I dropped into the Torres's house, I got a rather frosty reception from Señora Torres, who had always been like an aunt to me. But Rosalia was as cheerful as always.

The seasons changed and the year changed and a new semester began – with more difficult classes, of course. I found that without social distractions, I could keep up with the schoolwork, and occasionally even enjoy it. I was particularly enjoying Government, because the professor was so engaging. I wasn't just frantically scribbling notes and trying to keep up, I was comprehending the material and considering the implications. One day the professor asked a question, and I shot up my hand to answer it – but he called on a *señorita* whose hand had gone up at the same time. I didn't remember seeing her before, but she answered in a clear, confident voice – not only giving the same answer I'd had ready, but making comments very similar to what I'd been planning to make. Rather than being upset, I was delighted! It was good to see a young woman with such an alert, dynamic mind.

On the way out of class, I made my way over to her and introduced myself. I told her how impressed I'd been with her answer, and how much I loved the class. She seemed a little wary at first, but when I asked her to the café to discuss the day's assignments, she agreed.

That's how I met Valeria.

I hadn't seen her before because she'd just moved to town to continue her studies. She wanted to go all the way through college, and possibly on to graduate school. She was interested in the same things I was, and soon we were talking and laughing like old friends. She wasn't a stunning beauty like Liana – her features were a little heavy, and her looks weren't helped by her big black-rimmed glasses that kept sliding down her nose. But after an hour's discussion, you didn't notice Valeria's looks – what was beautiful about her was her intellect.

We met before classes the next day, and stayed on campus to go over our assignments. Valeria was a better listener and note-taker than I, so I picked up a lot from her. Soon we were meeting regularly to study, and when we weren't studying, we were talking of other topics of interest. I was thrilled, for I'd never been much for intellectual discussions, and found them quite stimulating. Valeria was full of new ideas and exciting concepts, and seemed delighted to talk about them over coffee while I sat and listened.

One evening over supper, Mama dropped a broad hint about not seeing me around home so much anymore. I enthusiastically explained how I'd met Valeria and how interesting and intellectual she was. I thought my parents would be excited that I'd found someone to help me with my studies, but they seemed tepid.

"That's nice, dear," Mama said. "You must bring her to supper some time."

Papa said nothing, but I could have sworn I saw him roll his eyes.

About a week later, when Valeria and I were sitting over coffee and she was expounding on some ideas she had about economics, I did something impetuous. I was so excited to be with her, and my mind was so full of bright new ideas, that on impulse I leaned across the table and kissed her mid-sentence. Of course, that stopped her speaking, but when I drew back she was looking at me with wide, startled eyes.

"No – nobody has ever done that to me before," she whispered.

"Well," I shrugged, a bit startled at myself for doing it. "Their loss."

"Could you," she asked shyly, "do it again?"

My love for Valeria was a strong, challenging, intellectual affair. I saw now that my earlier "loves" had been shallow and immature, based on nothing more than bedazzlement with appearance or emotional need. I realized that a man needs more than an arm decoration or a sympathetic ear. He needs a mental equal, someone with whom he can share thoughts and exchange ideas. Some men may want insipid, stupid wives, but not I. I loved being challenged and stimulated by the discussions I had with Valeria.

Valeria also seemed to appreciate my company, though it seemed for more reasons than just conversation. I didn't ask outright, but I guessed that she hadn't had much masculine attention in her past. She was shy, and seemed inept at the social graces, but she loved it when I'd pick her up or pay for dinner. She'd be thankful almost to embarrassment at even the simplest courtesies. I appreciated her appreciation – it was a welcome change from my recent experiences with women. Her kissing was also improving.

Mama and Papa noticed that my studies were doing better, and nodded when I credited Valeria's help. But, just like clockwork, Mama didn't miss her chance to drop a reminder.

"You know, Rosalia is a smart girl, too," she mentioned one evening after supper.

"I know she is, Mama," I replied, kissing her cheek. "I can't count the number of times Rosalia has helped me with my schoolwork."

"Just so you remember," Mama said.

Just a few days earlier, Valeria and I had been discussing how in certain circumstances passive resistance could be much more effective than active confrontation.

As Valeria and I spent more time together, I began to seriously think about marriage in a way I hadn't with Julieta and certainly hadn't with Liana. I considered spending my life with Valeria and pondered the practical aspects of being married. I knew I'd have to talk to Papa about working more in the shop, and I'd have to decide where to draw the line on my education.

But before I let my fancy wander too far, I knew I'd have to propose to Valeria. I was fairly confident of her affections, but one thing recent experience had taught me was not to assume anything. That same experience made me a bit nervous about broaching the topic, but one evening I pulled my courage together as we sat outside our favorite café. I decided to ease into the topic, approaching it by the path most familiar to us: discussion.

"So, my dear," I asked. "Do you think it's time to begin discussing our life together?"

Valeria looked up from her espresso with a guarded look in her eyes. "'Life together'?" she asked.

"You know – marriage," I replied, then quickly qualified myself. "Nothing immediate, of course. Plenty of time to talk things over. But I didn't want to be making any one-sided assumptions about our relationship."

"No," Valeria replied, biting her lip and staring at the table. "You wouldn't want to be doing that." She was quiet for a while and then drew a deep breath. "You're right, of course – we should be talking about our life together, if only for – we should be discussing it." She drew another breath and then looked at me with a strange expression in her eyes. "I'm sorry, Ramón, this has taken me quite by surprise. Can you give me a little time to think?"

"Ah – sure," I stammered, surprised in turn. Time to think I could understand, but why the topic should surprise her was beyond me.

"Can we meet here for lunch tomorrow? I should be more composed by then."

Composed? "Um...sure," I replied, a model of eloquence. "Lunch tomorrow."

I felt a strange foreboding as I waited at the café the next day. My experience with girls returning to discuss things hadn't been good, and Valeria's behavior had been strange. I was certain I wouldn't be getting a poem about a butterfly, but I had no idea what I would be getting.

I found out when I saw Valeria striding across the plaza toward me. I rose and held her chair, but she didn't sit down. Instead she walked up and looked at me with red, puffy eyes.

"I'm sorry, Ramón," she said in a choked voice as she handed me an envelope. Then she turned and strode away with a determined pace and without a backward glance.

I stared at her, then at the envelope, then back at her. My heart sank. Whatever was in the envelope, early indications weren't promising. Bracing myself, I opened it and scanned the short letter. It read:

Dear Ramón,

I apologize for leading you on and toying with you. I have enjoyed our time together – so much that I lost sight of my primary goal. I hope to make my mark in the world, to make a difference. I intend to be at least a full professor at a university, and possibly hold elected office someday. I intend my schooling here to be only the first rungs of a very tall ladder that will take much time, determination, and effort to climb.

Your proposal put me between the sword and the wall. I do care for you deeply. You are happy here, and I am glad for you. I have been happy with you, but I could never be satisfied as the wife of a provincial shopkeeper. I have set my sights higher than that.

You are an honest and honorable man, which I like about you. You are much more honest than I, for had I been honest I would have forced myself to acknowledge that of course your goal was marriage. I knew all along that my goals were incompatible with that, but I enjoyed your company too much, and I was lonely. In my selfishness and cruelty, I refused to face the inevitable, pretending that one more day wouldn't matter. I acted as if the day would never come when your intentions would collide with my dreams, for I knew which would be shattered.

But that day has come, and I am exposed for the selfish manipulator I have been. I cannot be your wife, I could never have been your wife, and I am sorry I led you to believe I could.

I have sat awake all night lamenting my weakness and trying to think of a way to explain all this to you. This is the best I can do. Goodbye, Ramón. I wish you well. You will find a woman to love and marry. I am not that woman.

Tears blurred the final lines of the letter, and I crumpled it in my hand as I struggled to control myself. My insides were collapsing into cold blackness. Part of me wanted to scream and stamp, but my lips and limbs felt leaden.

Was I that poor a prospect? Would no woman ever consider me suitable for marriage? Or was I just choosing the wrong ones? I was too insignificant for Liana, too domineering for

Julieta, and now too parochial for Valeria. Was there nobody for whom I was suitable?

I wandered the streets for some time, alternatively grinding my teeth at women and blinking back hot tears for myself. Rejected by three women within a year – maybe I was no good. Maybe I should just resign myself to – what?

I looked up and found myself by the church. I never thought much about church – I went with Mama and Papa, of course, but otherwise never came except on holidays. But the sun was approaching its hottest, and I knew it would be cooler inside. So I slipped in a side door and found myself in quiet dimness. The racks of votives glowed and flickered around the statues, but there were no lights on, and the place looked empty. I threw myself in a pew and buried my head in my hands, sinking into a black depression. It felt like my heart lay in pieces at the bottom of my stomach.

I sprawled back in the pew and groaned. I dreaded going home. Of course, Mama and Papa would know something had happened – again. But they would be too polite to say anything, or even glance significantly at each other, at least when I was around. They would go about their normal routines with exaggerated indifference, as if nothing had changed. Their nonchalance would speak volumes: that none of this had been their idea, that they'd suggested something different from the outset.

Perhaps they were right.

I opened my eyes and found I was sitting right before the statue of St. Joseph. There weren't as many votives around him as there were at the feet of St. Mary in the grotto on the other side of the church, but there were enough to bathe him in mottled, flickering light. He stood there, holding his lilies and carpenter's square, looking down at me with a paternal half smile. I'd never noticed how much he looked like Papa. It was the most sympathetic smile I'd seen in a long time.

"¡*San Jose!*" I cried. "Why does everything have to be so difficult?"

I leaned back and sighed, obviously not expecting an answer. Even now I'm not sure whether I got one – I just know a crystal-clear thought flitted into my head, seemingly out of nowhere.

It's not so bad, you know. I got told whom to marry, and look how that turned out.

I blinked in surprise and looked up at the statue. There he stood in the flickering candlelight with his benevolent half-smile, unmoving, but the thought was as clear as if he had spoken. Silly though it was, I cocked my head sideways to squint at his face, and strained to listen, just to be sure. I think it was because of that that I heard the rustle of fabric, and caught the shadow of movement out of the corner of my eye. But when I looked, there was nothing but the votives glowing at St. Mary's feet. Surely it was my imagination that made the flames waver as if someone had just passed by them.

"Is anyone there?" I called timidly. There was no answer, but I rose to investigate. Walking over to the grotto, I found it empty – but at the feet of St. Mary's statue lay a single white rose.

The trudge homeward seemed endless. I slammed the door heavily and hung my hat on the hook without calling a hello to Mama. She seemed to have guests in the kitchen, for I heard voices from that direction, but she must have heard me come in because she came bustling out, wiping her hands on a towel, concern etched about her eyes.

"My boy, my boy," she cried. "How are you? Are you all right?"

I guessed that, somehow, Mama already knew that I'd suffered another rejection, so I abandoned the idea of pretending nothing had happened. I hugged her and gave her a kiss. "I've been better, Mama, but I'll be all right."

"Come in, come in," she urged me toward the kitchen. "Let me fix you something to cheer you up."

I started to object that I didn't want to intrude upon her and her guest, but when we got to the kitchen there was nobody there. But there was a mug of fresh cocoa and a plate of warm cinnamon sugar tortillas.

"Oh, Mama," I sighed, "you're the best."

"But I –" she began, then smiled. "Thank you."

I took the cocoa and tortillas to my room. I ate them, and thought, and cried a bit more, and came to my decision. When dinnertime came, we gathered as if nothing had happened, but afterward I sought out Papa in his chair on the patio.

"All right, Papa," I said. "You can talk to Señor Torres. I'm willing to marry Rosalia, if you think it's a good idea – and if she'll have me."

Papa grinned. "A wise choice, son."

The months that followed were something of a blur. The parents took over all the wedding arrangements while I buried myself in my studies, trying to bind up my bruised heart and finish my semester well. I caught glimpses of Valeria in the few classes we had together, but she tended to slip in late and sit in the back, and then duck out early so I didn't see her. It didn't matter – even when I saw her briefly across campus or along a walkway, I felt nothing good or ill. My feelings were dead. Even the prospect of the wedding or my looming married state aroused neither fear nor excitement. My outlook had not changed from the day Valeria had handed me that letter. The rest of my life stretched before me as a drab, featureless terrain across which I was doomed to trudge.

Rosalia seemed to fit into this perfectly: she'd do. The thought of her as my wife didn't disappoint me, but neither did it excite me. She was who my parents had chosen, and I'd accept that, like I accepted the plain tortillas Mama served with dinner. Rosalia would do, I assured myself. She certainly couldn't be worse than the choices I made when left to myself.

I didn't see much of Rosalia during that time – apparently there was some old superstition about it being unlucky for the bride and groom to see too much of one another in the time leading up to the wedding. We did see each other occasionally, usually at dinner parties hosted by our parents, at which we were seated together like matched centerpieces and made much of. It was more like playing roles than being old friends, much less an affianced couple. But after one of these Rosalia caught me in the kitchen, grabbing my wrist and looking at me keenly.

"Ramón, was this your idea, or your parents?" she asked.

"Theirs, originally," I replied, "but in time I warmed to it – that is, if you'll have me."

She gave me a curious, piercing look. For a moment I feared that she'd say she wouldn't, but then she gave her familiar dimpling smile and patted my cheek.

"I'll have you."

Shortly thereafter the wedding date was announced, and the weeks ground on toward it. The semester ended, and I heard through the grapevine that Valeria had transferred to some university. The news had no effect on me – that chapter of my life was closed. Papa gave me more hours and responsibility at the shop, since I would soon need the earnings. The dinners and fiestas became more common, with Rosalia and me the toast of them all. The wedding gifts began to pour in, the most generous from Rosalia's parents: a year's rent of a small cottage on the edge of town. Rosalia and I would have our own home in which to begin our life together.

Finally, the day arrived. As Mama fussed about my *guayabera*, I felt not so much excitement as resignation. I was bustled to the church, where I allowed myself to be pushed and placed and instructed where I should go. Eventually I found myself standing at the front of the church with the Padre, having no clear idea of how I'd gotten there. I looked out at the pews full of people – about half the town, for my parents and the Torres' had many friends – and felt I was looking upon a crowd of strangers who had little to do with me. I was only anxious to get the ceremony over with.

Then I saw Rosalia, coming down the aisle on her father's arm. Her dress and mantilla were classic and very beautiful, but her face was what caught my attention. It was the same old Rosalia, with her eyes a little too squinty and her mouth a little too wide, the Rosalia of childhood lizard hunts and river bank mud, but there was something more. I felt like I was seeing her for the first time. I saw what the poets had meant when they spoke about how a face could glow. Part of my heart nudged me, suggesting that I might be able to do more than just settle for Rosalia.

I remember only brief images of the ceremony or the fiesta that followed. Rosalia's hand in mine, firm and familiar. Her shy, dimpled smile as she recited her vows. Her graceful form walking back from the traditional placing of the rose at the Virgin's feet. The padre blessing us and turning us to face our family and friends, and their cheering. The procession to the reception site, the music, and the colors. Seemingly hundreds of faces, most of whom I barely knew, wishing us joy and happiness. Neither Rosalia nor I were very hungry, but we smiled and returned all the toasts and danced the dances and leaned on one another. At last we were bundled into the carriage my godparents had rented, which took us to our cottage.

I was hoping that the bustle of unloading our scant luggage would provide a delay to cover my nervousness, but I was beaten to it by the carriage driver. He gave me a wink and a grin, and nodded toward the doorway, reminding me of my duties. Of course! I rushed to the carriage side, helped Rosalia down, and carried her over the threshold. After the expectable fumbling coming through the door, I brought her into the little living room and set her in the middle of our new home. We stood there shyly looking at almost anything but one another, hearing the carriage driver bundle our suitcases through the back door. Then it closed, and shortly thereafter the horses drove away. We were well and truly alone with each other.

My mouth was dry, but Rosalia reached up to pat my cheek and swept off, her gown rustling. I didn't know where she'd gone, and didn't care. I was nearly in a panic. I sat down on the edge of the loveseat. My palms were sweating and my heart was pounding so badly that I could hear the blood in my ears. Of course, I knew what was supposed to happen on a wedding night

– who didn't know that? But now that it came to it, I was terrified. And with Rosalia! What if I disappointed her? What if I was a clumsy fool? I wrung my hands – it wasn't like I could suggest we go out for coffee!

A door closed, and in another rustle of fabric Rosalia stood by me again. She'd changed into a sweeping white thing that looked like a dress but was obviously a nightgown. It was beautiful, all layers of gauzy fabric, but Rosalia was even more so. She'd let her hair down, and it cascaded around her shoulders in rich black curls. The gown was perfect – alluring but not racy, and utterly feminine. Her dark eyes were glowing but guarded – she, too, was unsure of the situation.

She sat down on the sofa beside me, and we were silent for a tense minute. Over her shoulder stood the bedroom door. She was watching her hands in her lap, occasionally shooting me a timid glance. Finally, I cleared my throat and took the chance.

"Ah – are you nervous?" I asked.

"A little," she admitted with a shy grin that relaxed into a tentative smile. "All right – a lot."

I relaxed a bit. "Me, too," I assured her. We both chuckled.

"But…I'm curious, too," she continued boldly. I grinned back.

"So am I, but –" I stumbled for words as I looked into her face. Something strengthened inside me, and I took her hand. "Look, Rosalia, we've only been husband and wife for a few hours, but we've been friends for years, haven't we?"

She smiled her familiar smile. "Yes, we have."

"And as friends, we learned how not to hurt each other, right?"

Her smile broadened and she cupped my face in her hands. "You're right, we did."

"Then, let's just be careful not to hurt each other now."

And we didn't.

The next morning, I awoke alone in an empty bed, but heard clattering in the kitchen. I stumbled out to find Rosalia cheerfully cooking breakfast.

"Ah, good – I was just about to come wake you," she said. "Don't count on all this every morning, for your mama has told me you know how to fix your own meals, but I figured we'd start out easy. Sit!" She waved a spatula at the table, where there were two places set and glasses of fresh juice. Whatever she was cooking smelled wonderful.

"Something to get you started," she said, placing a mug of cocoa and a plate of hot tortillas before me. I gasped with pleasure as the aroma of cinnamon wafted up from them.

"Rosalia!" I exclaimed. "My mama used to make me cocoa and cinnamon tortillas at home!"

"Why, yes," Rosalia replied with a curious smile. "So she did. Eat up – your eggs are almost ready."

Settling into our tiny cottage wasn't difficult, since neither of us had many things. But it did require some organizing, which included sorting through our boxes of books – by far our most abundant possession – and shelving them in some semblance of order. I was attending to this one afternoon when I noticed we had two copies of Virgil's *Aeneid*. One was familiar, for I'd gotten it for my Classics class, but I didn't recognize the other.

"Honey," I called, "is this volume yours?"

Rosalia wandered in and took the book from me. "Yes, it is," she confirmed. "I took Classics from Professor Arroyo, and started with that translation." She pointed to my volume. "But after a week, he recommended I try this one. He said it was more difficult, but that it better preserved the cadence of the original Latin. So I traded in my first volume, and you know what? He was right."

I stared at my wife in surprise. I'd had no idea she loved the Classics! We spent the evening discussing what we'd learned, and all our favorite myths.

Shortly thereafter, while Rosalia was off on an errand and I was still sorting through our books, I dropped one of her volumes of poetry. Out of it fell a folded piece of paper. I recognized Rosalia's compact script, and saw that it was a poem she'd written. Ironically, the poem was about a butterfly, but it was very different from the last butterfly poem I'd heard. It started off as a reflection on a butterfly she'd found dead on the grass, and how she'd seen that butterfly alive earlier in the spring. It had its mournful parts that meditated on why beauty had to die, but there was also joy and wonder that beauty should exist at all, and hope that beauty would always last. I was impressed.

I fetched my guitar and tried a few chords. Rosalia's simple verses fit into a tune I had floating around my head, so I toyed about with putting them together. By the time she returned, I had the rudiments of a song roughed out. She was a little embarrassed that I'd found her poem, but was glad I'd liked it and was interested in my composition. She suggested a few wording changes to make it scan more smoothly, and I made some changes to the music, and when we were done, we had a passable song. I played, and Rosalia sang in a nicely controlled alto. I hadn't known she could sing so beautifully.

"It was Mama," she explained. "She'd been professionally trained. Though I lacked the talent, she insisted that if I was going to be singing about the house, at least I was going to do it well. So she taught me."

I was impressed – I'd never known that Señora Torres was that accomplished a singer.

A few nights later we were sitting in the living room. Rosalia was crocheting while I sat at her feet reading. I was tiring of my book, so I pulled together the courage to pose the question my ego had been nagging me to ask.

"So," I said, affecting nonchalance, "While I was making a total fool of myself running about after every girl in town, were you patiently waiting at home for the day I'd come to my senses?"

"Honestly, Ramón?" she looked up at me over her hook. "No, I wasn't."

That took me aback. "No?" I asked as casually as I could.

"No. Truthfully, I wasn't all that keen on marrying you. Nothing against you, obviously, but I saw you as you saw me – a good friend, but not spouse material."

"Oh," I said, somewhat deflated. "Well – I'm glad you didn't miss me."

"I missed you somewhat," she explained. "Mostly our chats and fun times as friends. But I didn't lack for company – Lucio Mendoza came around quite a bit, and a few others."

I was shocked, and looked at her sharply. "Mendoza! That stuffed shirt! What did he want?"

"Why, time with me, of course," Rosalia said with slightly raised eyebrows. "And I know he's full of himself, but he's not too bad once you get to know him. Kind of lonely, actually."

"Well, it's good to know you had someone to comfort you in my absence," I said with more petulance than I'd intended. Rosalia gave a silvery laugh and rapped me on my head with her wedding ring. "Hey, silly, who got me in the end? As I said, I missed our friendship, and you were on my mind – I was worried for you."

"Worried?"

"Worried. I may have been unsure about marrying you myself, but I could see at a glance that those other girls were all wrong. Especially that prima donna, but the drama queen and the career girl weren't much better."

"You saw them more clearly than I did," I admitted.

"Obviously," Rosalia said archly. "I was primarily worried that you'd do something foolish, something you'd always regret. I said quite a few novenas for you. Mama was ready to write you off, and sometimes I came close, especially when you seemed to be changing girlfriends as often as you changed shirts. It was really Papa who counseled patience. He said you came from a good family, so we knew how you'd been raised. He was sure that these were just youthful flings, and that you'd come to your senses sooner or later. And you did."

"Well," I said, bemused by this torrent of unexpected intelligence. "I'm glad you waited for me to come around."

"Oh?" asked Rosalia, tucking her hook into her yarn and giving me a taunting smile. "How glad?"

So I showed her.

It wasn't long afterward that Rosalia and I walked up the street to meet my Mama and Papa at the Torres' house. Seated in the living room with both sets of parents, we delivered the joyous news. As we expected, the place exploded in cries and laughter. The mothers swept Rosalia away to talk womanly things, while Papa and Señor Torres shook my hand and grinned and deluged me with fatherly advice. Glancing across the room, I caught sight of my bride, all rich curls and shining eyes. Looking back at me, she gave me a smile that lit up the room.

My beautiful Rosalia, I thought. Sometimes it's wise to listen to those who know us best.

Many readers appreciated how my fictional account of the Magi in From Afar *brought those Scriptural characters to life, and asked for more. Here you go.*

Zakkai

- Yoses -

Zakkai flinched a bit as Yoses upended his sack, creating a small cloud as the little leather purses tumbling out disturbed the dust on the table. This was unusual, Zakkai thought. Normally his agents set their sacks on the ground and drew the purses out as they were asked for. He waved the dust aside as Yoses sat down across from him.

"Well, then, let's get to it, shall we?" Zakkai said cheerily, trying to pep up the unusually somber Yoses. "First, the South Yarden District." He picked up the applicable scroll and his stylus. "Two hundred denarii."

"That's these two," Yoses replied, handing over two purses for Zakkai to place on the scales.

And so it went, down through the list of districts for which Yoses was responsible, the assigned collection amount and the filled purses containing the collected taxes. Zakkai carefully recorded the weights and counts, for his supervisor was sure to audit him. Finally, the last bag was noted and tucked away, and Zakkai turned to his collection agent with a knowing smile.

"So," he asked. "How's this month's spillage?"

"No spillage," Yoses replied, holding up the empty sack at his feet and shaking it. "Everything I collected, you have."

"But...are you certain?" Zakkai asked. This was usually the best part of the monthly accounting, when Yoses would dip into the sack on the ground and pull out some of the "spillage" from his collections to share with his boss. It was expected. It was how things went.

"Quite certain," Yoses assured him.

"But what will I say to Archelus? He'll be expecting spillage from me!" Archelus was Zakkai's genial but demanding immediate superior.

"Tell him there was no spillage this month, nor will there be next month," Yoses said, spreading his hands.

"No spillage? Come on, Yoses!" Zakkai said with some sharpness. This wasn't how things were played at all!

"Look, Zakkai, you assigned me a collection quota," Yoses replied, pulling out a small scroll and waving it before Zakkai. "I have fulfilled it to the drachma. Do you have any complaints or charges against me?"

"Well...no, of course not. You're one of my most diligent collection agents," Zakkai blustered.

"Thank you," Yoses said, standing. "Since I have done my job, I'd appreciate my wages."

"Of course, of course," Zakkai replied, and busied himself counting out the proper number of denarii and recording the disbursement. "Here you go, and here's next month's quota." He handed Yoses the coins and another small scroll.

"Thanks, boss. See you next month."

"Certainly. Send Yudah in, will you?"

Shortly thereafter Yudah, his second collection agent, came into Zakkai's office. Rather than placing his sack beside his chair, Yudah emptied it onto the table just like Yoses had, dropping the empty sack to the ground.

"Oh, no," Zakkai said with foreboding. "Not you, too!"

- Yochanan -

"I think my collection agents might be holding out on me," Zakkai grumbled into his cup.

"Oh? All of them?" asked Philopater. They were sitting on Philopater's rooftop terrace, the latticed screen blocking the westering sun, sipping wine and waiting for the evening breezes to start flowing down the hills to cool the muggy valley. Philopater was one of the few citizens of Yericho with whom Zakkai could talk casually, and almost his only friend. Philopater was a merchant, and even wealthier than Zakkai. He, too, had Jewish roots, and his Hebrew name was Sh'mon, though he hardly ever used it. Like many who had taken the "Greek path," Philopater dealt almost exclusively with Gentiles, and thus was shunned by pious Jews. Of course, Zakkai was even worse, as one who worked for the hated *publicani*, firms that secured the contracts to collect the taxes from the provinces of Rome's far-flung empire. This gave the two men a bond as fellow outcasts sharing a common ostracism, and they met often to commiserate about their struggles.

"No, not all, just two – but they're my most reliable men," Zakkai replied.

"Then what makes you think they're holding out?" Philopater asked, so Zakkai told him how they'd both come in that month with no spillage to share.

"Well, maybe they are holding out," Philopater admitted. "Or maybe they've been down listening to Yochanan."

"Yochanan? Who's Yochanan?"

"They call him the Immerser. He's a revivalist of the primitive stripe. Apparently, he's a Levite, but he doesn't go near the Temple. He's been living in the Perean wilderness, but of late has been coming down to the river to preach and call people back to God."

"Oh," Zakkai muttered, taking another drink. "One of those."

"I don't know," Philopater replied cautiously. "This one sounds different than the run-of-the-mill rabble rouser, or at least so I've heard. He started up north, in Herod's territory, and apparently some of the soldiers came down to hear him. One of them asked him how they could be good law-followers, and do you know what he said?"

"Let me guess – stop serving the pagan overlords and use your weapons to drive the godless from the Holy Land?" Zakkai ventured.

"No, and that's the odd thing. He told them not to bully or extort, and to be content with their pay."

"Really?" Zakkai asked in surprise. "And he knew they were Herod's soldiers?"

"They were wearing his livery," Philopater replied. "Anyway, this Yochanan has been working his way up and down the Yarden, preaching to any who come out to him."

"Yeah, that's always the way with these religious nut cases," Zakkai said. "You have to go to them, they never come to you. Why do they call him the Immerser?"

"He calls for everyone to have a *t'vilah* to profess the changing of their heart and their resolution to follow *Torah*, though he uses the river instead of a *m'kveh*."

"That sounds inconvenient, getting all wet in that muddy water. He can't be very popular."

"I don't know. I've heard that he's drawing crowds so large that the *P'rushim* are getting nervous about him – you know how they hate it when people start listening to anyone but them," Philopater said.

"That's for sure," Zakkai replied. "And you think my agents might have gone to listen to this teacher?"

"Perhaps. He's come south, and is preaching down by the Twelve Stones these days. Your agents might have gone down to hear him."

"Hmm," grunted Zakkai. Be content with your pay, eh? That had a familiar ring to it. What else was this Yochanan saying? Zakkai drained his cup and stood. "Well, thank you for the wine, my friend. I'd best be going before the streets get too dark."

"Yes, you wouldn't want to be caught out, would you?" Philopater said.

"My place next time – I just got a new shipment of Arabian figs I'd like you to try."

"Looking forward to it!" Philopater called.

Zakkai bustled through the dusky streets. It was only a quarter mile to his home, but Philopater was right, he wouldn't want to be caught in a darkened street for a number of reasons. Other pedestrians passed him, but never looked at or greeted him. That was how faithful Jews treated the likes of Zakkai – by averting their eyes, not seeing, not acknowledging. He was a shame and a disgrace, a blot on the name of Israel. He was unseen, invisible – unless, of course, if night fell with him alone in the street. In that case, some faithful Israelites might just notice him long enough to deal harshly with the sellout, the betrayer, the craven collaborator who stole their livelihood to hand it over to the pagan occupiers – always, of course, keeping a little spillage for himself.

But nothing happened this evening, and Zakkai reached his gate without incident.

Two days later Zakkai had his burro saddled, donned his less extravagant clothes, and headed out the city gate toward the river. He didn't tell anyone in his household where he was going, not even his wife, and nobody pressed him. His work routinely took him on discreet errands here or there.

But his work had never taken him on an errand like this.

There was no mistaking the road Zakkai had to follow. For one thing, there was only one main road from Yericho down to the Yarden River crossing, and for another, there was a steady stream of people going down the road, a stream that grew as other paths joined it. Zakkai had never seen this much traffic, not even during the Holy Days when the roads were thick with pilgrims heading up to Yerushalem. But this crowd was mostly locals heading down from Yericho toward the river – Zakkai could tell by the way they studiously ignored him.

It was easy to tell where Yochanan was from the crowd along the river. Normally people didn't linger long on the banks because of the smell and the bugs, but as Zakkai descended the last slope he could see a crowd gathered in a semicircle along the water's edge, attending to some figures in the water. He tied his burro to a bush and worked his way into the crowd to get closer.

Zakkai could tell that news of his identity had gone before him, from the half-glances in his direction followed by the concerted efforts to hinder his progress and occlude his view. The occluding wasn't difficult because Zakkai was short even for a Jew, and Jews were not tall people. But he hadn't gotten where he was by acquiescing, so he pushed and nudged and elbowed (and got elbowed in return) until he was near the front of the crowd, close enough to see the river.

Some people were coming up out of the water, most of them dripping wet. One of them looked more tattered than usual, and Zakkai guessed that this was the famous Yochanan. He didn't look very impressive – almost as short as Zakkai, hair and beard unkempt, clad in what looked like a cast-off skin of some sort, and using a rope for a belt. He'd apparently just given some of his hearers one of the immersions he was famous for. He walked to a pile of large rocks on the bank and stood beside it, scanning the crowd that had gathered in the morning air.

Zakkai could see why Yochanan had chosen this place to preach, for the attraction of that pile of stones was clear. According to legend, it was made up of stones taken from the bed of the Yarden, brought up and piled here on the shore by the Twelve Tribes on the occasion of their crossing the Yarden while the Ark was placed in the middle, holding back the river's waters. Y'shua had been their leader then, and their next stop had been pagan stronghold Yericho, whose high walls threatened the Israelite march into the Promised Land. Zakkai knew the story as well as any other Israelite, though he doubted that the rocks in that pile were the very ones handled by the followers of Y'shua. Twelve hundred years was a long time for any such memorial to stand. But the symbolic significance was important, and Yochanan made good use of it.

"So, it's a kingdom you want, is it?" Yochanan asked the crowd. "A kingdom like your ancestors had, and a leader like Y'shua to lead you, is that what you want? Someone to take you up to Yericho and drive out the heathens, then down to Hebron, then across the Judean plains, and ultimately to Yerushalem to cleanse the Holy City? Is that what you hope for?"

A modest cheer rose from the crowd, and someone called, "Drive the pagans from the Holy Land!" That kind of zealotry could be found anywhere Jews gathered these days. Zakkai began to feel a little nervous.

"Ah, yes," Yochanan warmed to his message. "How many of you look back on those days, and wish you could have been there? 'If I could have stood at Horeb and been sprinkled with the blood of the Covenant! If I could have seen the face of Moishe glowing, and tasted the manna! If I could have walked dry-shod across the Yarden, right past the Ark, and seen the stones piled up! If only I could have been there!'" As he recited this fantasy, Yochanan's voice took on the rhythmic sing-song style used by cantors, and Zakkai guessed that the teacher was reading the hearts of many in the crowd.

"But let me remind you," Yochanan's voice turned harsh, and he swept the crowd with a fiery gaze. "That the Israelites who piled up these stones weren't the ones who stood at Horeb, or heard the law, or saw the face of Moishe glow, or walked through the Red Sea. Those Israelites, that favored generation, died in the desert, all but two of them. And why did they die there, forbidden to enter the Holy Land? Because of their rebellious hearts, that's why! They never came into their kingdom, the inheritance promised to Avraham, Yitzchak, and Yakob, because they rebelled! Their names and bloodlines were Israelite, but their hearts were Egyptian!" Yochanan paused, letting this thunderous denunciation hang in the air.

"And hasn't that been our sorry history?" Yochanan continued after a moment. "We boast of our pedigree, and diligently track which tribe we come from, and trace our lineage back to Avraham, but our hearts are in Egypt – or Babylon, or Greece, or Rome. When *Hashem* looks upon us, He sees not our garb or our houses or our genealogies, but our hearts. Followers of Moishe? Rubbish. Children of Avraham? Pah! *Hashem* can raise up children for Avraham from stones like these!" He slapped the pile of great rocks. "The purity of your bloodline means nothing if your heart is in Egypt!

"You want a kingdom? One is coming; in fact, it's right at the door! The citizens of this kingdom will be those with the hearts of true Israelites. Its King will know who his subjects are. Do you want that King to come? Do you want to see His reign? Then get busy preparing His kingdom. Turn your hearts from Egypt and Babylon and Rome, and resolve to be true Israelites. Wash away your worldly uncleanness, as *Hashem* intended those who crossed this river to have done. This is what I proclaim, and this is what I offer."

"But what is the *Torah* of this Kingdom? How can we prepare for it?" a voice called from the crowd.

"Have an Israelite heart, not an Egyptian one," Yochanan answered clearly. "Is your brother without a cloak while your second-best one hangs on a hook by your door? Give it to him. Is the family next door subsisting on scraps while you have seconds at dinner? Feed them. That is the heart of a true Israelite!"

This talk was novel to Zakkai, but encouraging. This rabbi did not propose an endless list of niggling laws to obey, nor dwell upon the ethnic purity of the Jews, but proposed a different sort of living. Hope rose in his heart, lending him boldness. "And what of tax collectors?" he called out. "What should they do?"

The crowd gave a quiet gasp, and those around Zakkai drew back a little to distance themselves from this embarrassment. Here was a test of Yochanan's ideals – could a tax collector have the heart of an Israelite?

Yochanan did not flinch, instead looking right at Zakkai with those burning eyes. "Collect your quota and no more. Deal honestly with all."

This evoked no small amount of murmuring among the crowd, and many dark looks, most directed at Zakkai but quite a few aimed at Yochanan. Here was this supposed man of God, speaking of Israelite hearts yet seeming to sanction the systematic plundering of the Holy Land to enrich the conqueror. Zakkai saw a cluster of *P'rushim* off to one side, with their long brown robes and tassels and staffs, muttering among themselves. But the rabbi looked at them all soberly, while Zakkai fidgeted and bobbed his head.

"Thank you, rabbi, thank you," Zakkai said, backing toward the crowd. He never liked having that many eyes upon him.

"I invite you to come and have your hearts washed," Yochanan pitched his voice so the whole crowd could hear. "Wash away the filth of Egypt, of Babylon, of Rome. Restore true Israelite hearts in preparation for a true Israelite King. You are all welcome." Yochanan turned his penetrating gaze directly on Zakkai. "Every one of you."

Zakkai was shocked. He had come simply to investigate, and here the prophet was inviting him personally. But – to go down for a *t'vilah*, as if he were a proper Jew? He shook his head slightly. No, no. Yochanan watched Zakkai expectantly, saying nothing but making a small inviting gesture with his outstretched hand. No, no, Zakkai thought. Not him, not here, not now. The morning sun was getting warm and he needed to find some shade. He needed to get back to his burro before someone made off with her. He needed to go home and think this over. Maybe tomorrow, or the next day, but not today. No, no.

Zakkai could see the prophet's *talmidim* working the edge of the crowd, ushering those who were stepping forward down toward the river bank. But Yochanan himself stood still, transfixing Zakkai with those dark eyes, even as Zakkai kept backing away, muttering to himself and shaking his head. Only when Zakkai reached the crowd and let it close in around him did Yochanan finally turned away with a small sigh. Once through the crowd, Zakkai turned and fled to his burro, and the safety of his house.

Back within his walls, Zakkai tried to put the morning's events behind him. He had accounts to cast and people to visit. The prophet's words were unusual and compelling, but he needed to sleep on them. He spoke to nobody of where he'd gone, except for a casual comment to Philopater over a late supper a few days later.

"So, I went down to hear the latest sensation, this teacher named Yochanan. Quite a guy. He had some interesting things to say. I've been considering going down to hear some more soon."

"Oh, haven't you heard?" Philopater asked. "He's left the area. Headed north along the Yarden, back the way he came."

Zakkai's heart chilled. "Oh?" he asked with exaggerated indifference. "Are you sure?"

"No," Philopater replied. "I just heard a rumor. I haven't time to track every religious crank that comes and goes."

The next morning Zakkai slipped away from his office. Once out of sight of his house, he bustled as quickly as his short legs would carry him, out of the city gates and down to the river. To his dismay he saw no crowds and no prophet there, just the brown river idling past the empty banks, with the ever-present flies buzzing about. Zakkai had missed his chance.

In weariness and despondency Zakkai turned to trudge back to the city. He'd meant to come back, he really had. There had been no way of knowing that Yochanan would leave that quickly. But then, Zakkai tried to reassure himself, that was the way of these wandering preachers. They come, they go, they come again. Maybe Yochanan was just making the rounds, working up and down the river. Surely, he'd be back, probably within a couple of months. Zakkai would just keep his ear to the ground in anticipation of his return.

It was a few months later, when Philopater was over for evening wine, that Zakkai next heard word of the rabbi.

"Did you hear what happened to your prophet Yochanan?" Philopater asked.

"Is he back?" Zakkai asked.

"Not hardly," Philopater snorted. "He's been arrested by Herod."

"For what?"

"For the same reason people are usually arrested by Herod – getting on the wrong side of Herod."

Zakkai's heart sank. Few who entered Herod's prison emerged again, unless they had wealthy friends, which Zakkai doubted Yochanan had. On the other hand, maybe –

"Though I've heard that the truly offended party isn't Herod," Philopater continued.

"Who is it?" Zakkai asked.

"Herod's wife."

"Oh, you mean Phillip's wife?" Zakkai guffawed at the standard joke about the embarrassingly public marital situation, but his heart was sinking even more. The fiery and vengeful

Herodias was notoriously sensitive to criticism about her questionable divorce. Someone who fell afoul of Herod might have a shred of a chance of acquittal or ransom; those who drew the wrath of the vindictive queen had almost none.

And so it proved. Many months passed, and Zakkai had heard nothing, when one day he encountered Yoses, who was looking unusually downcast.

"Haven't you heard?" Yoses replied when Zakkai asked him what the matter was. "The prophet Yochanan has been killed by that butcher Herod."

Zakkai was quietly devastated. Yochanan would never be coming back. Zakkai had been offered an opportunity, and had squandered it. That night he lay awake, alternating between rage at the injustice of the world and sadness that he'd lost his chance. He was haunted by the image of Yochanan smiling at him and gesturing for him to follow. The offer had been made, and he'd backed away out of fear. The invitation would never come again.

In the months and years that followed, Zakkai tried to distance himself from the painful memory. He busied himself about his work, addressing his administration and oversight and account management. He had staffing problems to solve as well. Yoses left him, taking his family down to a small community by the Salt Sea named Q'mran, there to try living a life of simple *Torah*. Yudah also left eventually, after trying for a while to carry himself with the honesty that the prophet had encouraged. But as time had worn on, the old Yudah had cropped up more and more often, with his coarseness and cruelty. He again began to frequent the taverns, and Zakkai caught hints that he was again collecting spillage from his territory. Finally, he quit, wandering off southwest to seek work. Zakkai had no trouble replacing both men. Despised as tax collecting was, it was a job, and there were few enough of those.

For his part, Zakkai tried to continue his life as if it had never been interrupted. He sponsored grand parties at his mansion, drawing his guests from the Greeks and Greek-friendly population, since no good Jew would darken his door. When he tired of the parties, he hosted philosophical discussions, led by itinerant teachers brought in from Alexandria and Antioch. These were engaging for a time, but eventually Zakkai ceased holding them. The discussions were mentally stimulating while they lasted, but never went anywhere, and left him feeling empty and desolate when they ended.

To please his wife, Zakkai sent agents to Joppa and Damascus to find the finest in Roman and Eastern goods – silk garments and exquisite porcelain and fine jewelry and other exotic things. These would delight her for a week or so, after which she would tire of them and start pining for some other novelty.

As busy as these distractions kept him, at times the dreary, dusty repetitiveness of his life so wore on Zakkai that he'd dream of casting it all away – selling everything and moving elsewhere, someplace nobody knew him. Tyre, perhaps, or Cyprus, or Alexandria. But no, his wife would never leave, and there was nobody to buy his property. He'd douse these flaring fantasies with buckets of cold reality and return to his work. He was who he was, and his destiny lay here in dusty, backwater Yericho, to live out his days in obscurity, unknown, unnoticed, and forgotten. It was no more than he deserved. He'd been offered a chance, and he'd wasted it. All that remained for him to do was die.

- Y'shua -

The first word Zakkai heard was from a Roman. Decius was the territorial supervisor, to whom Archelus reported. He kept his office in the provincial capital of Caesarea Maritima. He traveled throughout his territory, dropping in on his city chiefs to get the feel for what was happening in the region. While working the northern regions, one of his stops had been Herod's palace, and Decius was telling Zakkai about it.

"It was opulent enough, and Herod spreads an exquisite table, but he was behaving strangely. I think he has a tender conscience."

"If I were Herod, I'd have a tender conscience," Zakkai quipped. For some reason Decius thought this tremendously funny. "What was he doing that made you think that?"

"Well, there's a new wizard wandering about up there in the Galil, right in Herod's territory, talking about your Jewish god and drawing a rather large following."

"We call them rabbis or *Torah* scholars, not wizards," Zakkai explained.

"Well, apparently this one does more than just teach," Decius went on. "There are rumors that he heals people, and casts out demons, and some talk that he's even raised people from the dead. That's what has Herod spooked – he's half convinced that this wizard is the ghost or reappearance of some other prophet that he had killed not long ago. Yokoman, or something like that."

"Yochanan?" Zakkai asked, his heart chilling.

"Yes, that was it," Decius confirmed. "It doesn't help that Herod caught wind that the new wizard is some kind of kin to this Yochanan. I think that Herod is worried that he's going to show up at the palace gates someday, powers and all, to demand an accounting for his kinsman's life."

"Does this *Torah* scholar have a name?" Zakkai asked.

"Yeshuus, or something like that," Decius replied.

"Probably Y'shua, after an ancient Israelite hero," Zakkai said.

"That sounds right. Anyway, this wizard is spending a lot of time up in the Galil, which struck me as odd, because I'd think that any good Jew who wanted to make his mark would come down here to Judea."

"Lots of competition down here – and scrutiny."

"Well, he doesn't seem to be struggling in the competition department, if Herod's agents are right," Decius explained. "Draws crowds wherever he goes, which always worries rulers like Herod, and is getting quite a number of regular followers. In fact, I think he might be the same man who lured away one of my best supervisors up there."

"Really? Who was that?"

"Man named Mattityahu. The only word I got through my channels was that some preacher came up to his collection table and told him to come along. Mattityahu just walked off, following the preacher and leaving his accounts in complete disarray. I had to really scramble to replace him. Later when I heard about this wizard that has Herod so worried, I got to wondering if it could be the same person."

"Wait," Zakkai said, startled. "This *Torah* scholar is taking tax collectors as *talmidim*?"

"As what?"

"Close followers and students. Our name for them is *talmidim*."

"Ah. Well, it would seem so, though I wish he wouldn't take my best supervisors. Is that unusual?"

Zakkai snorted. "Come on, Decius, you ought to know Jews by now. Nobody anywhere loves the tax man, but for good Jews it's also theological. The whole region is the Holy Land, granted by God Himself to our forefathers. That pagans like you are here at all is a disgrace; that you run the place and take wealth away to your idol-filled cities is next to sacrilege – in fact, some devout Jews see it as just that. Those of us who assist in the plundering are not considered Jews at all, and indeed are barely considered human."

"Ah, yes – I see your point," Decius said uncomfortably. Zakkai understood his detachment. Caesarea Maritima was essentially a Greek city, culturally isolated from the land it ruled. Those who lived there might as well be living in Anatolia or Italy for all the interaction they had with the Jews around them. But this was a reality Zakkai had to deal with every day.

"That's why it's so unusual to hear of a *Torah* scholar taking on a tax collector as a *talmidim*. But here, you're yawning your head off and you've got to go back to Yerushalem early tomorrow. I'll call the steward to send you to your room."

"Thank you. Good night, Zakkaius," Decius said with another yawn.

Zakkai stayed on the terrace for a little longer, sipping his wine and staring into the charcoal embers glowing in the brazier. A teacher, perhaps a wonder worker, kin to the murdered Yochanan, who took on tax collectors as *talmidim*. What kind of scholar would do that? Unbidden in his mind rose the image of Yochanan smiling and beckoning him to follow, the image he'd sought so hard to forget. Zakkai finished his wine and headed for bed, hoping he'd be able to sleep.

Over the next few weeks Zakkai made discreet and indirect inquiries regarding this teacher up in the Galil. What little he discovered confirmed much of what Decius had said: his name was indeed Y'shua, and he was gaining quite a reputation as a preacher and, indeed, as a wonder-worker, which was something Yochanan had never been known for. This Y'shua stayed mostly in the Galil, but had been seen in Yerushalem occasionally, somewhat to the consternation of the Temple officials.

Yerushalem.

Hope surged in Zakkai's heart no matter how hard he tried to push it down. Someone who had traveled to Yerushalem might do so again, and one of the main pilgrim roads up to Yerushalem led right through Yericho. Maybe, just maybe, Y'shua might come this way. If he did, Zakkai might get a chance to see him! He had no hope of meeting or speaking to him, as he'd had with Yochanan, but if he could just get a glimpse, that would be something. But he dared not get his hopes up.

The months slipped by and Zakkai heard nothing further. His fiscal schedule was run according to the Roman calendar, which was based on solstices and equinoxes, not the Jewish religious calendar, which followed the moon phases. That, plus his ostracism from the faithful Jewish community, meant that he was almost completely out of touch with the rhythm of the Jewish festivals. What little he minded them was usually because the traffic through town got thicker as the crowds of pilgrims passed through. Thus Zakkai was barely aware that Pesach, the Passover festival, was coming around again.

It was late one morning when Zakkai was out and about on errands that he noticed a clamor on the main road of the city, down near the eastern gate. It looked like a lively crowd of pilgrims, and Zakkai began to ponder which side streets would serve as alternative routes home – he didn't want to get caught in a jam of out-of-towners. For some reason these ones were being unusually boisterous. There was lots of yelling and running, but it wasn't the ugly sound of a mob. These people were whooping and – dancing? What was going on?

Zakkai watched as the crowd came up the main street. Those he could see appeared to be the vanguard of some kind of procession or parade. Locals were starting to come out of their houses and side streets to see what the fuss was about. Just then one of the revelers came dashing up the street, his face aglow with excitement and – joy?

"Hey," Zakkai called to the man. "What's going on?"

"Haven't you heard?" the man called over his shoulder. "It's the prophet from the Galil, Y'shua! He's headed for Yerushalem, and he's healed a blind man!" The man said a few other things, but was running away so quickly that Zakkai didn't hear him.

Not that Zakkai was listening.

Y'shua?

From the Galil?

Coming right through Yericho? Not half a mile from where Zakkai was standing?

Without even thinking, Zakkai began running toward the crowd. He had to get through, he had to see! But the crowd was so thick, thicker than it had been on the riverbank when Yochanan was there. And even worse, many locals were now lining the streets, locals who knew him and would close ranks to shut him out. It was happening already! Zakkai noticed a townsman catch a glimpse of him, then deliberately look away while moving to hinder Zakkai's path and occlude his view. The man muttered to his neighbors, and they pulled together to block his way.

Zakkai was nearly frantic. He couldn't miss this chance, he just couldn't! He glanced one way, but the crowd was already too thick. Another path was being blocked by his neighbors, studiously ignoring him but still managing to hinder his progress. In desperation he glanced behind him and spotted a sycamore by the side of the road. It had a branch that hung low enough for even him to grasp, and a good spread of higher branches reaching over the street. He dashed to the tree and, heedless of his dignity, was soon scrambling up the branches like a street urchin. Some looked at him and snickered, but he didn't care – he'd be able to see from a vantage point that could not be blocked.

Zakkai was ecstatic – his view was perfect. Looking right over the crowd of pilgrims and townsfolk, he could see the rabbi coming along the street, smiling and nodding at people. Behind him came about a dozen men, undoubtedly his *talmidim*, but beside him walked a dirty looking man in tattered clothing who was nonetheless grinning and hopping about like a lunatic. Why, that was Bartimaeus, one of the beggars who sat beside the wall outside the city gate, hoping for generosity from locals or pilgrims! Zakkai knew him well, having occasionally dropped a few drachmas in his bowl. His eyes had been milky white and sunken into their sockets for as long as anyone could remember. Yet here he was, dancing down the crowded street in broad daylight, as clearsighted as anyone!

A hint of fear gripped Zakkai – who was this Y'shua?

The parade was getting closer, with the crowd now surrounding the trunk of the tree. Y'shua and his *talmidim* came on steadily, and even at fifty yards Zakkai could see the family resemblance to Yochanan. Wavy brown hair, bright eyes with perhaps a bit less intensity to the gaze, and a ready smile. He and his men were passing close now, their attention fixed on the people by the road who were calling out and reaching to touch the holy man. Zakkai could see it all from his perch.

The parade had nearly reached the sycamore when Y'shua stopped and looked up. He gazed directly at Zakkai, right into his eyes, and a broad smile spread across his face. Everyone else was looking at Y'shua, but Y'shua was looking only at him.

"Ho, Zakkai!" Y'shua called in a clear, hearty voice. "What are you doing up there? Hurry down now, for I have to come to your house today!"

Zakkai was stunned. Him? The rabbi was talking to him? Zakkai's mind may have been in shock, but his body responded promptly, scrambling down the branches and into the street beside Y'shua.

"My...my house?" Zakkai asked in amazement, staring at the rabbi and gaping like a hooked fish. There was a moment of silence before Y'shua spoke with a grin.

"If you have room."

"My...but...of course I have room, Rabbi," Zakkai babbled. "Room aplenty for all. This way, please, this way. I'll take you right there." Zakkai scurried through the streets toward his mansion, not noticing that the crowd had thinned substantially since the rabbi had hailed the tax collector. Y'shua didn't seem to notice, either, walking along easily, smiling and chatting and inquiring about life in Yericho.

When they reached the gate, Zakkai sent the guard scurrying to find the steward while he seated his guests on the benches in the outer courtyard. Since the guard was on his errand, Zakkai went to close the gate himself. The crowd had mostly dispersed, but he spotted Bartimaeus wandering around, still in wonder at what had happened but obviously unclear about where to go now. Zakkai beckoned him in and called a servant girl over to take the beggar off to be washed, groomed, clad, and fed.

By this time the steward had arrived and set the servants to washing the travelers' feet. Then Zakkai formally welcomed them into his home, and gave orders for a feast to be readied for sunset. Y'shua graciously thanked him. Glancing over the band of *talmidim*, Zakkai saw that they looked weary and travel-worn, and offered them the use of his bath. It was more a Roman custom than a Jewish one, but Zakkai assured them he would keep all his female servants away while they bathed. Y'shua and his men accepted the offer, so the steward escorted the men to their chambers and Zakkai ordered the water to be heated. As host, Zakkai had many duties to fulfill, but as he bustled about them, he couldn't shake the sense that one of the *talmidim* looked vaguely familiar.

A couple of hours later Zakkai was taking a rest on one of the benches of the inner courtyard, satisfied that preparations were on track for a magnificent feast to honor his guests. He was startled to see Y'shua stroll in, clad in one of the house robes that had been provided while Zakkai's staff washed (and mended, and patched) the men's travel garb.

"Hello, Rabbi," Zakkai said, jumping to his feet and bowing. "I trust everything is to your satisfaction?"

"Exquisite, thank you, Zakkai," Y'shua replied. "My men are relaxing in your garden. The bath was refreshing, and the wine and cakes you sent were perfect. We've been on the road for a long time, and a little taste of civilization was appreciated."

"You're more than welcome, sir."

"I also want to thank you for taking care of Bartimaeus," Y'shua went on, fixing Zakkai with a piercing gaze that was even more intense than his cousin's. "It was, if I may say, about time."

Zakkai felt distinctly uncomfortable under those steady eyes, and wrung his hands in distress.

"You didn't have to wait for him to have his sight restored to do all this for him," Y'shua continued. "When was the last time you gave him more than a few drachmas?"

"Well...I...so many beggars," Zakkai stammered. "You know how it is."

"Yes," Y'shua said. "I know how it is." He stood and walked over to a pillar that was made of the finest Italian marble. Stroking the stone in admiration, he continued. "This is beautifully carved Roman stone. But I have to wonder, how much of it was erected with the uncompensated sweat of your fellow Israelites?"

Zakkai squirmed. *Torah* spoke most sternly about justly and promptly paying workers their wages, and not defrauding them. He thought of all the spillage that had paid for those columns, and what that spillage had actually been.

Y'shua returned and sat beside him, still watching with those fathomless eyes but speaking in a gentler tone. "To live in a home of beautifully carved stone is one thing. To have that stone make its home in you is quite another. Governments will have their taxes and somebody has to collect them, but that carries the risk of seeing your countrymen as denarii, not kin. It carries the further risk of using your power to collect what is not yours to take."

Zakkai said nothing, his head bowed, his heart crushed with guilt. This man could see to the bottom of his soul, and his simple words lay bare the magnitude of Zakkai's sin, the sin which he had run from, and tried to bury with pride and indignation. He felt vile and untouchable, but Y'shua touched him nonetheless, reaching over and laying a hand on his shoulder.

"There is still hope," Y'shua said gently. "What does the prophet say? 'I will take from your body your heart of stone—'"

"'And give you a heart of flesh,'" Zakkai picked up, the lessons of his youth returning to him. "'And I will put My Spirit within you, and cause you to walk in My statutes and be careful to obey My laws.'" He was sobbing now, tears of remorse streaming down his face. Y'shua said nothing, but simply sat beside him and waited until he'd regained his composure.

"I had a chance before," Zakkai choked out at last. "Yochanan offered it, but I didn't take it, fool that I was."

"I know," Y'shua said. "But now you are being offered another. Will you take this one?"

Zakkai looked up into Y'shua's eyes and nodded firmly. "Yes."

"Good," Y'shua said with a smile. "Now, I must go look to my men, who are hungrily anticipating this feast you've promised."

The dinner was magnificent, with the cooks and staff outdoing themselves. The wine flowed and the delicacies were savored and the evening air was filled with laughter. Zakkai's wife made a brief appearance in honor of the guests, but quickly retired to her rooms, shy creature that she was. Even so, Y'shua treated her with deep respect, which seemed to be his habit with everyone, even the servants. Zakkai sat beside him in wonder, still amazed that the renowned rabbi had come to his very house to offer him another chance.

When came the time that it was customary for the host to honor the main guest, Zakkai rose to his feet and cleared his throat. His eyes were still red and he struggled to keep his voice level, but he had to say this.

"Blessed be this day, that has brought such guests to my home," he choked. "I vow by *Hashem*, the Holy Name, that this day I give half my goods to the poor, and if I have defrauded anyone, I will make fourfold restitution." He could see the *talmidim* glancing at one another. This far exceeded the one fifth restitution premium stipulated by *Torah*, but Zakkai was determined. Tremendous generosity called for a tremendously generous response.

"And this day you have welcomed another guest to your home: salvation," Y'shua added, then turned to his *talmidim*. "See, here is a son of Avraham. For this very reason the Son of Man has come: to seek and save the lost."

Zakkai had to step away from the table to regain his composure. To have Y'shua himself, rabbi and healer and holy man, affirm him as a son of Avraham, was more than his heart could bear. When he returned to the table, he had a question for Y'shua.

"Should I take my *t'vilah* now, as Yochanan offered? We could use the pond in the garden, or go to the river if that would be more suitable."

Y'shua paused, as if thinking or listening, then replied, "Let us wait. The *t'vilah* of Yochanan is passing and soon things will be different. Within the year Philip here will return to your home bearing a new *t'vilah* to which you may be joined." Y'shua nodded at Philip, who looked mystified but nodded back.

The feast continued for a little longer, but all the travelers were road-weary and wished to retire early. After they had gone to bed, Zakkai wandered about the house, still dazed from the events of the day. That the renowned prophet would come to his house, dine at his table, bring him back to *Torah*, and even call him a Son of Avraham – he could still hardly believe it.

There was a stir behind a column that startled Zakkai, and he called sharply, "Who's there?"

"Don't fear, it's just me, admiring your columns," came a familiar voice. "You always did well for yourself, Zakkai." At that a man stepped from the shadows into the flickering torchlight. It was one of Y'shua's *talmidim*, and at once it all came together for Zakkai. No wonder he'd looked vaguely familiar.

"Yudah?"

"The very same," Yudah admitted with a slight theatric bow. "It's good to see you again."

"And you," Zakkai replied. "How did you end up in the company of Y'shua?"

"It's a long story. After leaving here, I wandered back to K'riot for a while, but it was still as short on opportunities as it was when I left the first time. So, I left again, and wandered up the coast and into the Galil. There I came across some old *talmidim* of Yochanan who were following this new rabbi, so I tagged along."

"Really?" Zakkai asked eagerly. "What is it like? How is it to live so close to him, and speak with him every day?"

Yudah shrugged. "It's good, I guess. I can definitely feel some of the old fire at times, like when Yochanan used to preach. But he says strange things, and can be morose at times. He's been particularly depressing on this pilgrimage. We're headed for Yerushalem now, and frankly, I hope this settles matters once and for all."

"Settles matters?" Zakkai asked. "What needs settling?"

Yudah laughed. "Yericho really is a backwater, isn't it? Haven't you heard the talk surrounding Y'shua?"

"I've been a little out of those circles," Zakkai admitted. Yudah leaned in to speak in lower, more conspiratorial tones.

"It's the big question – is he the *Meshiach*, or not? The *P'rushim* and temple agents keep pressing him, but he plays coy, or gives them one of his maddeningly indirect answers."

Zakkai felt a thrill of excitement. Y'shua was surely a wonder worker and holy man, but – the *Meshiach*? The one to restore the Throne of David, to cleanse the Temple, and resume the provision of manna? Zakkai could easily believe it, and put the question to Yudah. "Well, is he? You're one of his *talmidim*."

Again, Yudah shrugged. "How should I know? I'm not in the inner circle – ask Yochanan or Ya'akov or Shim'on. He's always calling them aside for the truly intimate conferences. I tell you one thing, though – matters are coming to a head. We're bound for Yerushalem, where he's either going to deal with the corrupt temple establishment or else."

"Or else what?"

Once more Yudah shrugged. "I don't know, but something had better happen. I'm not like you, Zakkai. You've got the patience to build slowly, to wait and attend to details for years until you end up here." He slapped the carved marble pillar. "I'm not like that. I want quicker results." Yudah gave a great yawn. "But, I fear, the only results I'm going to get tonight will be from that decadent pillow you've provided. Good night, old boss."

"Good night, Yudah," Zakkai called as his old employee slipped into the shadows. Zakkai shook his head in wonder. How strange! Imagine Yudah ending up in the company of the prophet. Zakkai turned toward his own bedroom, feeling strangely sullied by the conversation. Somehow Yudah had changed, but yet he hadn't. Zakkai had never been able to figure out what drove that man. For that matter, maybe Yudah didn't know himself.

The next morning dawned fresh and clear, and Zakkai insured that there was a generous breakfast laid for his guests. His excitement was still high enough for him to dare approach Y'shua with an offer.

"Sir, if you and your men wish time to rest from the road, you are welcome to stay here as long as you wish."

Y'shua smiled and clapped him on the shoulder. "Thank you so much for your generous offer. Unfortunately, we must decline." He looked southwestward, toward the heights where Yerushalem lay, and his face grew somber. "I have appointments that must be kept. We intend to make it to Bethany before sundown, to celebrate *Shabbat* with some friends."

"That's a full day," Zakkai said sympathetically. "And uphill all the way."

"Indeed," Y'shua grinned. "But my men are accustomed to it. Here they come now, clad in the garments your staff so graciously washed. Please thank them for us."

"I shall," said Zakkai. The *talmidim* were clustering about now, and the group began walking toward the gate. "I...I don't know how to thank you for all you've done for me, Rabbi."

"You can thank me by keeping your word, Zakkai. Once I leave, things will seem easy for a while, but in time the fears will crowd around, seeking to dissuade you from your intent. Do not listen to them. Listen instead to the cries of your brethren, such as Bartimaeus here." Y'shua gestured to where the healed beggar came running out into the courtyard from the room that had been found for him. Y'shua stepped over to greet him privately. The man fell at Y'shua's feet, but the rabbi lifted him up and spoke quietly to him for a few minutes. Then they both came to the gate, where there were embraces and farewells, as well as a few tears, then the rabbi and his *talmidim* were gone, his face set toward Yerushalem. The two men stood side by side watching them until they passed out of sight, then Zakkai turned to Bartimaeus and clapped him on the shoulder.

"My friend, I would be honored if you would join my household for *Shabbat* this evening," Zakkai said. The beggar's eyes, now clear and bright brown, widened, and he began bowing repeatedly and muttering what sounded like "master". Zakkai halted him and made him stand straight. "After that, I would deeply appreciate your help with a task."

"Anything, master," Bartimaeus replied, attempting to bow but being stopped by Zakkai's hand.

"Please help me prepare my house for *Pesach*, which is next week. It has been many years since I celebrated that holy festival.

"All get what they want: they do not always like it."
Aslan, *The Magician's Nephew*

The Narrowing

The room was starting to darken in the gathering twilight, and she heaved a great sigh. No good sitting here any longer, she might as well check the rest of the house. With great effort and much puffing, she heaved herself up out of the recliner and braced herself against the wall until she stopped swaying. It never got any easier.

Looking around the small room, her eyes fell on the big TV screen. It was mostly dark now. There seemed to be something wrong with the power button. She could push and push on it but the set usually wouldn't come on. Once in a while she managed it, but it didn't do any good – there was only static and white snow on the screen. Something was wrong with the stupid cable. She'd have Ben call about that when he got back. But some days she tried anyway, just to see if the idiots had fixed it yet.

But not this evening. Trying to turn on the TV was maddening enough, and even if she managed to succeed, staring at the incompetence of the cable company made her even angrier. Tonight, she was too tired. She weaved her way down the hallway to the kitchen. She was so very hungry – tonight she'd make something to eat. Nothing elaborate, just some crackers and soup, maybe with a glass of cold milk. That sounded good.

Bother. There wasn't any milk. In fact, there wasn't much in the fridge at all. Oh, she'd noticed that yesterday, and had intended to do something about it, but it had totally slipped her mind. Now it was too late. Tomorrow, for sure. Tonight, she'd get by with water. Not as good as a glass of milk, but she was so thirsty that it didn't matter. She reached for the faucet and pushed the handle, but it didn't budge.

Blast! That's right, the faucet was broken! It had been getting stickier and stickier, and she'd been after Ben to fix it, but he hadn't yet. It totally seized shortly after he left. Another thing for him to look at when he got back, whenever that would be. Shouldn't they have called about that by now? Maybe she could

113

get Steve to look at the faucet to get it working a little until Ben could fix it properly.

No soup then. Just as well, since she couldn't see any cans in the cupboard. Pick up milk and soup tomorrow, then. Crackers, too – she could have sworn there were some in the pantry, but she couldn't see any. And she was so hungry, and thirsty. Perhaps the bathroom faucet worked.

She worked her way back down the narrow hall toward the bathroom. Part of the wall was the sliding glass door that opened to the back yard. She looked out it and saw the debris on the patio, the debris they had left when they'd run off. She ground her teeth in rage.

It still made her blood boil when she remembered that evening. She'd been trying to get some rest in the TV room when she'd heard the noise outside. It was a gang of punks, half a dozen or so, who'd just come up on the patio and were sitting around drinking beer and smoking – something. They were making enough noise to wake the dead. They were only young toughs from the neighborhood, but the nerve of them, sitting around her patio as if they owned it, drinking and smoking and swearing.

Of course, she was scared, but she was even more furious. She knew she should call the police, but she couldn't find the handset. All the time the laughter and the swearing went on, and she got more and more furious, until finally she decided to give the punks a piece of her mind. She stormed to the door, knowing she was doing something very foolish, but she was unable to contain herself. But the lock chose that moment to jam, possibly because of the angry force with which she tried to throw it. As she struggled to free it, she hammered on the door and yelled at the kids.

That had gotten their attention. They'd turned to look, then suddenly started yelling and scrambling to flee. They'd dashed away across the back yard, leaving behind their tipped-over beer cans and cigarette butts. Their reaction had amazed her, but it was also a relief. As she'd calmed down, it had begun to dawn on her what a dangerous thing she'd almost done. Had she managed to free the lock, they could have opened the door, shoved right past her, and gotten into the house. She couldn't have that.

At least they'd never returned, not even to pick up their litter – not that she would have expected that. The beer cans still rolled around the patio, rattling in the evening breeze. Looking beyond the patio, she saw the garage. That's where the freezer was, and the pantry shelves. Maybe there was some soup and crackers out there! And surely there was something in the freezer she could bring in – not for tonight, but she could get it thawing for tomorrow's dinner.

She pressed against the glass doors, gazing longingly at the garage, then sighed in resignation. Not tonight. It was already too dark, and she'd have to leave the back door unlocked while she was out there, and who knew who might come along? Those punks might return, and lock her out of her own house! Best not to chance it. First thing in the morning. When Steve came over – was he due to come tomorrow? She kept forgetting which day it was.

Sighing, she turned and limped to the living room. It was getting quite dark now, which meant that the lamp would come on soon. She eased into the chair beside the lamp and looked up at her collection of dolls. The glass front cabinet was full of them, and there were some on top and on the buffet as well. There were Dutch dolls and Mexican dolls and Polish dolls and Brazilian dolls and Russian dolls. There were '50s dolls and square dancing dolls and disco dolls and western dolls – all sorts of dolls that people had given her, and she'd collected through the years. She loved her dolls. She even kept little ones tucked here and there about the living room. She looked around and sighed with contentment. Her living room. Everything just as she wanted. The couch and chairs, the doilies, the hangings, her doll collection – just the way she liked it. Her living room in her house.

They'd tried to take it from her, but she hadn't let them. Ben's pushy kids, first trying to move them to another state, and then into one of those care facilities. They'd talked all concern and caring, but she knew what they wanted – her property. Ben had wavered, but she'd put her foot down. In the end they'd all gone away and left her alone.

Becky had tried it, too. Becky had brought over brochures for those facilities, and driven them to inspect some of the nearer ones. They were all very nice, and again Ben had wavered. But all she'd had to do was point out how terribly expensive they all were. She didn't have to state the obvious: that they'd have to sell the property to afford them. So, they'd thanked Becky, and stopped going around to look at facilities, and threw away the brochures, and that had been the end of that.

Even Steve and Marci had hinted from time to time that maybe it was time to consider moving. Once or twice she'd even gotten sharp with Marci when they'd gotten near the topic, so it had been quietly dropped.

Yes, her property, her house, and she'd fought off all attempts to wrest it from her. Sure, it was old, and not everything worked perfectly – but that was true of her, too, she chuckled. Ben would be able to attend to those minor repairs when he got back.

The last of the sunset was fading from the sky, and the room was getting very dark. When would the lamp – oh, there it came. The lamp came on every night for a few hours. She liked to sit beside it, looking around her living room, before it shut off.

She looked over by the door and saw her walker leaning there. That reminded her of something – what was it? The mail! She'd forgotten to get the mail today. The driveway was so long that she needed the walker to make it to the mailbox. That was so much trouble that some days she just plain forgot, or decided it wasn't worth it. She parted the blinds and looked down to the end of the driveway. It was certainly too dark, and too far, to try it tonight.

There were two men out in the road under the streetlamp. She'd seen them walk by for several nights now. They weren't punks – they looked middle-aged, maybe about as old as Steve. She guessed they were out for a walk around the neighborhood. They seemed like nice men. Maybe if she asked them, they could bring her the mail when they came around on their evening stroll. That would be a neighborly thing to do, and not much trouble for them, she hoped. She looked again, and saw they were stopped in the road at the end of the drive. They seemed to be talking and looking at the house. Perhaps now was a good time to go out, introduce herself, and maybe ask that favor.

But no, not tonight. She sat back in the chair. Tonight, she was too tired. Tomorrow night she'd be more rested. Tomorrow she'd get the mail and talk to the men. Maybe tomorrow they'd bring Ben back, or Steve would drop by, or Becky would call. Tonight, she just wanted to sit in the living room. Her living room, which she wouldn't leave no matter who pressured her. She'd just sit here by the lamp until it went out and she was left in the darkness again.

Tom enjoyed these late evening walks around the neighborhood with Randy. It was just the level of exercise the doctor had recommended and they mixed up the route enough to make it interesting. Randy was an intriguing guy who had lived in these parts for years and seemed to know everyone and everything, so there were plenty of good stories to pass the miles. For the past week they'd been walking this loop of the subdivision, keeping a brisk pace as the day's heat faded.

They were just rounding the corner past the lot with the house trailer when Tom saw a light come on in one of the trailer's windows.

"Oh!" he exclaimed. "I thought that trailer was vacant, but apparently not."

Randy stopped and gave him a curious look. "Actually, it is vacant. That light is on a timer."

"Really? That's unusual," Tom said. Their walks took them past many vacant properties, some with the foreclosure notices still taped to their doors. Usually utilities were shut off.

"It is," Randy said in an odd tone, looking at the shadowed property with an enigmatic expression. "That's not all that's unusual about that trailer."

"What do you mean?" Tom asked. Randy was silent for an unusually long time, gazing into the deepening gloom, before he spoke again.

"Anita and I know Steve and Marci Lorenz through our bridge club. They live just a few lots down the road here."

"That guy we spoke with the other evening? The one out doing yard work?" Tom asked.

"The very one. He and his wife were close to the couple who lived here – saw them through their final days, as much as they could," Randy said.

"'As much as they could'?" Tom asked.

"The couple was pretty independent – foolishly so, as Steve tells it. At least she was. They were well into their eighties, in failing health. Several years back she almost died from heart problems and a subsequent infection, then he had a heart attack and a stroke. Steve helped as much as he could by driving them around, fetching groceries, and tending the yard," Randy explained.

Tom whistled – he'd had to contend with aging parents. "Two elderly folks in sketchy health living alone in that little trailer? That's a recipe for trouble."

"That's what his kids thought. They're scattered across the country, but after her problems they tried to move them a couple of states away to live with one of them. But she wasn't having it, and insisted on staying in the trailer. When he had his stroke and heart attack a couple of years later, they again tried to get them moved into a local care facility. Again, they refused, and returned here."

Tom looked at the trailer in amazement. "That place? It's a house trailer, for Pete's sake – thirty years old if it's a day."

"Closer to forty," Randy said. "Though apparently it's been well maintained."

"So – what happened?" Tom asked.

"What you'd expect," Randy shrugged. "One afternoon he died in his chair of congestive heart failure. She was napping, and didn't even hear him go. But even after they buried him, she wouldn't hear of moving. One day she didn't answer the phone, so Steve went over and found her slumped at the kitchen table. Official cause of death was renal failure, but apparently it could have been any one of half a dozen things."

"When did this happen?"

"She died just over a year ago. It's been vacant ever since."

"That long? The property's in pretty good shape," Tom said. "I'm surprised it hasn't been abused by the local kids." The problem of vacant properties being used by short- and long-term squatters was epidemic in the area.

Randy gave Tom a curious look, as if deciding whether or not to continue. The light from the streetlight overhead cast sharp shadows across his face, giving him an eerie appearance. "Actually, there are some strange stories about this property," he said.

"Strange?" Tom asked.

"Yes – as in spooky," Randy continued. "The first I heard of it was from Steve, who helped Becky – that's the daughter-in-law – clean out the trailer. He said they both felt a strong animosity, an 'unwelcome' as he put it, that was almost tangible. He says he still feels it when he looks in on the place from time to time. Furthermore, he and Becky have both noticed odd little things when they drop in – like the TV on, or some of the dolls moved around, or a faucet dripping, or cupboard doors that had been closed standing open. They both secure and double-check the place every time they leave, but they still find these things."

A chill ran down Tom's spine as he looked at the dusk-shrouded trailer. Come to think of it, there did seem to be a slight air of hostility that hung about the place – or was it his imagination? And did he just see the blinds in that window move a little?

"Are they sure nobody is getting in? Squatters are pretty common," Tom said.

"They're pretty sure, and that's the other odd part," Randy replied. "Seems that some months back a group of kids realized the place was vacant and decided to use the back porch for an evening party. They were just getting rolling when one of them noticed an old woman glaring out through the glass doors. Frightened the wits out of them, and they took off in a hurry."

"Was it the lady who'd lived there?" Tom asked.

"Well, nobody could get a detailed description, because none of the kids would officially admit to having been there. But the word that got around was that she was a 'mean-eyed old witch'. When Steve heard about it, he went over and checked it out. But there wasn't any sign of anyone inside, and all the doors were still securely locked. That's when he put the timer on the lamp, so the place appears occupied. Doesn't matter much, though – the neighborhood tales are much more effective. There's been no trouble with trespassers ever since."

"Wow," Tom said. "So that trailer is reputed to be…haunted?" Did those blinds just move again?

"That's the rumor," Randy confirmed. "But not for much longer."

"How so?"

"Steve tells me that shortly after he and Becky did the preliminary clean-out of the trailer, Becky's own mother got sick and needed all her attention. So, they essentially locked up the place until they could deal with it. Well, now Becky's mother has died and her estate is settled, so they can attend to this property. They plan to sell it to a developer who wants to clear the lot. Since nobody's interested in sorting through the trailer, they engaged one of those salvage outfits."

"Salvage outfits?" Tom asked.

"Yeah – they pay a flat fee for the rights to all contents. A team shows up with a truck and a dumpster and strips the place to the walls. Whatever they think they can resell goes on the truck, everything else goes in the dumpster. Apparently, they're quite efficient – they plan to empty both the trailer and the garage in a day. After that the crane and dump truck show up to take down the structures."

"When is this due to happen?"

"The salvage guys should be here this week or next, and the demo crew shortly after that. A month from now this lot will be leveled, ready for new construction."

There are two prominent Marys in the New Testament. One exemplifies the perfect response to the call of grace, another illustrates fall, repentance, and acceptance of salvation. If we allow it, our souls can be made like the first; until then we live like the second - in tension, our hearts wooed by many conflicting voices...

Miriam

Miriam was walking down the beautifully paneled hall when she heard the music. At first, she thought it might be coming from the garden. But it was too delicate to have come from the hammering guitars of the rock band playing for the party. There it was again! Just a few bars, fading quickly, but clearly from a piano or keyboard – and also somewhat familiar.

Had it been merely a random melody, she would have ignored it and continued on her way. Perhaps it was a guest who had wandered away from the party, or a family member enjoying a little quiet. But the tune was hauntingly familiar. From where did she know those notes? They stirred yearnings, pleasant memories long dormant, yet at the same time unsettled her with feelings she'd forgotten – or had chosen to forget. What was that music?

Hesitant and torn, she halted at the intersection of two hallways and clutched her purse. She'd been intending to follow this hallway to the right, but the music seemed to be coming from a hallway further up on the left. There it was again! Her curiosity prodded her to follow the music to the next hall.

Her search was rewarded. From the head of the hallway she could hear the music dimly but steadily. The long hall was lined with doors, all closed except for one double door that stood ajar toward the far end. The music seemed to be coming through that door.

She walked tentatively down the hall, searching her memory. Why did the music seem so familiar? Perhaps it was the melody, which seemed something between classical and slow ragtime, but what seemed most familiar was the style. Unlike the cacophony she'd just left, this was gentle and alluring. The strains seemed to float along the hallway, now soft and delicate, now swelling in a lively allegretto. The theme sad and somber, not quite a lament, but there was an underlying thread of joy and hope that kept bubbling through. Whoever was playing knew much more than how to play notes off a sheet – he knew how to bring a piece of music to life, to make it express the artist's heart and soul. She hadn't met many who could do that. In fact, the only one she could remember was...

She came to the doors and cautiously peered around the corner. Seated at a concert grand was a young man with his back to the door, playing with grace and passion. She could only see the back of his head, but the cut of his wavy brown hair and his posture were familiar enough – could it be? Her breath caught in her throat and her hand flew to her mouth, but her heart was racing. What if it was? Could she – after all this? Part of her wanted to turn away and return to the party, pretending that she'd never followed the music down the hall. But a stronger part wanted to know, to at least see if it was he.

She walked quietly into the room, trying not to distract him. If she was quiet enough, maybe she could catch a glimpse without his noticing her, and then leave without having been seen. She could see more of the pianist's profile now. He was playing from memory, his eyes closed, swaying as he played, entranced with the music. She was almost alongside him now, and could see most of his face. He was still caught up in his music, oblivious to everything else. Her heart raced faster – it was him.

Images raced through her mind, images from a life she'd almost forgotten, a life she'd tried to leave behind. His deep brown eyes smiling into hers as they walked along the beach. His slight wisp of a smile, with the ever-present edge of sadness. The brief touch of his hand – all the contact he'd ever ventured, yet, somehow, all the contact he'd ever needed. No, no – her heart turned away from the images, and she made a slight turn back toward the door.

"Hello, Miriam," he said without opening his eyes.

"Oh!" she caught her breath at the sound of his voice – that familiar, comforting, yet slightly disturbing voice. "Hello, Josh. I heard the piano...that is, I was just wandering by, and the music – I didn't know you were here. That is, I didn't see you at the party."

"I wasn't invited to the party," Josh replied, opening his eyes and looking at her as he continued to play. "But I'm an old friend of the family, and I have a standing invitation to their home. I'm staying in the guest house, and happened to be over and decided to try tickling the ivories a bit."

Miriam heard him speaking, but was only half attending. She'd forgotten how penetrating his eyes could be. When he looked at you, you felt like you were the only person in the world. Yet at the same time it felt like he could see things you'd rather remained hidden. Josh was the only man she knew who could comfort and unnerve you with the same glance.

"Yes…ah, that is, you play beautifully, as you always have," Miriam said, dropping her eyes from his and looking nervously around the room. They were alone, weren't they? She felt like she should say something else, but didn't know what. Josh's fingers swept over the keys with effortless skill, and the haunting melody filled the room.

"That – what you're playing – it sounds familiar," Miriam ventured. "Have I heard it before?"

"I doubt it," Josh replied, then corrected himself, "but then, maybe you've heard bits of it. I just made it up tonight, but it contains themes I've used before."

"Yes, I can see that," she replied. "It's very beautiful."

"Thank you," Josh nodded slightly and played for a bit more. "So – how have you been?"

Miriam dropped her head and smiled. She should have expected that – it was the expectable Josh question. Almost every meeting, phone call, letter, or even e-mail would include that little question; so casual yet so probing. How had she been. How had she been? Let's see, Josh – how long has it been? Years now? A lot of water under the bridge, a lot of distance between her and – oh, just about everyone. Lots of acquaintances, lots of cards in the box on her dresser, lots of memories that blurred together, lots of faces but no names to go with them, lots of meetings but few friends, lots of parties...

"Fine, Josh, I've been fine," she answered. "It's – I'm a little tired these days, but otherwise I'm doing well. And – and you?"

"You're looking good," he volunteered, his hands still sweeping across the keys. "Nice dress."

"Thanks. Nick got it for me, and since he brought me here, I thought I'd – you know, wear it," she answered. It was a nice dress, but in Josh's presence she was suddenly conscious of how short it was, and how low the neckline was cut. It certainly complemented her dancer's legs and the trim figure she worked so hard to maintain. She could always tell that male eyes were watching her every move when she wore it. It certainly was sexy. Sometimes men would come and talk to her. And keep looking at her. It was attention, but…they weren't the nicest men.

"You've always looked good in red," Josh continued.

Looked good in red. Yes, she did – everyone told her so. But then, she also looked good in white. Even more people told her that, especially when she wore the white dress that Josh had gotten her years ago. It wasn't at all like this red party dress – it was more a cool weather dress, with long lacy sleeves, a tea-length skirt, and a beautiful collar that framed her long neck. She'd joked with Josh about his taste running toward Victorian wedding dresses, but there was no denying that it made her look and feel more feminine and beautiful than anything else she had. When she wore that dress gentlemen would open doors for her with little bows, and women would come up to tell her how beautiful she was, while Josh just looked on and smiled. Goodness, she hadn't worn that dress in ages. Just last month she'd spotted it in the cleaner's bag at the back of her closet and had taken it out. Why was she still keeping it? She pondered donating it, but she just – couldn't. She'd hung it back on the bar.

"Thank you," Miriam answered, tugging at her hem. "I…thank you." The silence fell between them again, full of the melody and so much more. "How have you been?"

"I've been well," Josh said lightly. "Here and there, plenty to keep me busy, of course. You remember how it was."

"You always managed to make time for me," Miriam said, startling herself. Why had she said that?

Josh looked back at her with one of his small smiles. "It's easy to make time for the truly important things."

The music again filled the room, but now it was interrupted by another sound – feet in the hallway outside, accompanied by a loud male voice. Josh kept playing. "Miriam! Are you down here?" The voice was at the door now, and Miriam turned to it with a forced smile. "Oh, there you are, baby! We were wondering where you were – oh, sorry, I didn't know you had company."

"Um – hello, Nick," Miriam said, suddenly aware that she was still tugging on her hemline. In his party clothes Nick looked like he'd just stepped out of a *GQ* advertisement – but then he always looked like he'd just stepped out of a *GQ* advertisement, right down to the three-day stubble. He was grinning and holding a beer bottle, just as he'd been when she slipped away. Feeling uncomfortable and embarrassed, she looked back and forth between Nick's grinning face and Josh, who kept playing gently.

"Hey, sorry, I didn't mean to barge in," Nick continued, walking up to her and slipping his arm around her waist. "It's just that – oh, hello there, Josh."

"Hello, Nick," Josh gave Nick a brief glance and continued playing.

"Long time, no see! I brought Miriam to the party," he pulled her close to his side. "What are you doing here?"

"Playing the piano," Josh answered with the slightest of smiles, not bothering to turn his head.

"Well – ah, right. Anyway, baby, the band's about to start another set. I thought you might want to get out on the floor with some of those signature moves of yours. Whaddya say?"

"Um, I dunno, Nick," Miriam hedged. Difficult as it was to stay here with Josh, feeling all the turmoil his presence caused, the prospect of leaving filled her with bleak despair. She felt she could not face the pounding rock music, the empty laughter, smoke and flickering lights from the mirrored balls. "I've got a bit of a headache coming on."

"Oh, come on, baby, don't be a spoilsport," Nick urged, tightening his arm around her waist and grabbing her elbow with that grip of his that was just a little too firm for comfort. "I know how much you love to rock and roll, and the band's well warmed up now. I was looking forward to the chance to – y'know, get down a little." He gave a little dance wiggle, his tight grip on her forcing her to do the same.

"I don't know, Nick," Miriam repeated, trying to wrench her elbow free from his grip. "I was hoping to lie down for a while."

"Baby, baby," Nick chided with one of his perfect grins, "I didn't bring you to this party to have you lie down in a room by yourself. I brought you to show you off, and have a little fun! That's why I asked you to wear that dress I got you. Great dress, eh, Josh?"

"We were just talking about the dress. It's beautiful," Josh said, not turning, continuing his beautiful playing in a more subdued key.

"See, baby? Even ol' Josh here doesn't think you should be hiding in a corner! So c'mon!" Nick slipped his arm from her waist but grasped her hand in an iron grip. "I'm not leaving without you." He was looking into her eyes now. His lips were smiling but his eyes were cold and determined, almost reptilian. She knew that look – Nick used it when he intended to get his way, and he always did. Resistance flared within her, but old habit overruled it. Her heart collapsed – she was too tired to fight right now.

"All right, maybe for a dance or two," she dropped her eyes with a sigh. "I really am getting tired, Nick."

"That's my girl," Nick said triumphantly. "Come on, let's go. See ya, Josh ol' man!" Nick was tugging on her hand now, pulling her from the room. Tugging back and looking over her shoulder, Miriam called to Josh.

"You'll be here for a while, will you?"

"Can't say for certain," Josh answered quietly. "A little while, at least." But then she was out in the hall, pulled by a Nick who was almost running. The piano music followed them, a little sadder now.

Nick pulled her back to the main hallway and was dragging her toward the garden. They reached the hallway to the right when she remembered why she'd come here. Stopping dead, she pulled her hand clear of Nick's grip. He turned with an angry look.

"What is it, baby?"

"I need to go to the powder room. That's why I came in here, and I think it's down this hall."

"Yeah, it's down here. C'mon, I'll show you."

"Nick, I think I can find a bathroom by myself," Miriam bridled. "You go on ahead, I'll be along in a few minutes."

Nick looked at her like a rancher might look at a mustang. He glanced quickly back up the hall toward where the faint piano music could still be heard, then at her again. "You sure?"

"Yes, Nick, I'm sure. I'll only be a minute."

"All right, then," he conceded, though it was clear he wasn't pleased. "I'll get you a drink and then we can get the good times rollin', right?" He pulled her to himself and gave her a rough kiss.

"Right, Nick," she said, pulling free and starting down the hallway to the restroom.

"Whiskey sour, right?" Nick called as he headed toward the party.

"Right!"

"I'll make it a double! And if you're not along in five minutes, I'll be back with the bloodhounds!"

"I'm sure you will, Nick," Miriam sighed as she opened the bathroom door.

When she emerged a few minutes later, she was half surprised not to see Nick waiting for her at the main hallway. It was the sort of thing he'd do, but for whatever reason he wasn't there. She walked back to the hallway, still tugging at her hem and feeling dismal about going back to that damned party. She stopped for a minute and listened. She could still hear the sound of the piano coming from the hallway to the left. At the end of the main hallway, where it opened onto the garden, she could hear the drums and guitars beginning to warm up. Still no sign of Nick. She started walking toward the party, then stopped and turned. She looked back up the hallway toward the piano music, then back down toward the party.

The initial draft of this story was written for an online forum that was frequented by young people whose understanding of spiritual warfare was formed by comic books and fantasy movies. It was there that I learned of some of the struggles that young people face in the spiritual desert that is modern culture. I hoped the story would help them see connections they hadn't seen before.

Catherine's Triumph

"Are there any questions?"

A couple of hands shot up, and Guillermo was selected.

"Dr. Kirkland, is Cho-kan-tee their name for themselves, or was that name given to them by the Spanish?" Guillermo struggled with the name.

"Xoqanti," Dr. Kirkland pronounced carefully. "Interestingly, it was neither. We don't know what they called themselves. What we have is a corrupted form of the name given them by a neighboring tribe. The closest translation we can get is something like 'murderous bloodthirsty enemy'. We know next to nothing about what the tribe thought of themselves, because little remained of them after the neighboring tribes banded together and destroyed them. Even tribes we know were enemies for centuries joined forces against the Xoqanti and wiped out every trace."

"Wow," quipped Peter. "They must have been really bad neighbors."

"Even to this day," Dr. Kirkland replied. "Descendants of local tribes are normally very protective of any land where their ancestors lived, resisting any incursion onto it. But when local developers wanted to put a shopping center on a site that was known to have been a center of Xoqanti activity, nobody said a word. The silence was deafening."

"You mean the new strip mall? Up on old 170?" asked Peter.

"The very place."

Looking at the clock, Sister Marie Ellen stood up. "Ladies and gentlemen, let's give Dr. Kirkland a big thanks for coming to speak to us today." The youngsters applauded while the doctor nodded, smiled, and started packing his materials away. Katie swung her backpack over her shoulder and made her way to the doorway with the rest of the kids. Local anthropology and archeology interested her, but it was always hard to stay awake during last hour – and she was ravenous. Maybe she'd take the long way home.

Her cell phone rang. "Katie?" came a familiar voice.

"Hey, Denise," Katie smiled. "What's going on?"

"Nothing, really, just called to say hi. How did the day go?"

"Good, good. We had a guest speaker from the University today – talked about local tribes and stuff. I had trouble keeping my eyes open."

"Heading home?"

"I thought I'd drop by Abuela Herrera's first – she sometimes bakes this time of day."

"Hungry?"

"Starving!"

"Great! Give me a call tonight, okay?"

"'Kay!"

At Abuela Herrera's, she didn't even bother knocking. She could smell the baking masa, so she just walked around to find the elderly *señora* stooped over, slapping another tortilla flat while three baked on the rock before her.

"*Abuela!*" Katie called. The wrinkled old lady looked up and her eyes lit up with excitement.

"*¡Ay, mi Katie! ¡Me veniste a ver!*"

"Yes, I have, Abuela! It's been too long," Katie gave her a hug.

"*¿Que preciosa, mi vida, mi linda, te has engordado, si? Ven a comer algo...* Sit, sit here and eat!" Abuela Herrera pushed her down at the picnic table and lay a plate of hot, fresh tortillas before her. Katie rolled one up to better devour it while her adopted grandmother bustled about muttering. A tall glass of lemonade and a bowl of black beans appeared. Katie sighed as she wrapped another tortilla around a spoonful of black beans and bit into it.

"How is your school, your studies, *mi* Katie? The good sisters, they are well, *si*?"

"We had a doctor from the University come down today," Katie said around her bites. "He talked about the local tribes. He mentioned one I'd never heard of before – the Xoqanti."

Abuela Herrera turned and spat viciously into the dirt, then ground her foot on the spittle. "Them!" she snarled. "In a church school, they teach you these things? Why do they do this?"

Katie was startled. She had never seen friendly, easygoing Abuela like this. "Abuela, it was just class. The doctor said that they –"

"Pah!" Abuela Herrera spat again. "These doctors and smart men, who think they know so much! So many things there are, not in their books. Never should be in their books! I tell you, *me preciosamente* Catarina, I tell you, and may *la Madre Maria* forgive me for what I must say to young ears." She crossed herself a couple of times and sat down across from Katie. Her usually smiling eyes were black and hard as obsidian, and her smile wrinkles were gone.

"Mrs. Bertrand?"

"Yes," the woman replied.

"And this must be – Jennifer?"

The teenager at the woman's side gave a small nod but said nothing, keeping her gaze fixed on the floor.

"Who were those – people out there?" Mrs. Bertrand blustered.

"Just our local fanatic fundamentalists," the receptionist said lightly. "They're there most afternoons. You'd think the pavement would get hard on their knees, but they keep coming. You learn to ignore them."

"You'd think they'd respect other people's privacy," Mrs. Bertrand muttered angrily, taking a clipboard from the receptionist.

"You'd think," agreed the receptionist. "The procedure will be five hundred fifty."

"Five hundred fifty dollars!" Mrs. Bertrand said. "But...our insurance–"

"Yes, ma'am," the receptionist replied with the smooth familiarity of one accustomed to such protests. "With your coverage, we prefer you pay up front and apply to them for reimbursement. I've put a claim form and instructions there on the clipboard. We accept cash and major credit cards."

"But – well, if you insist," Mrs. Bertrand muttered, digging in her purse. "Let's just get this over with."

"Thank you," the receptionist replied. "If you'll have a seat over there, a technician will be along for Jennifer shortly."

"Bye, Abuela!" Katie called, waving as she walked away. The tantalizing smell of fresh tortillas rose from the bag she carried, but she didn't notice. She was turning over in her mind what the Abuela had told her, wondering how much was just legend and how much might be true. But even if only half of it was, it was still terrible. Right here in this area! It had been quite a story, and she'd stayed longer than she intended, listening in horrified fascination as the old woman told the tales that her grandfather had told her. She shivered and offered a quick prayer.

She reached back and fished her cell phone out of its pocket on the side of her backpack. Two messages – and both from Mom. Oh, no! She'd forgotten to call – well, she'd be home shortly.

"Hi, Mom!" she bounced through the back door to find her mother seated at the kitchen table.

"Catherine Anne!" her mother cried. "Where have you been? Why didn't you answer your phone?"

An old, bitter part of Katie rose up at the accusation in her mother's tone. She felt the same old sting of anger and hurt, and sharp words sprang to her lips. But then she saw the redness around her mother's eyes, and the rosary gripped tight across her knuckles.

"Mom, Mom, I'm sorry," Katie said, dropping her backpack and sitting down by her mother. "I dropped by Abuela Herrera's after school, and must have put my backpack down on my phone. I never heard it ring. I saw your messages, but thought I'd be home soon enough. She was baking tortillas, and she gave me some! See?" Katie held up the paper bag.

"You were gone for so long!"

"We got talking – she was telling me stories about local tribes, and I was eating tortillas and beans. We just lost track of time."

"So – you've had supper?"

"Oh, Mom, have I had supper," Katie groaned for effect. Her mother smiled through her tears. "You know I can't resist Abuela's tortillas, and she stuffed me full. But I'll eat more, if you want me to!" Katie grinned as she made to open the bag, but her mother took it from her.

"No, I believe you. What kind of stories?"

"Pardon?"

"Stories. You said the Abuela was telling you stories – family stories?"

"No," shuddered Katie. "They were – creepy."

"Creepy?"

"Yeah, creepy," Katie replied, looking out to where the sky was getting dark. "I'd rather not talk about them just now, if you don't mind. I've got studying to do." She pulled her backpack onto the table and began dragging her books out. She would have told her mother about the guest lecturer, but that would have led back to the Abuela's tales, and that's just what she didn't want to think about. Trigonometry, now – that would take her mind off things.

It was the darkest part of the night, and only the keenest of ears could hear the rustling, or the low snarl that occasionally escaped through the Beast's fangs as it prowled the underbrush. It could hear the little creatures as they skittered away, terrified at its approach. They were nothing. Animals could be frightened, but they couldn't be terrified as men could. The panic of animals could never provide the same heady intoxication as the black terror of a cornered man.

Soon the Beast would know that again. It was growing stronger. The blood was flowing again. It wasn't the same, not like the old times, but it was blood and that meant something. It could feel his strength building with each passing day. Soon it would again be able to leave this hollow and roam abroad. Even now it wondered if it would be strong enough, if the right prey strayed across its path. Maybe, just maybe. It drew itself up and gave a roar. It wasn't much, not like it was once able to do, but some dogs answered him in the distance. It snarled again and swiped at a branch with its claws. A mark – it could just see it on the bark in the dim moonlight. Not much, yet – but soon.

Katie rolled over. There were those dogs howling again! What on earth was troubling them? They never used to howl. She knelt on her bed and looked out her window. The moonlight blanketed the land in a quiet, ghostly glow. On the bluff to the west she could see the lights of the strip mall that had gone up recently. She shook her head, remembering what Abuela Herrera had told her about what had once taken place atop that bluff. Below it, closer and a little to her right, was the gully, all overgrown with brush. There were paths through that brush, including one that brought you out right behind the school. She used to take it to school, back – before. It was down by there that the dogs were yammering, behind some of the homes that backed up to the gully. Now some were throwing themselves against the chain fences of their kennels as they barked – she'd never heard them this agitated!

Glancing to her right, she could see hanging on her wall the small plaque that she'd been given for her birthday years ago. St. Catherine of Siena – her namesake. She reached over and gently stroked the placid face of the icon. St. Catherine always seemed to be wearing a quiet, cryptic smile that looked like she was either sharing a joke or hiding a secret, or both. Katie had read a book about St. Catherine while she was in the Center. There was a strong woman for you! If only she could be as strong. She wondered if she would ever be a heroine like Catherine.

Katie looked out over the moonlit landscape and shuddered to remember what she'd learned that afternoon. Then she gave St. Catherine another nod and lay back down, knowing that she was well guarded.

"You're not forgetting that you're walking Abby and Liam to school this morning, right?" Mom asked.

"No, Mom," Katie replied as she stuffed her books into her backpack. "Kevin, too?"

"No, he's got a dentist's appointment."

Katie was tucking the final items into her backpack when she noticed beside the toaster the small plastic bottle of holy water that Mom kept there. It was an odd thing to keep about a house, but Katie knew that Mom had only started doing so about the time Katie had been going through her difficulties. She wasn't sure when or how Mom used the holy water, but it looked like it hadn't moved in months. On a whim, she picked up the bottle. It was about half full. Glancing over to see that Mom busy with Abby, Katie tucked the bottle into one of the outside pockets of her backpack. She wasn't sure why - there were plenty of places to find holy water at school - but she was feeling a gentle urging. No harm - she could top it off and return it this afternoon. Mom probably wouldn't even notice it was gone.

The twins were now ready, complete with Dora and Spider Man backpacks. Katie bustled them off to school, one on each side. It was a lovely morning, sunny but not yet hot. It would be May in a couple of days, and May was her favorite month.

They were just past Hanson's house when Katie felt the trails calling her. The brush came closest to the sidewalk here, and she knew that just beyond that elderberry bush was the head of a trail that would take her to the one that led up to the school.

"Hey, kids," she asked, "how about taking a short cut to school today?"

"A short cut! Cool!" Liam said with enthusiasm, but Abby was less excited.

"Will it be scratchy?" she asked.

"No – I know the paths. Come on, it's a new way to school," Katie urged her. They rounded the bush and she parted the branches to show the trail. Liam bounded ahead in glee while Abby took some coaxing. Soon they were working their way along the familiar ways, and Katie was breathing the scent-laden morning air with nostalgia.

"Why are we going this way, Katie?" Abby whined.

"Oh, just for some variety," Katie said. "Liam, come back here! Hold my hand." Truthfully, she wasn't sure why she was obeying the urge to take this old shortcut. It was true that she liked variety, and the roundabout sidewalk way to the school was getting well-worn, but there was something more – almost like she was fated to walk this way today.

It heard the rustling, and the chattering voices coming toward where it was hiding. It knew it should stay out of sight, especially in the growing sunlight, but its hunger was too great. It had been too long, too long, and those were children's voices. It began to follow alongside, moving through the brush alongside the path.

Not far along the path, Katie's casual confidence began to fade. Why had she come this way? Dark doubts and shadows of old fears began to flit about the edge of her mind. She quickened her pace a little. A vague menace seemed to pervade the morning air – coming from somewhere over there? She glanced to her right – had she heard a rustle in those bushes? The sense of menace intensified, and she hurried a bit more.

"Katie, you're squeezing me," whined Abby.

"Why are we running?" asked Liam.

Why were they running? Abruptly, Katie stopped short, as if someone had shaken her. Why was she running, indeed – and from what? She turned toward her right. There was something there, she was sure of it. Something that was hiding, trying to scare them. Katie realized that she could be frightened if she chose, or she could face whatever it was.

"You!" she called. "In the bushes! Show yourself!"

"Who are you talking to, Katie?" Abby asked.

The path had just entered a grassy clearing. An acacia bush stood just to Katie's left. She was looking across the clearing at the scrub on the far side when she saw it, rising out of the ground, fixing her with glowing red eyes. She gasped, watching in horror as the thing seemed to keep growing and growing until it towered over her, tall as a house. It was massive, with great bare arms and large hands that had nails long enough to be claws. The huge head had a short forehead, a flat nose, and jutting jaw. Its mouth was gaping, showing a set of long fangs that were dripping as the Beast snarled. It was staring right at her and, when it saw that she was looking back, leaned over and snarled, showing more of the jagged teeth. Its mottled skin was hairy and covered with vile, tumorous growths. Katie was petrified.

"Why are we stopping, Katie?" came a small voice beside her. Abby was tugging at her hand insistently. Clearly the children could see nothing – thank God for small favors.

So, this was it. This was what lived here. It was still looking at her, snarling and reaching out with those claws. It wasn't coming any closer, but she suspected that if she turned and ran, it would be on them.

"Katie!" the tugging was getting insistent. Now Liam was looking up at her in puzzlement.

"Here, kids," she said, backing up and keeping an eye on the snarling thing. "Why don't you just sit under the tree for a minute here."

"But Katie," Abby whined.

"Just sit down, Abby," Katie pushed them to the ground and dropped her backpack beside them. "I'll be right with you."

"But where are you going?"

The Beast was still there, looming over the clearing while it snarled and slashed the air. It was terrifying, but there was something about it that annoyed Katie – almost as if the thing were posturing. An unfamiliar determination rose within her and she strode forward.

"I see you've graduated from annoying dogs to accosting schoolchildren," she snapped at the thing, surprised at the strength of her own voice. "You're a brave one. What's next? Shoving little old ladies?"

"Silence, vermin!" snarled the thing, leaning over and making a grab in her direction. "Or I'll not tear out your throat quickly, but gnaw on your arms while I listen to you scream."

Katie's eyes narrowed. Whatever this tough talking thing was, it had probably been lurking in the brush around here for centuries. She remembered parts of the tales that Abuela Herrera had told her – perhaps this was what lay behind all those atrocities. "I don't scream easy," Katie snapped back. "And we need to get to school, so why don't you just go away and trim your fingernails or something?"

"Ah, a feisty one," the Beast laughed cruelly. "I like that. Feisty ones struggle harder as you're taking bites out of them. That's unusual for a girl – girls usually just scream and faint. Boys at least try to fight. That's why after I deal with you, I'll save that little boy for last. Maybe I'll let him run around for a while before I end it."

Katie thought fast. She was certain that if this thing could actually harm them, it would have done so already instead of standing there jabbering. The fact that the children couldn't see it meant something, though she didn't know what. But she didn't want to risk letting it get to them. She had to drive it off or at least hold it back, and she wasn't going to do that with just sarcasm. Could she fight it? If so, how? And with what? She glanced around, but couldn't see so much as a stick on the ground.

Then she remembered something from the Abuela Herrera's stories. Maybe if she could…

"You're not going to be running anywhere after anyone until you deal with me," Katie said, "in a blood circle."

It was the Beast's turn to be surprised. How could this whelp, this stripling woman, know about that? A blood circle? Here, in broad daylight? It licked his lips in anticipation – it had been so long, so long. It remembered the circles that had been drawn years ago – not down here in the hollow, but up on the bluff. The memory almost brought back the scents to its nostrils: the smoke of the ceremonial fires, the sacrificial incense, the tightly packed men, the stench of fear, and ultimately the tang of blood. It could almost see the flickering torchlight edging the circle that had been marked with blood poured from the ceremonial bowl. They'd used the children for that, since they were useless in the ceremony itself. There would be the priest in the jaguar mask, crouching within the circle and holding the obsidian-edged club. The prisoners, bound and piled nearby, brought one at a time to be hurled into the circle. Most tried to run at first, and were mystified when they couldn't pass the invisible wall formed by the blood. Then some had tried to fight, while others had just collapsed and screamed for mercy. If it was early in the evening, the priest would play with them, goading them to run or try to fight. If it was a woman, he might have his fun with her. But as the night wore on and he got tired, he wouldn't waste the effort. It all ended the same anyway – the prisoner's head yanked back, the bare throat, the club falling as the worshipers howled.

And it got another meal.

Another meal. The Beast's insides growled at the prospect. This recent trickle of blood was something, but it wasn't proper food – more like leavings, spiritual offal. The people didn't even know what they were doing, who they were feeding.

But this girl – she had just offered to step into the circle, freely and of her own will. Oh, what that meant! Real food, for the first time in centuries! And she was the guardian, so after defeating her, it could get the children, and with the strength from that...

"Very well, whelp," the Beast leaned over and snarled, trying to hide its eagerness. "You mark out the circle, and I'll enter it."

"Since I'm the only one here with blood," the bitch snapped back as she turned away.

Oh, we'll see about that, the Beast thought. We'll see about that, indeed.

Katie stepped back to grab her purse, to find the children asleep on their backpacks. "Thank you," she whispered a prayer as she dug in her purse for something to nick her wrist with. It would be difficult – she wasn't allowed to carry even a nail file, and Mom went through her purse regularly to enforce that. She didn't want to have to use a sharp rock... ah, this would do. A small pair of fingernail clippers, but they had one of those mini-nail files under the handle. She extended it and looked about for a rock. A couple of quick swipes got the hooked end just sharp enough for her purposes. She half turned, but then remembered the small plastic bottle. So, this was why! "Thank you very much," Katie whispered as she slipped the bottle into her pocket. Somebody had known this was going to happen – in fact, had led her here – and that meant...

Katie stood up with a predatory smile and turned back to where the Beast stood rocking on its stumpy legs. It hissed as she approached. She found herself at a bit of a loss – she didn't know how to mark out one of these circles – but then, oddly, she did know. It didn't have to be a round circle. Somehow, she knew that all she had to do was mark off four corners. The four points of the compass would be best, but any four would do. She'd start – right there.

Katie knelt in the dust and dug at the base of her palm with the nail clipper. Snarling and slavering, the Beast crept closer. "Back off!" she snapped, and to her surprise it did, though it kept staring at her hand with those glowing eyes. There! She broke the skin a little, and a few drops of blood oozed out. The creature started panting and running its tongue over its lips – it couldn't seem to get its eyes off the bright redness.

Katie brushed her palm on the grass, leaving the smallest hint of blood. Somehow, she knew it would suffice. She stepped off about twenty paces and did it again, then turned to mark off the next point. This would bring her closer to the Beast than she wanted, but she figured that she would soon be doing that regardless, so she strode toward it.

"Back off, I said!" Katie yelled, and again, it did, at least far enough to let her mark the third corner. The little cut wasn't bleeding much anymore, so she had to dig at it a little, which stung. The Beast was gasping and slobbering again, and it gave her the creeps to think of it looking over her shoulder. She was glad to walk away from it to mark off the fourth corner. Then she returned to the first spot – oh, yes, it was right over there by the path. She turned to face the Beast, whose shoulders were heaving with the intensity of its breathing.

"Are you ready?" she called out.

"I've been ready, whelp," snarled the thing.

"Do you enter this circle of your own free will?" Katie was puzzled at herself – why had she asked that?

"Just get on with it!"

"Answer the question!"

"Yes, I do," the Beast roared, stepping forward.

"And I, too, enter of my own free will," Katie said, mostly to herself as she stepped forward into the area she had marked off.

The scent of the fresh blood was intoxicating. A willing victim! It had been millennia since anyone had willingly come to the Beast! What power it would gain from this meal! Quivering with anticipation, it was barely able to contain its excitement as the girl stepped into the circle she had drawn – for her own execution. The second she was inside, it leapt forward and reached for her.

She crossed the invisible line and stopped. All she had to do was stand – she knew that with the mysterious certainty that had told her how to mark off the circle. The hideous Beast was bounding for her, reaching out with those grotesque arms to catch her in its claws. She wanted to run, but somehow knew that she couldn't leave the circle. She felt like vomiting, but instead stood straighter, closed her eyes, and drew a deep breath.

"Father, Son, and Holy Spirit, be with me now," she whispered. "Jesus, Mary, and Joseph, stand by my side. Gabriel, Raphael, and Michael, be my defenders. St. Anne, St. Margaret, and St. Catherine, pray for me."

The Beast's talons closed around her.

From the darkest places of Katie's mind all the dark, familiar feelings came rushing back. Like sewage welling up a drainpipe, the self-loathing, fear, disgust, and anguish surged up and overwhelmed her mind. Everything went black, and she was tossed about by the maelstrom of emotions she thought she'd left behind. How weak she was! How disgusting she was! How fat she was! She reeled where she stood, having nothing to cling to but the words which her lips were reciting.

"Jesus, Mary, and Joseph" she whispered. "Gabriel, Raphael, Michael…"

Now images were flitting past her, images from the past, bringing with them the full force of who Katie had been. She could see her face looking back at her, as out of a mirror – the pale white skin, the black lipstick and nail polish, the ironed black hair. The gaunt cheeks and bright eyes. How fat she was! How ugly! Her insides cringed.

"Father, Son, and Holy Spirit," she clung to the words. "St. Margaret, St. Catherine..."

Miles away, her mother gasped and pulled the van to the side of the road.

"What is it, Mom?" Kevin asked.

"It's Katie." Mother grabbed the rosary from the rearview and put her head down on the steering wheel, sobbing as she clutched the beads. "Please no, God. Please no."

"Is she all right?" asked Kevin.

The images were shifting quickly now, and the old feelings they brought with them were tossing her like a scrap of rag in a windstorm. The ironed hair, and the ironed skin. Pulling back the black skirt to expose the white, white skin of her thigh. Lowering the blade and drawing it slowly along, watching the skin peel back and the blood well up. The delicious pain, the red blood on the white skin, now dripping down. Another cut.

The girls had concluded their study and were standing in a circle holding hands. One of them stumbled and moaned. Her friends caught her.

"What is it, Denise?"

"It's – it's Katie," Denise answered. "A girl in my support group. She goes to St. Agatha's."

"Your support group? Is she…you know…"

"I don't know. It doesn't matter. We need to pray, guys, we need to pray hard."

Katie was dimly aware that the Beast was standing right over her, gripping her in its claws. It seemed to be bending down, but her consciousness was overwhelmed by even more images. "Father, Son, and Holy Spirit," she whispered, as more memories deluged her. Mother, her sleepless eyes red from weeping, pleading with her at the kitchen table. Dad yelling and storming out of the family room. A tearful Kevin looking at her with bewildered eyes and pleading with her not to make Mommy cry. Yelling and slamming doors. Fear and pain and hatred. Her grade school friend Joanie turning away in pain after some sarcastic comment that was meant to wound.

How fat she was. How disgusting she was.

"Jesus, Mary, and Joseph."

In her office at the school, Sister Marie Ellen's heart heard the call and she bowed her head to pray for young Katie. In the chapel, Padre Mendez lifted the chalice and said the ancient words, "Take this, all of you, and drink from it, for this is the chalice of My Blood, the Blood of the new and eternal covenant..."

Katie felt so battered that she could hardly stand, yet something seemed to be holding her up. She sensed that the Beast was leaning over now, opening its jaws to take her in its putrid mouth, but that didn't matter. She could feel the blood pounding in her ears as a memory came back so vividly that it was like she was there.

"St. Catherine, St. Margaret."

Thub, thub, thub went her heartbeat.

The room was dark, like most parties that she went to in those days. The glowing cigarettes were scattered about the room, and there were black lights and strobe lights. Everyone was dressed in black, and she was following a girl through the crowd. Movement looked sharp and staccato in the strobe lights.

Thub, thub, thub.

"Michael, Gabriel, Raphael," her lips whispered.

She was coming to the back of the room. Hunger and smoke were making her head spin, but back here was what she had come for. There were several people clustered around a pool table. A kid in a muscle t-shirt was taking a stiletto to his forearm. Everyone was watching in fascination as the pointed tip sliced into the skin. Two parallel cuts, then a cross cut to connect them.

"Jesus, Mary, and Joseph."

Thub, thub, thub.

The kid then slid the knife under the cut end and slowly peeled back the skin, exposing the raw tissue beneath. Katie could see the muscles in the kid's jaw clenching, but he kept peeling back until everyone could see the red muscle. There were gasps and cries, but Katie watched in silence, noticing that despite the depth of the cuts, no blood was flowing from them.

Thub, thub, thub.

With a look of triumph, the kid turned and looked right at Katie. Slowly, deliberately, he held the stiletto out to her.

In the chapel, kneeling for the Consecration, Abuela Herrera bowed her head. "*Mi Katie, mi Katie preciosa,*" she murmured.

She could take the knife. Everyone was watching her. There was bright anticipation in all the dark eyes. Would she do it? Would the worthless, disgusting, putrid, detestable slime do it? The strobes flickered along the bright edge of the red-edged blade. Slowly she reached out. The kid's eyes dared her, and those around the table leaned a little forward. Her hand drew close. Would she do it? The choice was hers.

The choice was hers.

Thub, thub, thub.

Jesus, Mary, and Joseph.

Suddenly she seized the kid's wrist and shoved the knife away. Light! She craved light! As she turned to run from the dark, smoky room, the vision broke and dispersed. She found herself standing in the sunlight, breathing the morning air. The Beast was before her, but it was drawing away, wearing a frustrated look. A foul smell lingered, but the freshening breezes were blowing it away.

"So, you are stronger than I thought you would be," it snarled in a disappointed tone, "though I suspect you had help. It appears I shall have to wait for my meal."

Katie wobbled and felt like fainting, but knew she couldn't. This wasn't over. "St. Joseph, St. Catherine," she murmured.

"I have done my worst," the Beast growled. "Now, you must do your worst – unless you have already done it."

"My worst?" Katie asked. Her hand slipped around to the pocket that held the small bottle.

"Yes, whelp," replied the Beast, folding its arms cockily. "The worst you can do – not that I expect it will be much."

"You're right about that," Katie said, holding the bottle in her palm and thumbing the cap open. "I can't do much – but my God can! In the name of the Father, Son, and Holy Spirit, I curse you, demon!" Sweeping her hand up, she splashed the holy water in two great arcs; one vertical and one horizontal.

The demon screamed and reeled, holding its arms before its face as the droplets fell on the vile skin. Wherever they touched they seemed to burn, for smoke rose up and the demon cried out in agony. Katie felt no sympathy as she advanced toward the Beast, slashing with words and bright water that glistened in the morning sun like polished steel.

"My Lord defeated your foul master two thousand years ago, Beast! You have no power over me or over those I love," Katie was screaming as she stalked forward. The demon was literally shriveling beneath the onslaught, screaming and writhing on the ground as more and more smoke rose from wherever the holy water struck. Now it was no larger than a tall man, and she could see it shrinking even more as it twisted in the dust. "The glorious company of apostles praise You! The noble fellowship of prophets praise You! The white-robed army of martyrs praise You!" Katie didn't know where the words were coming from, but they seemed to be tormenting the thing as much as the holy water was.

Finally, she could feel the bottle getting low. She was standing over the thing now, which was no larger than a small boy. She twisted off the cap and dumped the last of the water on it, which caused it to howl and scrabble in the dust. It sure wasn't much, was it? But now what should she do?

With the curious certainty that she'd felt thrice before that morning, she knew that there was a presence nearby. It was a powerful but loving presence that seemed oddly familiar. It was asking her – permission to speak? She mentally assented, and found words coming from her lips that were not of her forming.

"Monster, you have entered this circle of your own free will, and here you have been defeated," Katie heard her voice saying. The words were heavy with authority, and the demon just lay face down in the dirt and quivered. "Hear now your doom: in this circle you will stay, until this world is remade and you face your final judgment." Katie started backing out of the circle, toward the children. "You shall not leave it, nor shall any come in to you. It is sealed until the end of this age." Katie was now on the path, and she swept her hand in an arc. The air before her started to mist up, but she could see that it was more like a wall. Before her eyes a great globe of opalescent mist was forming, roughly around the edges she had marked out with blood. The mist was thickening as she watched, and even now she couldn't see the small form of the demon. Now the globe was pearly white and completely opaque. Then it started to shrink, or sink into the ground, she couldn't tell which.

She felt something like a tug – it was hard to describe – and felt the presence departing. Glancing about, she thought she saw the slightest image of a woman's face – a kind, somewhat familiar face, wearing a gentle smile – drawing away from her. She was looking at Katie with eyes filled with infinite love.

"Hey," Katie called, but the vision swirled and was gone. Katie shook her head. Where did she know that face from?

Katie looked about the clearing, which didn't seem any different than it had when they'd arrived – except that now there were two children sleeping under the tree. She felt very weak, and ravenously hungry. She wondered if she'd been dreaming, but then looked down at the empty bottle in her hand. And at her watch.

"Mom, are you all right?" Kevin's voice was laced with panic as he shook his mother's arm. "Is Katie all right?"

The mother lifted her head, her heart suddenly lighter than it had been in years. She looked at her son. "Yes – yes, I think Katie is all right." She laughed briefly for sheer joy. "And I'm all right, too!"

The girls released their hands. The tension that had been thick in the room had suddenly evaporated, and everyone breathed easier. Nobody had said anything, but everyone felt the sense of completion – and triumph.

"Do you think she's okay?" someone asked.

"I don't know, but I'll try to find out," Denise started rummaging for her cell phone.

"Behold, the Lamb of God," Padre Mendez intoned, lifting the Host and chalice. "Behold Him who takes away the sin of the world. Blessed are those called to the supper of the Lamb."

"*Señor, no soy digno de que entres …*" Abuela Herrera lifted her eyes and muttered her prayers of thanks.

Her watch! O my gosh, what time was it? It seemed like hours had passed, but they were only about ten minutes behind. But she had to wake the kids, and they were sluggish and whiny. Katie felt that she'd been totally drained, and kept fighting off woozy spells as she got the children to their feet and hustling down the path.

Her phone warbled. "Hello?"

"Katie? Are you all right?" came Denise's familiar voice.

"I'm okay – a little worn, but okay," Katie replied.

"What on earth happened? You sound exhausted!"

"I don't have time to explain right now, but it was – good. Real good," Katie laughed. Her body was exhausted, but her heart felt as though it had finally emerged from a dark cave into morning sunlight. "Praise God, it was real good!"

Denise was stunned. Katie never talked like that. "Are you sure you're all right?"

"I'm fine, Denise," Katie assured her. "I'll call you later, okay?"

They were coming to the hill that led up to the school, and Katie could hear the bell. "Come on, you two, there's the bell!" she urged them up the slope and just made it into the doors as the second bell rang. Dropping them off at their classroom, she made her way to her locker. She was going to be late for first hour, but somehow, she felt that it wasn't all that important.

"Katie?" Sister Marie was standing outside her office door, watching Katie fumble in her locker. "Are you all right? You look wrung out."

"Hello, Sister," Katie stammered. "I...there was...I'm sorry I'm late."

"Has something happened, Katie?" The Sister knew Katie's history, and was stepping toward her with a look of concern.

"Yes, yes, something happened," Katie replied, not wanting to lie but not wanting to explain right here. "But it was a good thing – a very good thing." Part of her felt like laughing – everyone was so concerned about her doing terrible things to herself, while her heart felt so light that if she hadn't been so tired, she would have danced down the hallway. She was free! She felt like – a butterfly landing on the most delicate flower being carried on a cushion of finest gauze by a white-garbed maiden riding a high-stepping white mare! If only she didn't feel so hungry...

Sister Marie was still looking at her oddly, so Katie went out on a limb. "Sister, do you mind if I skip first hour today? I'd like to spend some time in the chapel this morning."

Sister Marie smiled. "That'll be fine, Katie. I think Padre Mendez is waiting for you."

Katie smiled and turned, then turned back. "Oh, Sister –"

"Yes, Katie?"

"Do you still go up to the strip mall to protest on Saturdays?"

"As much as we can," the Sister smiled.

"I'd like to come with you this weekend, if I may."

"Of course, you may."

It was a hot summer afternoon, and Katie was shucking corn with her mother on the porch when her cell phone rang.

"Hello?"

"Hey, Katie!"

"Hi, Denise! What's up?"

"What, you haven't heard the news? I thought you'd be calling me."

"What news?"

"About the clinic. It's closed."

"Really?" squealed Katie. "When?"

"Just this week. Apparently, everybody came to work on Thursday and the place was just locked. My dad says there's been word around that the owner got in some kind of trouble with the IRS."

"Yes!" Katie pumped her fist in the air.

"So, does this mean we get Saturday morning back?"

"You bet it does, sister!"

I've always wanted to write a story that would fit into The Arabian Nights...

The Queen's Request

Once upon a time there was a queen named Sophia. She ruled her small kingdom well and justly, and on the whole her people were happy and prosperous. But Queen Sophia wanted to be the very best ruler she could be. At times she felt she lacked the wisdom to rule her people as well as they deserved. So, one day she called her old friend the Vizier and asked him what she could do to be a better queen.

Queen Sophia and the Vizier decided to seek help from other kingdoms. They would find out what their kings did to rule well, and perhaps make alliances with them. The next morning messengers were sent off on swift horses. Each messenger bore a request asking the other kings to send emissaries to explain what was best about their kingdoms, and possibly to discuss alliances. One messenger went to the court of Dormin, King of Ranish, a nearby kingdom renowned for the might of its armies. Another was sent to King Laabeth of Nidos, a neighboring land known for its great wealth and many merchants. The third was sent to a far-off kingdom of which the queen had heard little, but which was rumored to be well ruled by a just and wise king. The queen asked that these emissaries arrive on Midsummer's Day, when she would hear what they had to say.

Several weeks later, when Midsummer's Day dawned, the Vizier stood outside the main gate of the capital, awaiting the emissaries. First to approach was a company of soldiers in close array, clad in shining armor and marching smartly up the road to the gate. At their head rode three officers on grand horses. The martial company came up to the Vizier and halted with a great shout. The three officers dismounted and saluted. It was a grand sight.

"We have come from the mighty Dormin, King of Ranish, in answer to your queen's request," announced the tallest officer with the richest uniform. "I am General Strongarm, commander of all the king's armies. I have brought with me two officers from allied armies. They can tell of the many benefits of alliance with our kingdom. This is Colonel Brut, and this is Major Sack. We have also brought a company of the king's own guard, to show your queen the honor she is due."

The Vizier bowed low. "We are honored by your presence, General Strongarm. I am the queen's Vizier. I have been sent to escort you to the queen, to whom you can deliver your message directly."

Even as the general was saluting the Vizier, there was another commotion on the road as a caravan approached the gate. It was a small caravan, but seemed very rich. There were mules carrying gold-trimmed chests and oxen pulling carts laden with goods. At the head of the caravan rode three men on great camels led by slaves garbed in satin. The caravan halted at the gate and the three men dismounted. The leader was a tall man with a curled beard who was dressed in velvet and hung about with golden chains and beautiful jewels. He bowed low to the Vizier.

"Greetings from my master, King Laabeth of Nidos," he said. "I am Count Pelf, chancellor of the king's treasury, and I have been sent in answer to your queen's request. With me are two lords who have prospered greatly under my king's rule. Allow me to present Lord Edacity and Lord Frill. King Laabeth has sent us with many gifts for your queen, to give her the honor she is due."

The Vizier bowed in return. "We are honored by your presence, Count Pelf. I am the queen's Vizier, and I have been sent to escort you into her presence. There you can deliver your gifts in person. This is General Strongarm of Ranish – General Strongarm, Count Pelf." The general gave a stiff salute, and the Count bowed slightly in the general's direction.

"Well, then," the general said, "If we are both here, perhaps you could lead on..."

"Actually, we expect another – in fact, that may be him now," the Vizier pointed down the road, where three swift riders approached. Deftly steering their nimble ponies between the soldiers and the caravan, they came before the Vizier, dismounted, and bowed.

"I am Ramus, and I have been sent by my king in answer to your queen's request," said the foremost rider. "I bring his greetings and best wishes. These are my assistants, Lord Virtus and Lady Pietus."

The Vizier struggled to hide his astonishment. This Ramus was young, clad neither in bright armor nor rich robes. He and his companions wore plain brown garb, clean and well fitted but with no adornment but a single white jewel on the front of Ramus's turban. They wore no weapons and brought no gifts, unless they had items in the travel bags at their sides. This seemed a most unusual emissary for a king to send to a queen. The Vizier wondered briefly if he should be offended and send Ramus away, but decided Queen Sophia would not wish that. He bowed to the young man.

"Welcome…ah…Lord Ramus. I am the queen's Vizier, and I have been sent to bring you into her presence. This is General Strongarm of Ranish and this is Count Pelf of Nidos. Gentlemen, Lord Ramus."

The general barely nodded and the count sniffed and looked away. They made no secret of what they thought of Lord Ramus.

"Now that we are all here, let us proceed," the Vizier said. "Welcome to our capital. Behold the Great Gate, which was erected by the queen's great-grandfather. No enemy has ever taken it."

The gate was indeed magnificent, towering far above their heads. Guards walked the battlements and sentries stood beside the mighty doors, which stood open in sign of peace and welcome.

"Most impressive," exclaimed Major Sack. "I can foresee battalions marching out through these gates, to defeat the queen's enemies in mighty battles!"

"And I," declared Lord Frill, elbowing his way forward, "envision great caravans laden with wealth entering in to fill the queen's treasuries."

Smiling at these flatteries, the Vizier waited for one of Lord Ramus' attendants to speak. When nothing came, he looked about and saw that Ramus had left his side and was attending to a sick man who lay begging beside the city gate.

"It's my leg, sir," the beggar was explaining. "It has a sore that won't heal, and I can't work."

"Let's have a look at it," Lord Ramus said, starting to unwrap the filthy bandage that bound the man's leg. "Here, Virtus, fetch some clean water, if you will. Hold him up, please, Pietus."

The Vizier gazed dumbfounded at these irregular proceedings. The beggar should not even have been by the gate where he could be seen by emissaries. The Vizier would have called the sentries to carry the man away, but he could hardly order Lord Ramus aside.

When the bandage was removed, the sore looked as bad as the Vizier had expected. He could only imagine what it smelled like, but Lord Ramus paid no heed. He washed the sore clean, applied some ointments drawn from his travel bag, and bade his attendants wrap the leg in clean linen.

Behind the Vizier, General Strongarm and Count Pelf were muttering to one another.

"Embarrassing," growled the count.

"In my master's kingdom," snarled the general, "pathetic weaklings like that know better than to let themselves be seen, especially about the capital. We are a strong people, and the weak are – dealt with."

Count Pelf nodded approvingly.

Lord Ramus helped the beggar up onto his own horse. "Virtus, take him to his house, see to his care, and rejoin us."

"Yes, my lord," Lord Virtus replied.

"My apologies, gentlemen," Lord Ramus said as he rejoined them. "I hope that did not delay us too long."

"No matter, my lord, no matter," the Vizier replied. "Shall we proceed?"

The Vizier led the emissaries and their retinues through the streets of the capital, which had been cleared to allow them swift passage. Presently they came to the great marketplace which lay at the city's center. It had been impossible to empty out this bustling hub of activity, which was thronging with merchants and travelers and shoppers. The best they could do was to open a path through the crowd.

As they approached the center of the marketplace, Colonel Brut exclaimed, "I can envision this square filled with the queen's armies, bringing home the plunder of nations and the weapons of her enemies!"

"And I," proclaimed Lord Edacity, "can see this market filled with rich wares from faraway lands, a great center of trade, and the queen's court overflowing with wealth."

"Drop that, you little thief!" cried a loud voice from their right, just as a small figure dashed between the escorts and cannoned right into Lord Ramus. Staggering for balance, the lord caught hold of his assailant, who turned out to be a small and grubby lad clutching a large fruit.

The parade of dignitaries came to a jumbled halt. As the Vizier looked on in confusion, a merchant dashed up, spluttering and panting, to find himself facing the crossed spears of the palace guards. Abashed, the merchant pulled off his cap and began bowing profusely, muttering apologies while pointing at the lad with the fruit. He was starting to back away, reasoning that one fruit was not worth all this trouble, when Lord Ramus beckoned to him.

"If you please, sir," he said. The astonished guards glanced at the Vizier, who shrugged and nodded. They lifted their spears and the merchant stepped nervously though.

Lord Ramus knelt down and looked the lad right in his wide eyes. "Did you take that fruit from this man?" he asked. The lad nodded. "Did you pay for it?" After a moment's hesitation under Lord Ramus' stern gaze, the boy shook his head.

"Then you must return it, and apologize," Lord Ramus said. Eyes brimming with tears, the lad nodded. Ramus stood, his hand on the boy's shoulder, and turned to the merchant. The lad bowed, muttered something barely audible, and held out the fruit. With trembling hand, the merchant took it.

"There," Lord Ramus said. "Pietus, if you will..." He nodded to his attendant, who began fishing in her bag for a coin to pay the indemnity for theft.

"In Nidos," murmured Count Pelf to General Strongarm, "thieving urchins know better than to try their tricks in our markets. We are a prosperous people, and those who cannot make their own way are – dealt with." The general nodded approvingly.

Lord Ramus paid no heed to this. He looked at the boy's filthy face, now streaked by tears. Seeing his trembling lip and gaunt cheeks, he asked gently, "Are you hungry?"

The boy nodded, so Lord Ramus brought out from his bag a small loaf of bread. "Here, eat this," he said, handing it to the boy. His eyes wide with amazement, the boy took it and, without regard for manners, began wolfing it down.

Count Pelf and General Strongarm snorted in disgust, while the Vizier looked about helplessly. What was he supposed to do with a nobleman who acted so oddly?

The boy suddenly stopped gobbling, though the loaf was not half gone. Looking ashamed, he tried to tuck the remainder into a pocket that was too small.

"What's wrong?" asked Lord Ramus. "Are there more of you at home?"

The boy nodded, his lip trembling worse than ever and tears spilling from his eyes. "A-and m-m-my mother..." he stammered.

Lord Ramus stood and slung his bag from his shoulder. "Pietus, see the boy home," he said, handing her the bag. "There should be enough in there, but if not, you know what to do."

"Yes, my lord," Pietus answered, and she turned to follow the boy.

"Again, my apologies, gentlemen," Lord Ramus said as he returned to the group. The count and general took no notice of him, but the Vizier smiled wryly.

"It seems that things are rarely dull around you, Lord Ramus," the Vizier said.

"So I've been told," Ramus grinned.

The parade resumed, with the other emissaries surrounded by their assistants and keeping far away from Lord Ramus, who strode along by himself as if he hadn't a care in the world. They continued through the streets until they came before the palace.

"The royal palace," proclaimed the Vizier with a sweep of his staff. "Erected through the centuries and substantially improved by the queen, this is the pride of our kingdom." It was a very impressive palace, with a great arch, tall towers of white marble, and magnificent golden domes.

"I can see," cried General Strongarm, "with my king's help, this palace as a great center of mighty campaigns, home to generals and marshals, with messengers coming and going night and day, carrying orders to the queen's vast armies."

"And I can see," exclaimed Count Pelf, "with my king's help, this palace as a bustling center of commerce for the whole region, with the queen sending forth great caravans and fleets of ships to trade with the entire world."

The Vizier waited for Lord Ramus to say something, but was not surprised when he didn't. Looking around, he saw that the lord had noticed a couple by the palace gate. One was an old woman who was seated on a stool looking despondent, and the other was a young man with a large satchel at his side and a sheaf of papers in his hands. He seemed to be trying to accost people coming in and out of the palace gate. He brandished the papers at them, but nobody was paying him any attention.

"Is there some difficulty?" Lord Ramus asked as he approached the young man.

"My lord! My lord!" the young man cried as he rushed up to Lord Ramus. "Justice, that is all we ask! We have been wronged, my mother and I – terribly wronged! If only we could see the Queen, she would give us justice, I know she would! It is all right here, see..." He began to leaf through the papers in his hands.

"Peace, peace, good sir," Lord Ramus calmed him. "Justice shall be yours. Tell me of your complaint, and I will do what I can."

By now the Vizier had come over to stand with Lord Ramus as the young man poured out his story. His father had been a veteran of the queen's service who had been granted a small plot of land when he retired. He had died some years before, leaving the land to his wife and son. But in the province where they lived a group of large landowners had formed a guild and were snapping up smaller plots of land through trickery and deception. The widow and her son had been among their victims. They had lost their land and livelihood, and were now penniless and homeless.

"But I have them dead to rights, my lords, dead to rights," the young man assured them, riffling through his papers. "It's all here, witnessed and sealed. They are in clear violation of the law. Justice is on our side!"

"If that is so," asked the Vizier, "Why not take your case to the provincial court to be heard?"

"We have tried, my lord, tried desperately for many years," the young man explained. "But they will not hear our case. The rumor is that the landowner's guild owns the judges and court officials, and pays them to turn a deaf ear to our pleas. I do not know that, but I do know that our letters go unanswered, our appointments are canceled, and no official will give us a hearing date. We know not what to do – we do not have the money to bribe magistrates. Our only hope is to appeal to the Queen for justice."

"If the Queen," began Lord Ramus, but the Vizier interrupted him.

"My lord, a word, if you please." He drew Lord Ramus aside. "My lord, these supplicants at the palace gates are as common as flies in summer. If we were to trouble the Queen with every real or imagined complaint, her schedule would be filled with nothing else."

"My lord Vizier," answered Lord Ramus, "there seems nothing imaginary about the widow's complaint. The son is confident that his suit will stand in court."

The Vizier sighed. "Perhaps we could find a court official to hear the case..."

"My lord, if this guild is able to corrupt a provincial court, they will certainly have a presence here in the capital, and will have influenced the court officials. Your Queen's reputation for justice, even for the least of her subjects, is renowned far and wide. Do you not think that she would wish to try this widow's appeal immediately, if she knew of it?"

Again, the Vizier sighed, for he knew that the Queen would want to do exactly that. "But my lord," he pleaded, "this is most irregular. There are channels, there are procedures. The queen's time –"

"You let me worry about the queen's time, my good Vizier," grinned Lord Ramus. Turning to the widow and her son, he said, "Come – I will bring you before the queen. Bring all your documents and stay quiet and close by me."

The Vizier rolled his eyes and returned to where General Strongarm and Count Pelf stood muttering and looking on with disdain. They sniffed when they saw the shabbily dressed couple joining their company, but the Vizier just shrugged.

"Shall we go in?" he asked, gesturing them into the palace.

A guard of honor snapped to attention just inside the gates, and heralds called out the names of the dignitaries. All the nobles of the kingdom had assembled in their finery to welcome the emissaries. First to enter was General Strongarm, marching smartly at the head of his company. Then came Count Pelf in his opulent dress, leading his parade of riches. Last came Lord Ramus, walking as easily as if he'd been out for a morning stroll. The Vizier, coming behind them all, noticed that the widow and her son tried to shrink away into the crowd, but Lord Ramus insisted they walk beside him.

The honor guard led the emissaries into the throne room, where Queen Sophia waited to receive them. Here most of the crowd had to turn away, for only the most favored courtiers had been invited to the audience. The Queen sat on the Great Throne, well above the heads of the assembly. She wore her ceremonial crown, and her scepter was on her arm.

The Vizier stepped forward and bowed low. "Your Majesty, the emissaries you requested have been good enough to come. It is my honor to introduce General Strongarm from the Kingdom of Ranish." He bowed again and stepped aside, clearing the center of the floor for the general and his retinue.

The general stepped forward and saluted sharply. "Queen Sophia, I bring greetings from his royal Majesty King Dormin. He was delighted to receive your request and has sent me, the commander of all his armies, to convey his message." A whisper ran around the room – the king had sent his supreme commander to speak to their queen? "But first," continued the general, "a small display in your honor."

The company of soldiers launched into a very precise ceremonial drill. They marched in intricate patterns and twirled their weapons expertly. After they finished, Major Sack stepped forward and testified how alliance with Ranish had benefited his kingdom. With the help of King Dormin's armies, his king had been able to march on a neighboring kingdom with whom they had had a border dispute, soundly defeat their armies, and impose terms upon them. Then Colonel Brut told of how Ranish troops had helped his king suppress an internal rebellion and strengthen the throne.

Then General Strongarm spoke at length of the benefits of an alliance. He told how fearsome the armies of Ranish were, so that none dared attack their allies. He spoke of how the queen could secure her borders and expand her territories with the help of their military might, and how she would never have to fear another enemy.

When he had finished, Queen Sophia bowed and thanked him. She said that she had heard much of the might and prowess of Ranish, and that she would carefully consider their offer.

Then the Vizier introduced the delegation from Nidos. Count Pelf stepped forward and bowed low. "Your Majesty, I bring greetings from my sovereign, King Laabeth. He was honored to receive your request, and sent me, the supreme minister of his treasury, to bring you his reply." A louder murmur swept through the room. A military chief was impressive enough, but here was a member of the king's own cabinet! Smiling, Count Pelf bowed again. "But first, in your honor..."

He called forth his servants, who began a most impressive display of tumbling, juggling, and gymnastics. The court had never seen such skill or agility. Once everyone was thoroughly impressed, Lord Frill stepped forward. He testified how an alliance with Nidos had opened up many new markets for his country's goods, and had greatly enriched his king and court. With their new wealth they were able to purchase the many wares that the traders of Nidos brought to their land. Then Lord Edacity spoke of how his seafaring nation had profited from alliance with Nidos – how their ships were in demand for carrying trade goods, and investments from Nidos were funding new, larger ships. All this activity had made the entire country wealthier, especially the king and his nobles.

Then Count Pelf spoke of the vast wealth of Nidos, and how they insured that all their allies prospered as well. He assured Queen Sophia that enough wealth could buy anything at all – allies, military expertise, scholars, doctors, and lawyers. With enough wealth, the queen and her court would never have to worry about anything.

Queen Sophia nodded and thanked Count Pelf. She assured him that she had heard wonderful things of the glory and wealth of Nidos, and that she would carefully consider his offer.

Now came the moment the Vizier had been dreading. He stepped forward, fidgeting with his staff, and bowed nervously. "Your – your Majesty," he stammered, "The third delegation from the far kingdom is also present. Their lord brought two attendants with him, presumably to speak as these others have, but they have been – diverted."

"'Diverted', Vizier?" the queen asked in astonishment. "What do you mean?"

Glancing at Lord Ramus, who stood smiling with the widow and her son by his side, the Vizier wrung his staff in his hands. "Well, your Majesty, it's like this," he began, and explained how they had found the sick beggar at the city gates, and Virtus had been dispatched to take him home and tend to him. The courtiers hushed at this, and the queen tipped her head to one side in wonder. Then the Vizier told of the thieving urchin in the marketplace, and how Lord Ramus had fed the child and sent Pietus to tend to the boy's family. A murmur rippled around the room, and the queen cocked one eyebrow in astonishment.

"Which is why, your Majesty," concluded the Vizier, "Lord Ramus has no parties to speak on his behalf. However, he is here to speak for himself. Your Majesty, I present Lord Ramus of the far kingdom."

Without fanfare or show, Lord Ramus stepped into the center of the court and bowed low to the queen.

"Your Majesty, I am deeply honored to come before you," he said. "When my father received your request, he bid me choose two of my most trusted aides and come forthwith."

A rustle of amazed whispers swept the room as the courtiers grasped the import of what Lord Ramus had said. The Vizier stared in amazement. This unpretentious young man had just claimed before the queen and court that he was a prince.

Taking no notice of this, Lord Ramus again bowed low. "I thank you for allotting me time to speak of my father's kingdom. However, I have learned of a matter which I know will grieve you as much as it does me. A widow of your people has been gravely wronged, and has been seeking justice from your officials but has not been granted a hearing. Her son has all the documents in the case. I have reviewed the documents, and by the law of your land the matter seems clear. Your Majesty is widely renowned for your love of wisdom and passion for justice. Therefore, I crave your indulgence of a small request: to permit me to cede the time you have allotted for me to speak in order to hear the suit of this widow, and render her justice."

A gasp went up from the assembled court at the audacity of this request. The queen raised both eyebrows in wonder as Lord Ramus beckoned the widow and her son out to join him in the center of the court. The widow stood close by him, as if seeking to hide, but the son held his folio and stared around at the courtiers almost defiantly.

Off in a corner, General Strongarm and Count Pelf stood together, smirking at the scene.

"Well, you knuckle-dragging barbarian," Count Pelf said, "I may still have some competition from you, but at least there's no worry from that corner."

"I was thinking the same thing, you oily weasel," the general replied. "It takes true talent to insult the queen's judiciary, forfeit your audience, and put the queen in a touchy diplomatic position all within the space of one minute."

"Let's see what she'll do," Count Pelf said. "My king would have the guards run him and his sob cases right out of the palace gates."

Queen Sophia sat silent for a full minute while the courtiers whispered and muttered. Finally, she spoke in a clear voice:

"Very well, Lord Ramus – I grant your request."

Lord Ramus again bowed low. The queen did off her crown and laid aside her scepter. Descending the steps to the foot of the throne, she ordered her seat of judgment be set up on the dais there. Tables were brought and scribes were called. Queen Sophia took up her staff of justice and convened the court according to the ancient customs of her kingdom.

Messengers were sent to summon representatives of the landowner's guild, who indeed maintained offices in the capital. They came in great haste and consternation, for the summons was completely unexpected. The bribes and favors they distributed among the court officials were intended to ensure that they would never be brought before any judge, much less the queen herself.

Once they were present, the case was opened. The widow's son had researched the law and prepared his case well. The documents and statements he presented were impeccable, and his mother's testimony was perfect. When the guild representatives had their chance to respond to the charges, they stammered and bumbled. They had brought no documents, for the last thing they wanted was their records examined in the queen's court.

As the accused, the guild had the right of first questioning. They tried to discredit the son, maligning his character, but he was ready for them. He answered every question with facts and appeals to the law. When his turn came, he kept his questions focused on legalities of ownership and acquisition. They were again reduced to stammering and contradictions.

The case was swiftly decided. The queen ruled decisively in the widow's favor, restoring all her lands and the value of the yield for the years it had been lost to her. She levied a heavy fine on the guild, to be divided between the widow and the crown. A party of court officers escorted the guild representatives back to their offices, seized their records, and began an immediate investigation of their doings. And before she rose from her judgment seat, Queen Sophia dispatched a panel of judges to the province where the widow lived, there to begin an inquest into how the courts handled the cases brought before them.

When the queen laid aside her staff and rose from her seat, the widow was clinging to Lord Ramus with tears pouring down her cheeks. The son turned to him in triumph. "I knew it! I knew the queen would grant us justice, if only we could get a hearing." Bowing low to Lord Ramus, he continued, "My lord, I don't know how we can ever thank you."

Lord Ramus smiled and clapped his shoulder. "It was your own queen who granted you justice – my part was small. As for thanks, I only ask you to be just in all your dealings, great and small."

"That we will, my lord," the son assured him, bowing again. Then, bowing to the queen, he led his mother over to where the scribes were preparing the writ of judgment.

Queen Sophia lifted her hands for attention. "Honored emissaries, my lords and ladies, the morning's activities have been lengthy and...unusual. We are past due for refreshment. Fortunately, my chefs have been working hard to prepare a feast in honor of our guests. They tell me it is now ready. Let us repair to the banquet hall and enjoy it."

The feast was the grandest the kingdom had seen in many years. In addition to the many delicious dishes, there were tumblers and acrobats and jesters. The queen noticed that Count Pelf and General Strongarm and their assistants seemed to be trying to seek out the most influential courtiers. Lord Ramus spoke freely to all, even the servants, laughing and enjoying himself. Shortly into the feast two similarly clad people, whom the queen presumed to be his aides, slipped into the banquet hall to join him.

After the feast, the emissaries were escorted to apartments where they could rest for the night. In the morning the Vizier came to summon them into the queen's presence.

They gathered in the queen's private chambers. First Queen Sophia welcomed General Strongarm and his assistants. She thanked him for his embassage, assured him that she would soon let King Dormin know of her decision, and gave him gifts for himself and his king. She likewise thanked Count Pelf, presented him with gifts, assured him that King Laabeth would soon know her decision. The emissaries bowed and departed.

Then the queen turned to Lord Ramus, attended by Virtus and Pietus. To the Vizier's surprise, she did not offer him gifts and send him on his way. Instead, she bade them all be seated.

"So, my lord," Queen Sophia said, fixing her gaze on Lord Ramus. "The sick are tended, the hungry are fed, and justice is delivered to the poor. You must tell me more of your father's kingdom."

This dystopian-edged long short looks at our times from a different, and sometimes uncomfortable, vantage point.

Kateri's Sentence

"Bah!" scoffed Kateri. "Monica, I don't believe that for a minute, and I'm amazed you do."

"But he swears it's true," Monica replied eagerly. "He's talked to people who've seen the records. It used to happen commonly!"

"Monica," Kateri answered. "That's just ridiculous. How could a giant thing made of metal that weighed more than five houses fly through the sky faster than any bird? That's sillier than a Paul Bunyan story."

"Well, I see why he warned me not to tell anyone," sniffed Monica. "He told me this would happen, and he was right. He said this is how the Church keeps people under control – by hiding the history of the Old Times, and encouraging small and narrow minds."

"Monica!" gasped Kateri, shocked.

"He's right, though," Monica replied defiantly, but with a hesitant edge in her voice. She seemed to know she'd gone too far. "Not that all churchmen are bad, of course, but the Vatican archives are full of records of the Old Times – as are cathedrals and universities throughout the world. They keep them hidden so that the people will stay ignorant. The Counselors are in on it, too!"

"Monica!" cried Kateri, now truly frightened. Her friend had always been one to push boundaries, but now was speaking with a sharp bitterness that was unlike anything Kateri had ever heard. "Please stop talking like that! It's not true! It's poison, all of it!"

"He's right, he's right!" taunted Monica. "He said you wouldn't listen, that you'd be too scared to accept the truth!"

"No, no," Kateri answered, covering her ears. "I won't hear any more! Against the Holy Church, and the Counselors, too! I won't hear it!"

"Of course, you won't," Monica said smugly. "He said you wouldn't – that you'd rather live in ignorance and slavery. But I know the truth!"

"Monica," Kateri gasped, seizing her hand and glancing around the shed where they were sorting eggs. "Monica, where have you been hearing this? I mean – you haven't been meeting up with Richard, have you?"

"No, no – of course not," Monica replied, somewhat too casually. "Just here and there about town." Townsfolk were allowed to talk casually with strict exiles if they met them in the course of the day, but they could not interact regularly with them unless duty required it.

"You seem to be discussing a lot during these casual encounters," Kateri pressed. "He hasn't – told you his true name, has he?"

The quick flicker in Monica's eyes told Kateri all she needed to know. However, Monica withdrew her hand and stepped back with stiff dignity. "Of course not – our conversations involve other things."

"Good," Kateri replied. "I've heard more than enough, and don't want to hear any more of this – ever."

"Why? Are you scared of the truth?" Monica scoffed as Kateri bustled off. "Are you going to tell your father?" she called as the door slammed. Kateri strode away with her head down, hoping people wouldn't notice her flushed cheeks or the tears in her eyes. She was shocked and ashamed and frightened and a little angry. Monica had once been her closest friend – they'd done everything together. But now it was like she was a stranger, someone Kateri didn't even know! Ever since Monica had started meeting that exile – she had to be meeting him, she couldn't be talking about such things on street corners – and that was against the law! Maybe she should tell Father. But this was Monica...

*   *   *

Kateri sat perfectly still on the bench in the waiting chamber, her head tipped back against the wall, staring at the ceiling. She was alone in the room, her insides hollow with an emptiness that had nothing to do with hunger – though she was hungry, too. But there was nothing to do for that. All she could do now was wait for them to come for her, to take her back to court to hear her sentence.

The trial had lasted all morning. It made Kateri weak and sick to think of it. She could have been present for the whole thing – it was her right – but she'd chosen to stay in one of the waiting chambers until she was called to testify. She'd been escorted into the court and sworn in, catching only a glimpse of Richard standing defiantly behind the bar, and Monica hunched over a table, hiding her face.

The prosecutor had asked several questions which she'd tried to answer clearly, hoping nobody noticed the quaver in her voice. Once her eyes had flicked up to where Father sat behind the judge's bench with the other governors. He'd looked as impassive as the rest, and she'd quickly looked down again.

The nature of the case made the verdict obvious. Kateri's testimony had simply confirmed how long the two had been meeting illicitly, and what they'd discussed. She knew it would also implicate her, which would have consequences. The alternative was to have her tried separately, and she didn't want that. She deserved to be implicated because she was guilty – not as guilty as Monica, but guilty – and deserved whatever sentence she got.

It couldn't be long now. Kateri knew the other two had been sentenced because she'd heard them being led away. Richard had gone first – she had heard him shouting and raving and struggling with the bailiffs as he'd been dragged down the hall. More heart wrenching had been Monica's wailing and sobbing as she'd been led away shortly thereafter. But all that had been some time ago, and Kateri began to wonder if she'd been forgotten.

Finally, there was a rattling of bolts, and Kateri stood and straightened her frock, bracing herself to return to court and hear her sentence. The bailiffs were waiting – Mr. Taylor and, because she was a girl, Mistress Sands – but when she stepped into the hall, she was surprised that they turned away from the courtroom.

"This way, please, miss," Mr. Taylor responded to her quizzical look, leading the way down the hallway. Kateri followed as they passed several doors, finally turning in to one that led to the smaller meeting hall.

Kateri saw that the hall stood nearly empty, its dozens of benches lined up neatly. At one of them, just about in the center of the room, sat a black-robed figure who stood when they entered. Kateri recognized him from across the room.

It was Brother Matthew.

Now Kateri was truly mystified. Brother Matthew had been one of her favorite lecturers, but she hadn't seen much of him since she'd left school a couple of years before. Why was he here? Whatever the reason, she'd probably learn it soon. The bailiffs took her directly to where Brother Matthew stood. He nodded to them and gave her a bow and a friendly smile.

"Miss Kateri – or Mistress Peterson, I suppose I should call you."

"'Miss Kateri' is fine, Brother Matthew," Kateri smiled in spite of her nervousness. Brother Matthew was one of the best loved and most rigorous teachers in the city, but he did have a tendency to remember students as students, even after they'd come of age.

"Thank you," Brother Matthew replied. "Oh, officers – of your courtesy – I need you as witnesses." The bailiffs, who had begun to withdraw, looked puzzled in turn but stayed nearby. Brother Matthew gestured Kateri to stand across from him, and on the table between them he placed a battered black book. Atop this he put the Crucifix from the great Rosary that hung at his side. He gestured her to put her hand on the items, and then he placed his great hand atop hers.

"Kateri Marie Judith Peterson," Brother Matthew asked, fixing her with a sober gaze. "Do you solemnly vow, by God's Holy Word and by Christ's Blood shed on the Cross, to disclose nothing of what we are about to discuss to any man without the express permission of myself or a Counselor?"

Kateri was surprised. This was a Blood Oath, even more solemn than a courtroom oath. But she knew the proper response.

"I do vow, so help me God."

"So help me God," Brother Matthew echoed, lifting the Crucifix to his lips and then offering it to her. "Thank you, officers," he dismissed the bailiffs, who withdrew to a corner of the hall. He set aside the Bible and pulled over a plate with a roll and butter, some cheese, and some dried fruit.

"Here," Brother Matthew nudged the plate toward her as he poured a couple of cups of water. "The judges are taking their luncheon now, and you haven't eaten since dawn. Don't worry about me – this," he held up his water cup, "is all I'm having."

Kateri tucked into the lunch while Brother Matthew paged through a sheaf of papers by his elbow. They looked freshly written, and Kateri could guess the content. When he noticed that she was slowing down, he fixed her with his sternest gaze.

"Serious business, this," he gestured at the papers. "Do you know what your greatest sin was?"

"Yes, Brother Matthew," Kateri replied, dropping her eyes in shame. "I knew that a crime was probably occurring, but did not notify those in authority."

Brother Matthew gazed silently at her for a minute. "No," he finally said. "That may have been your greatest crime, but your greatest sin was not loving enough. You listened to your fears and acted upon them, instead of acting out of true charity. You and Monica were old friends, were you not?"

"Since grammar school," Kateri confirmed.

"I remember you both. She was louder and more assertive, was she not? You were more often following than leading?"

Kateri nodded – that was a good characterization.

"So, when you learned that she might be taking terrible risks, you feared her scorn and rejection, and so kept quiet?" Brother Matthew continued.

Again, Kateri nodded.

"There was your failure to love. You knew your friend was playing with fire, and could get badly burned. You could have prevented or mitigated it by speaking up. But out of fear you kept silent, and now many must pay the price. That was your greatest sin – acting out of fear rather than love."

Kateri's head was still hung. She could see that Brother Matthew was right. In a corner of her mind she wondered if she'd chosen that, knowing how badly Monica might fail, in repayment for the numerous slights and insults over the years. Could she really be that petty and shallow?

"I...I understand, sir," Kateri mumbled. "I see that you're right. I'm sorry."

"Learn from it, Kateri," Brother Matthew said. "Be more courageous next time."

"Yes, sir," Kateri responded. "Please, sir – what will happen to Monica?"

Brother Matthew grimaced. It was no secret – the sentence would be posted in the square by sundown – but it was still hard to speak it. "It is the usual sentence for such cases. She will be sent into strict exile until the child she carries is born. The child will be adopted, and she will go to another town to finish her exile. Five years after the birth she will be eligible to return, if her behavior warrants it and if her family will take her back."

Tears slipped from Kateri's eyes. It was a severe exile indeed. She had heard of such sentences before, but to have it happen to a close friend! She tried to imagine six years without Monica, but it was just too difficult. Then she gasped.

"And – Richard?"

Brother Matthew said nothing and looked away. Kateri knew what that meant, and her hands flew to her mouth.

The treaties regarding exiles had been worked out as an arrangement between the Church and the towns to deal with more severe lawbreaking. The towns agreed to accept each other's malefactors for a time, to separate them from their families and give them a chance to reform.

Common exiles were those who had committed lesser crimes and were exiled from their towns for periods of six months to two years. They lodged with families, helping about the household to earn their keep. They were allowed to retain their names, but had always to wear an identifying yellow hood. Kateri's family had hosted an exile many years before when Kateri was a child. Her name was Bridget, and she was from a town across the Big River. At first, she had been withdrawn and sad, as could be expected, but she'd never shirked her duties. Over time she'd become more comfortable and opened up a bit. She had a lovely singing voice and had delighted Kateri and her siblings with her songs. By the end of her year, she had been almost part of the family, and there had been tears at her departure.

Strict exiles, or Red Hoods, were a different matter. They were guilty of major or repeated crimes, and were exiled for anywhere from two years to life. They were given new names during their exile, lived apart from the town population, and worked on tasks that kept them separated. Contact with town people was not completely forbidden, but it was discouraged for both parties. One reason for this was to deny the Red Hoods opportunities to commit more crimes, because if they did, things got serious.

Richard was a Red Hood who had committed a crime that would warrant exile. But the town governors could not exile him, because this was not his home town. This left them three choices: appeal to his home town to take him back, turn him out at the town gate, or execute him.

Appeals for the return of a strict exile were rarely successful – after all, the party had been exiled for a reason, and was hardly more welcome back home for having committed more crimes. Turning him out at the town gates meant either a cruel death from starvation and exposure, or having him turn outlaw and become a danger to everyone.

That left execution. The Church acknowledged that legitimate civil authorities had the right to execute criminals who had been found guilty by due process, but strongly discouraged it. From comments Brother Matthew had made in class, Kateri gathered that much of this opposition arose from the Church's experience just before the Collapse, when human life had been so devalued that people had been killed for convenience. But sometimes there was little choice, when all other avenues had been exhausted.

Brother Matthew's distress spoke volumes, and Kateri struggled to grasp the magnitude of the situation. An appeal would be sent to whatever town Richard had come from, but it would be mostly *pro forma*. When the refusal came back, Richard would be taken to the hidden courtyard one cold dawn and hanged. It would not be a public spectacle, but all the governors and male Counselors would be there. Father had had to attend several executions, and he always returned from them grim and silent. It was not a fate Kateri would wish on anyone.

"That is not your concern," Brother Matthew said at last. "We are here to discuss issues pertinent to your sentence."

"My sentence?" Kateri asked, her throat tensing.

"Yes," Brother Matthew confirmed. "Testimony during the trial made clear that not only had Monica and Richard been meeting illicitly, but that he had passed along information about the Old Times – information that Monica told you in turn. Given my training, and my relationship with you as your teacher, the court has asked me to talk to you about what you heard. I need to know everything Monica told you, in full detail."

"Yes, sir," Kateri replied, though she couldn't understand what this had to do with her sentence. "It was mostly crazy things, tall tales and outrageous legends. It would seem a waste of time to repeat them."

"Nevertheless, tell me everything," Brother Matthew said with an enigmatic smile. "Hold nothing back, no matter how outlandish."

So Kateri did, dredging her memory to recall the several clandestine conversations she'd had with Monica. From the first time that Monica had called her aside with a secretive whisper to relay the news she was bursting to tell until their last meeting in the egg shed, Kateri told Brother Matthew everything she could remember. From the tales of the giant metal ships that could cross oceans without sails or oars, to the magic devices that enabled people to speak to others miles away, to the final absurdity of great metal flying machines, Kateri told it all while Brother Matthew listened impassively. As she spoke, the ridiculous nature of what she was saying became even more obvious, and she became increasingly ashamed that she'd ever listened to Monica.

"Was that all?" Brother Matthew asked when she finally concluded.

"Well," Kateri paused, remembering Monica's accusation against the Church at their final meeting. She'd been hesitant to mention that, partly because it wasn't strictly about the Old Times, but mostly because it was so scandalous.

"Everything, Kateri," Brother Matthew urged.

"She said – or, she said that Richard said, that the Church had records of all the old things. She said that the records were being suppressed, covered up to keep people ignorant and enslaved. She said these records were in the Vatican, as well as cathedrals and universities around the world, but that they were controlling them so that the truth about the Old Times wouldn't get out. She also said the Counselors were in on the deception. I didn't believe her for a minute, but that's what she said."

"Ah," said Brother Matthew with a twinkle in his eye. "The oldest lie in The Book."

"Sir?" asked Kateri, puzzled.

"The oldest lie in The Book," Brother Matthew repeated, tapping the Bible at his elbow. "'Something is being withheld from you, and if you could just get hold of it, you would be free.' The oldest lie in The Book."

"I knew it couldn't be true," Kateri said, still a little mystified. "So, the rest of it – the flying machines and talking devices and all – that's a lie, too, then? Legends and tall tales?" She felt that if she could just get Brother Matthew to tell her it was all false, that would wash away the seeds of doubt and suspicion that Monica's gossip had sown in her mind.

Instead of speaking, Brother Matthew fixed her with an unusually direct gaze. He looked for a long time, as if evaluating her and making a judgment. Kateri started feeling uncomfortable and dropped her eyes to the table. "It was all nonsense, wasn't it?" she asked again, mostly to break the silence. "Tall tales for children and fools?"

To her surprise, Brother Matthew's solemn face cracked into a broad grin, and he buried his face in his hands. His shoulders started shaking as if he were – laughing?

"Brother Matthew," Kateri asked, now utterly lost. "It was all lies and nonsense, wasn't it?"

Brother Matthew looked up, laughter in his eyes and mischief in his smile. "Kateri," he said. "He didn't know the half of it. He didn't know the tenth of it. All that part was true – the flying machines, the metal ships, the talking devices – all those existed in the Old Times."

Kateri rocked back, aghast. From Richard, through Monica, those had seemed but fantasies for the gullible. But this was Brother Matthew – respected teacher, scholar, confidante of the governors and Counselors, official of the Church!

"In fact," Brother Matthew continued, "Richard didn't mention – probably because he didn't know – that not only were there great metal ships plying the oceans, but there were even ships that travelled under the ocean."

"Under the ocean, sir?" Kateri asked.

"Yes. As with many Old Things, we're not sure how they did it. Shipbuilders confirm that you could make a ship sealed tightly enough to submerge without sinking, but they have no idea how you could keep enough air inside for people to live. Yet the Old Ones knew how, and made ships that could travel beneath the waves for months at a time."

"And the great flying machines? The ones that flew through the sky at great speeds, even though they weighed tons? How could that be possible?" Kateri asked.

"Again, we're not sure. Some scholars may understand, but they only know the theory, and it is far from general knowledge. The machines were called airplanes, and flew great distances at high speeds. In fact, old accounts say that people would ride in these things, even as you or I would ride in a wagon, and go all the way across the continent from one ocean to another in the space of half a day. Furthermore, this used to happen routinely, several times a day."

Kateri sat stunned. This was like being asked to believe that the moon really was a green cheese, or that witches actually wore seven league boots.

"In fact," Brother Matthew continued, his mischievous smile looking a little reckless. "There's good evidence that the Old Ones did even more than that. Many scholars who study the records contend that they learned to fly above the sky, into the heavens themselves."

"Above the sky, sir?"

"Forgive me – do you remember from your classes that the earth we stand on is not as it appears to our eyes, but in fact is a giant round planet soaring through the heavens, circling the sun?"

"Yes, I remember that," Kateri confirmed.

"And do you remember learning that the air we breathe is actually a thin layer of gas wrapped around the earth, like the skin around an apple? Of course, to us it seems vast, extending for miles above us, but on the scale of the earth it is very scant and thin."

"I remember that part as well," Kateri said.

"Well, the airplanes flew within the air, staying aloft by some use of the properties of air, even as soaring birds do. But have you ever wondered what lay above the thin skin of air?"

"Why…no," Kateri answered. It struck her as odd that she'd never wondered about this.

"Few do," Brother Matthew grinned. "We just refer to it as 'the heavens' and leave it at that. But I know scholars of the old records who say that the ancients learned how to fly above the air, in those very heavens, even landing upon the moon and walking on it."

"The moon? In the night sky?" Now Kateri felt she was truly in the realm of fairy tales. "The Old Ones claimed to have walked there?"

"Yes," nodded Brother Matthew. "I must tell you that not everyone believes this, maintaining that the Old Ones were boasting beyond their abilities. But the scholars who know the records best contend that the Old Ones left devices on the moon, artifacts that could be detected by such tools as the Old Ones possessed. They do not question that this happened."

"So, I presume that this did not happen several times a day," Kateri said.

"No," Brother Matthew replied. "If it happened it was only a few times, and was considered one of the greatest feats of mankind."

"I can well believe that," Kateri replied. Her head was reeling from all this new knowledge. Ships that sailed underwater, great machines that could fly across continents in a few hours, men walking on the face of the moon – this was too much to believe. But something Brother Matthew had said was nagging her.

"Brother," Kateri ventured hesitantly. "You mentioned scholars of old records—"

"Caught that, did you?" Brother Matthew replied, his mischievous twinkle returned. "I thought you might. I was getting to that, once I'd finished bedazzling you with tales of the old times. You've been told a lie, but one which contained a partial truth. You deserve to hear the whole truth." He settled back and took of a sip of his water before continuing in his classroom style.

"As you know, study of the Old Times and the Collapse was my specialty at University. They both fascinated and repelled me. Without question the Old Ones made tremendous advances in knowledge and technology – "

Kateri's Sentence

"Excuse me, sir – 'technology'?" Kateri interrupted, mouthing the unfamiliar word.

"Ah, yes...um..." Brother Matthew stumbled a bit. "For our purposes, consider technology to be a combination of simple machines assembled for a specific purpose. The Archimedes screw at the town well, and the wheel that drives it, would be a simple technology."

"I see," Kateri smiled. The town well was normally driven by horses or donkeys pushing the great wheel, but Brother Matthew was not above assigning unruly boys a of couple hours in the yokes for misbehavior.

"The Old Ones were renowned for their knowledge and technology, but they were often very cruel and selfish. Many scoffed at God and ignored His law, with the inevitable consequences.

"In her wisdom and guided by the Holy Spirit, the Church saw the Collapse coming, and knew the destruction would be deep and widespread. She instructed her children around the world to begin storing away books and pages full of knowledge. The Old Ones had vast records of many things, but much of it was stored by technology that we do not understand, and those were lost in the Collapse. All that survived was the printed page, and many of those were destroyed in the dark and desperate centuries immediately following the Collapse. Almost all of what was preserved were the records kept and catalogued by the Church, which was the only institution to survive."

"So, the knowledge we have of the Old Times – and of all the centuries before them – was preserved by the Church?" Kateri asked.

"Even so. The books we use in school – the Scriptures, of course, but also the classic works like Euclid and Homer and Aristotle, as well as Newton and Galileo and Pasteur, were all preserved by the Church," Brother Matthew confirmed. "But even in the shadow of the Collapse, the Church was already debating how to manage the knowledge it had preserved. How could it keep, and reintroduce, the good things from the Old Times without bringing back the problems?"

"I don't understand, sir," Kateri said. "Wouldn't it just be better to leave it all behind?"

"There have been some who advocated just that," Brother Matthew replied. "But the Church maintained, and still does, that knowledge of its own is an objective good – knowing is always better than not knowing. The pivotal question is what is done with the knowledge, and how to guide the knowledge and technology in the hands of sinful humans. There is no question that the vast knowledge and technology of the Old Ones, unguided by the wisdom of God and the teachings of the Church, helped bring about the Collapse. But how to learn from that, and properly manage the knowledge and technology for good?

"Eventually the debate coalesced into two schools of thought. There were the Technologists, who thought that the problems which led to the Collapse were primarily fueled by the technology the Old Ones developed, particularly things like weapons. Those of this school are most cautious about reintroducing any of the technologies or techniques from the Old Times."

"I think I might be one of them," Kateri suggested.

"Perhaps," Brother Matthew acknowledged. "But it's a subtle matter. You use more of the old knowledge than you know. For instance, the Old Ones excelled at understanding the causes and treatments of diseases. Most of the habits and methods you have regarding things like household cleanliness and food handling were first developed in the Old Times."

Kateri was surprised – she'd always just done what her mother had taught her.

"Technologists are an interesting breed," continued Brother Matthew. "A few don't want to study technology at all, lest they become corrupted. But most delve into the records to learn as much as they can, and thus be forearmed. I know many of these, and they are interesting to speak with. They ponder the works of the Old Ones, trying to discern what these might say about those times.

"One friend of mine refers to the Old Ones as the Masters of Precision. They excelled at fine measurements and could work materials of all types. What few things survived are mostly metal, but they could make amazing things out of nearly anything – including materials that we have no idea what they were. He was the one who gave me this," Brother Matthew put on the table a small, surprisingly heavy thing. Kateri picked it up and saw that it was two rings of some metal that were separated, or connected, by a set of small metal balls that were fixed in a stiff frame. One of the balls was missing, leaving a hole in the frame. The metal was so finely worked that the rings and balls were smooth and shiny. She moved it a little and saw that the inner ring rotated, the little balls rolling as it turned, all of it moving smoothly. Delighted, she put two fingers in the inner ring and spun the outer one, watching it whir smoothly around on its bracket of balls.

"It's amazing – what is it?" Kateri asked.

"My friend says it was probably used to help wheels turn. If you were to affix an axle through the center ring, and attach a wheel to the outer one, the wheel would turn very smoothly."

Kateri thought of wagon wheels, and how they needed to be lubricated with tallow or beeswax. Something that spun as smoothly as this would surely be helpful, but –

"Isn't this a bit intricate for something as commonplace as keeping wheels turning?" asked Kateri. Brother Matthew laughed.

"It would be for us. An extremely skilled blacksmith would take a month to produce something even close to this, and wouldn't do as good a job. Yet these were common in the Old Days. My friend told me that things like this came in all sizes, from as large as buckets to so small that ten could fit in a thimble, all as finely made as this one. I find this one handy, since having lost one of the little balls, ten remain, making a very nice decade for me to finger while praying."

"It's wondrous," Kateri acknowledged, handing it back to him.

"Just one small example of how precise the work of the Old Ones could be," Brother Matthew said. "But another friend of mine refers to the Old Ones as Masters of the Miniature. Scholars have taken apart old devices to find parts of decreasing size down to the point that even our most powerful lenses cannot see their full detail. We have no idea how they could make such tiny things, much less what they were used for. But they also were commonplace in those days.

"But as amazing as these attributes are, I think that one of my university professors summarized the Old Ones best when he called them Masters of Fire. He is of the opinion that their control of fire was the key to nearly all they did."

"Fire, sir?" asked Kateri.

"Yes," Brother Matthew confirmed. "When we think of fire, we envision things like hearth fires or bonfires. But it seems the ancients could control fire in many forms and ways. For instance, you can imagine how hot a fire it would take to create and form steel of this hardness and precision," he held up the steel-ring device. "But that was only part of it. Scholars speculate that the airplanes could only be kept aloft by tremendous pushing force – and that was created by carefully controlled burning of some substance. Again, we have no idea how.

"But the greatest mystery and wonder, I am told, was that they learned how to harness the power of sky fire – lightning – and channel it to work for them."

"Lightning, sir?"

"Well – the same force as lightning. Somehow fire was involved in that as well, I'm not sure how. They managed to tame this force, probably with cables, and it was the key to almost everything about their world."

Kateri struggled to imagine binding the force of a lightning bolt with cables. Like so much she'd heard of the Old Times, it seemed more like something out of mythology than history.

"I don't understand that part, I'm afraid, sir," Kateri admitted.

"Neither do I," shrugged Brother Matthew. "I've heard it said that the scholars who study such things most closely know not only what the Old Ones called this force, but how it was manipulated. Needless to say, this is one secret the Church guards most closely and is most hesitant to make widely known. The control of this force was something the Old Ones only perfected just before their decline to the Collapse. It changed everything about their world in very short order, so everyone is very cautious about it."

"How did it change things, sir?" Kateri was intrigued despite the depths of her troubles.

"Oh, in thousands of ways," Brother Matthew replied. "We've been talking about big, dramatic things like undersea ships and possible journeys to the moon. Were you able to visit those times, you would probably most notice the day-to-day conveniences. For instance, the house you lived in would be sealed as tight as a drum, with no gaps for drafts. The windows would all have crystal clear glass of uniform thickness. There would be no need for open hearths or stoves – the temperature would be controlled by a wondrous device connected to subtle machines that would blow warm or cold air as needed. No more hauling logs or shoveling ashes, and you'd wake every morning to a house that was already warm. You would never get too cold in winter or too hot in summer. You would be able to illuminate rooms by touching devices that would make light without flame, smoke, or fuel. If you wished to speak to someone, you wouldn't even have to leave the house. You could pick up a device, manipulate it, and speak to him as if he were in the same room, even if he was on the other side of the world. How does that sound?"

"It sounds like we're back in a fairy tale, sir."

"It does, doesn't it? I must admit that the device which attracts me most is the one which would allow me to wear a small thing on my head and speak to a hall larger than this, full of people, in a normal voice without shouting," Brother Matthew said.

"But it gets better. Let's say you wished to go to the market. You could get in your carriage, which needed no horses, and ride to the merchants. The carriage was sealed against the weather, so you would always be as warm or cool as you wished. The roads were broad and flat, so your carriage could travel faster than the fastest racehorse – and go much further. When you got to the market, you could find all manner of goods from all over the world, because communications and transportation worked so well. Let me ask you this: do you like music and dances? And stories?"

"Of course," Kateri answered. "I never miss a dance if I can help it – I love the music and the fun. And we have a great story book at home, rich with pictures. Mother used to read it to us when I was growing up, and now I read it to my siblings."

"Then imagine, if you can," continued Brother Matthew. "A device that could capture the music from the dance so you could listen to it any time you wished, even after the musicians had gone home. Or imagine a device like a story book, except the pictures came to life and told the story for you."

"That – takes a lot of imagining, sir," Kateri replied.

"I know. I can barely imagine it myself, but that is how it was explained to me. The Old Ones had such devices for their amusement, as well as many other things."

Kateri sat pondering. Like everyone, she had wondered about the days before the Collapse, and what the Old Ones were really like. Now she was learning so much so fast that she felt like a field that had just received a downpour after snowmelt – she was having trouble absorbing it all. Had it been anyone but Brother Matthew telling her this, she'd be certain that her leg was being pulled.

"Sir?" Kateri finally asked tentatively.

"Yes, Miss Kateri?"

"If the Old Ones had all these wonders, and all this knowledge and mastery of things, then how was it that they weren't able to avoid the Collapse? Couldn't they have seen it coming, and done something to prevent it?"

Brother Matthew grinned to himself – this was the student he was accustomed to.

"Well, let me give you another example of their mastery of science: in the Old Times, toward the end, a woman could go to a physician's place to get potions and procedures in order to determine who the father of her child was." He tapped his metal trinket on the table as he gazed steadily at her, waiting for her to assimilate that historical detail.

Kateri's eyes grew wide as the implications of that information sank in. Brother Matthew was gratified, and a little amused, to see her puzzlement and shock increase the more she thought about it.

"But..." Kateri stammered. "If she...then...how could that be?"

"Be grateful that you find it incomprehensible," Brother Matthew assured her. "But let me back up. Remember that I mentioned earlier that there were two main schools of thought about what was the primary cause of the decline of the Old Ones, leading to the Collapse?"

"Yes."

"The Technologists suggest that it was the technologies they created, and the pace of change that brought about. The other group, the Philosophists, suggest that it was more due to changes in the way people thought and understood themselves.

"Though these two schools differ in their opinions of the primary causes of the decline and Collapse, everyone agrees that the two factors played off one another to drive the crisis that became the Collapse. Are you with me?"

"I think so, sir," Kateri replied, though she felt a bit bewildered.

"No, you're not, and it's my fault," Brother Matthew acknowledged. "Let me back up even further and give you a simple example, if I can think of one..."

Kateri nibbled some fruit while Brother Matthew thought. At last he looked up.

"Let's try this," he suggested. "Remember how I told you about their wondrous carriages that needed no horses or oxen, and how they would travel so quickly along the broad, smooth roads?"

"Yes, though I can hardly imagine it," Kateri admitted.

"What would you say if I told you that the Old Ones would sometimes get in those carriages and travel away to set up their homes hundreds or thousands of miles from their families?" Brother Matthew asked.

Again, Kateri struggled to understand, and again her eyes grew wide as comprehension dawned.

"You mean," she gasped, "they'd exile themselves?"

"Well, we'd think of it that way," Brother Matthew acknowledged. "But this is the point to understand: they didn't see it like that. Often, they considered that a freedom, a good to be desired."

"A freedom!" exclaimed Kateri. "Living that far from your family, all by yourself? I can't imagine a worse bondage!"

"Of course, you can't," Brother Matthew said. "But that would be an example of how the Old One's technology affected their thinking, and vice versa. Admit it: haven't there been times that you've gotten so frustrated with your family, or school, or some other situation, that you've just wanted to flee?"

"Indeed," Kateri answered. "More than once. Sometimes I've done it."

"We all have. But I imagine you'd flee to the town square, or maybe take a walk in the meadows, correct? But what if you had the ability to go further – miles further – to the next town, perhaps, or even across the Big River?"

"I might," admitted Kateri, remembering nights of hair-tearing frustration with her siblings.

"You'd probably find that if you had that ability, you'd soon be thinking differently about departures and distances. Can you see that?"

"I – I think so, sir," said Kateri.

"You'd be able to see it better if you could actually do it, rather than just ponder a hypothetical," Brother Matthew assured her. "The point is, the tools of the Old Ones influenced how they thought, and how they thought influenced how they used their tools. It changed how they looked at the world, until they achieved almost complete separation."

"Separation, sir?"

"Yes," Brother Matthew replied. "One of my professors at University, Msgr. Davis, is a prominent Philosophist and a brilliant scholar. He has focused his studies on the thought of one of the greatest men of the period preceding the Collapse: Pope St. John Paul the Great. Msgr. Davis contends that the key to understanding the days leading up to the Collapse lies in John Paul the Great's description of his own time. He referred to it as 'The Culture of Death'."

"A culture of death?" asked Kateri. "Sounds horrid – was there that much dying?"

"Well, there were terrible wars with atrocious weapons, as well as – other factors. Unbelievable numbers of people died. But that wasn't the sole issue. Do you remember your lessons? Can you recite the definition of human death?"

Kateri was curious as to what 'other factors' might kill as much as terrible wars, but she answered the brother's question: "Natural human death occurs when the soul separates from the body. The soul ascends to face the Lord while the body decays and returns to its natural elements. The soul remains separated from the body either in bliss, purgation, or torment, until the resurrection of the body. Then it will be given a new, everlasting body, and either united with Christ in His eternal kingdom or separated from Him in eternal damnation."

Brother Matthew grinned at his pupil. "Almost verbatim from the Lesser Catechism, even after all these years. Very good. But notice how often the word 'separated' occurs. That's the core of death and, according to Msgr. Davis, the key to understanding St. John Paul's diagnosis."

Kateri's eyes narrowed as she struggled to understand. "In what way, sir?"

"Msgr. Davis contends that even beyond the obvious carnage of war and other killings, the Culture of Death eventually led to separation from top to bottom. Once the Old Ones separated themselves from God, that separation kept spreading like a cancer, ultimately reaching every corner of their lives."

"How so, sir?" asked Kateri, again mystified but intrigued.

"Things that were intended to be united were fractured and separated. Families were separated by distance, husbands and wives divorced and then remarried, which made for families of fragile unity. Even within the marital act, union was separated from fertility, and—"

"Excuse me, sir," interrupted a startled Kateri. "But what do you mean by that?"

Brother Matthew looked sheepish and a little embarrassed. "Maybe I shouldn't have said that. But the Old Ones had ways, drugs and…ah…devices, that would render the marital union infertile. There have always been such things, but never so commonly as then."

"You mean," gasped Kateri, her eyes widening again. "That they voluntarily made themselves sterile?"

"Indeed," said Brother Matthew with a dark look. "According to Msgr. Davis, that was only the beginning of their perversions and cruelty. It would not be seemly for me, a vowed brother, to discuss with you, a maiden, some of the ways they put their technology to work. Suffice it to say that things were separated that were never intended to be separated: husband from wife, parents from children, union from fertility, even conception from the womb – and worse."

Kateri was a little alarmed. Her curiosity urged her on, but something in her heart, as well as the disturbed look which clouded Brother Matthew's face, warned her that they were on the edge of very dark matters, and she'd best hold her tongue. After a minute Brother Matthew rubbed his face with his hands and looked at her.

"I'm sorry," he said. "I've had to study those harsh and confused times far more closely than I wished. I'll try not to darken your heart with any more details. Now – where were we?"

Kateri stumbled for a moment. They'd discussed so much that she'd almost forgotten where they'd started.

"I'd asked why the Old Ones with all their knowledge and sophistication couldn't have headed off the Collapse. That took us to the issue of death and separation."

"Ah, yes," Brother Matthew confirmed.

"But, sir," asked Kateri. "I'm not sure how that ties together. I understand your point about separation, but I don't see how that relates to the Collapse."

"Yes, well," Brother Matthew struggled for a bit. "I can see how that wouldn't be an easy connection to make." He pulled his beard while staring off into space for a bit. "Let me illustrate with an example."

Kateri smiled – this was so classically Brother Matthew. He was always coming up with examples to illustrate things, most of which were very good.

"Let's say – let's say you had a heap of roots and branches. A big heap, as tall as you are," Brother Matthew began.

Kateri's smile widened into a grin – she couldn't wait to see where he went with this one. "All right," she said.

"If you wanted to pull out one branch – one that went deep into the pile – how easy would that be?"

Kateri thought back to brush piles she'd had experience with. "Not easy at all."

"Exactly! And why not?"

"Because all the twigs and tendrils intertwine," Kateri answered. "They'd hook and catch on each other as you pulled."

"So, if you wanted to remove a branch more easily, what would you probably do?"

"I suppose," Kateri said. "You'd break off the twigs, and maybe strip away the bark, so it wouldn't catch as much."

"That's what I'd do," Brother Matthew confirmed. "Now, think of your life as one of those branches, and your family and town like the pile. The twigs and tendrils are like all the relationships that bind you to those around you – bonds of kinship and friendship and citizenship. They support and define you, but they also bind and constrain you. If you wished to be free of these constraints, you could break away the twigs, as you point out. With me so far?"

"Yes, sir," Kateri assured him.

"But doing that would have at least two effects. One has to do with the person. What would it mean for a person to 'break off twigs' in order to be less bound and constrained? What would that look like in real life?"

"I suppose," Kateri responded slowly, thinking hard. "It means severing those relationship bonds, right?"

"Precisely – that's my girl!" exclaimed Brother Matthew. "Those natural bonds get strained and broken. Think about it: as Monica went further and further in her dalliance with Richard, how did that affect her friendship with you?"

"She withdrew," Kateri admitted sadly, remembering those dark and painful weeks.

"Of course, she did. Your friendship was a constraint she didn't want, so she broke away the 'tendrils' that bound you, thus separating herself from you.

"Now imagine, if you can, entire cities full of Monicas, people so determined to do only what they wanted without hindrance or constraint that they broke away or stripped off anything that connected them with others. What would such a pile of brush look like?"

"I imagine," Kateri said. "It would look like a pile of straight, smooth sticks."

"Exactly so," Brother Matthew confirmed. "Imagine further what would happen to such a pile if a strong wind blew up, or something pushed at the pile."

"It would fall over, of course, and scatter all over the place."

"Well, that was essentially the state of society just before the Collapse, except Msgr. Davis compared it more to a pile of polished wooden balls. People so separated themselves from one another that ultimately events caused the social order to completely disintegrate, and people were scattered. The Church, being Christ's Body, was the only thing that survived."

Brother Matthew fell silent for a minute. Kateri nibbled a slice of apple while mustering her courage.

"Sir," she finally asked. "I've always wondered – how did the Collapse happen? I mean, what exactly were the events that caused the 'pile to collapse'?"

Brother Matthew smiled gently. "The inevitable question. Sooner or later, everybody wants the particulars – what happened to whom, where, when, and how? Have you ever wondered why that particular history isn't taught? We teach ancient history, Scriptural times, Rome and Greece, the Middle Ages – but fall quiet about the years leading up to the Collapse. Hasn't that ever made you curious?"

"Well, a little," Kateri admitted.

"I'd be surprised if it hadn't. To men like Richard, it's *prima facie* evidence that the Church is suppressing knowledge to keep the population in ignorance and subjection. The reality is more mundane and more subtle.

"Detailed records exist of the history leading up to the Collapse, and are studied by scholars and churchmen – in fact, it's a particular focus of Counselor training. But we don't make the records generally available because we don't want people focusing on the wrong things."

"'Wrong things', sir?" Kateri was puzzled.

"Yes. If people learn only of the circumstances and events, then it's easy to think that if you can just avoid those circumstances or change those events, you could build a civilization insulated from the possibility of collapse.

"The Church knows that so long as societies are constructed by sinful men, the weaknesses will be built right in. However, that does not mean we cannot learn from a catastrophe as great as the Collapse, so we can at least avoid making the same mistakes over and over. So, when the Church started rebuilding society, she tried to examine where mistakes were made and to construct structures that avoided those mistakes. With me so far?"

"I think so, sir," Kateri said. "Though it seems a little—"

"Abstract, I know," Brother Matthew admitted. "To explain it completely would take a year-long University course. You would have to understand thoroughly how people thought just before the Collapse, and that's always difficult. But let me try one narrow example. We've just been talking about the separation that permeated the pre-Collapse society: how in the name of freedom people would strip their lives of anything that connected them with one another."

"Yes," Kateri said.

"It's very hard for us to imagine just how complete that separation was. Between their thinking and their technology, the Old Ones saw that separation creep into the smallest corners of their lives. For instance, it became possible – even common – for a man to be able to wake up in his house, get into his sealed wagon, travel more miles than you or I could in a week, enter another building to do his day's work, and then return to his home in the evening – all without ever walking under the open sky or feeling the fresh wind on his face or placing his feet on plain earth."

Kateri stared in disbelief. "How could that be?"

"The world and works of men," shrugged Brother Matthew. "They became so enamored of the works of their own hands that they cut themselves off from God's creation. They ate eggs they didn't gather laid by chickens they never saw along with bacon from pigs they never fed, much less slaughtered. They ate cheese never having milked a cow and ate bread never having kneaded a loaf. Having separated themselves from God, it inevitably followed that they became separated from His creation, one another, and ultimately themselves. Their disintegration was complete, and they lost all true knowledge."

"I'm confused," Kateri said frankly. "Haven't we been talking about the immense knowledge of the Old Ones? How can you say they lost all knowledge?"

"It is true," explained Brother Matthew. "That they accumulated many facts and skills, but the knowledge they acquired was mainly abstract facts, detached from daily life. They were consumed with what St. Thomas identified as *curiositas* – the desire for knowledge simply for the sake of knowing, rather than for God's glory or man's edification. They amassed knowledge to be inflated with pride, as St. Paul says, or to learn ways to manipulate Creation. Let me ask you, Kateri – your family still works your Forty directly, does it not?"

"Why – yes," Kateri confirmed, taken aback by the sudden change of subject. "Father is very traditional that way. Uncle Stephen and his boys prepare the fields in spring, and maintain them during the growing season, but at sowing and harvest we're all out there."

Father was indeed strictly traditional about the family directly working the forty acre plot that was theirs outside of town. Every family had one, as well as half an acre within the town walls. Though the plots could never be sold, they could be leased, so some families effectively turned them over to the tenants. They'd show up at sowing time to cast a symbolic handful of grain, and bring a scythe at harvest to gather a ceremonial sheaf, but for all practical purposes they let others work their lands.

But such families were few – most worked their own plots. Father was very insistent that his family be out sowing and reaping as was proper. It worked out well that Uncle Stephen and his family lived out on their land in the great house, because it allowed him to oversee both family's plots while the grain grew. But the vegetable patch needed constant tending, and that fell to Kateri and her sisters. The brothers got their workout come harvest time, swinging the great scythes and stacking the sheaves. Harvest was hard work, but it was fun as well, with the feasts and the dances in the barns. Of course, there was the garden in the yard as well, and the hogs and chickens and milk cows, but they were right outside the house, and didn't require an hour's walk to get to them.

"There you have the difference," Brother Matthew continued. "In the days leading up to the Collapse, you might be able to learn much about, say, pigs. You could get many books about pigs, and study the varieties and diets and habits of pigs. You could study their diseases and breeding and uses. You could stuff your head with facts about them, to the point where you could be considered a pig expert. And you could do all this without ever laying an eye, or a hand, on an actual pig.

"On the other hand, you, Kateri, have worked with pigs as long as you could walk. You have lived near them and fed them and scrubbed them and helped with the slaughter. You know pigs with an intimacy that few scholars of the Old Times could match."

"But – I don't know about them as well as the town vet – and he's studied many books about pigs," Kateri answered.

"Right you are, young Kateri!" replied Brother Matthew, slapping the table. "That is the heart of what the Church kept in mind as it helped rebuild from the Collapse. There is a place and reason for all kinds of knowledge, and they must be integrated. Society must be ordered to keep together those things that should be kept together. As the Church helped society rebuild, she drew on her wisdom to craft laws and customs that would build up, not tear down, a proper understanding of human nature. From simple things like ensuring every family can grow its own food to more complex matters having to do with civil law and economic policies, the Church helped build the world you know. This is a much wiser way of avoiding another Collapse than simply looking for particular events and avoiding them.

"As Monica and Richard prove, this does not make men any less sinful. But building structures that lessen rather than worsen the damage caused by man's sin is at least pointing in the right direction."

Kateri felt very excited. She had known that the Church had been important to rebuilding society after the Collapse; she had not known that the Church had designed so much of it. She longed to learn more.

"Brother Matthew – how, exactly, did the Church do this? What laws and customs did she institute?" Kateri asked eagerly, then checked herself. "That is, if you can tell me."

"It's not restricted information, if that's what you're wondering," Brother Matthew assured her. "I can't tell you here and now because it would be impossible to do it properly. It would take a multi-year course of University study to learn even some of it, and our talk here has already run over time. But I can give you an example of one change implemented after the Collapse: the Order of Counselors."

Kateri's brow creased in puzzlement. "Counselors? But haven't there always been Counselors?"

Brother Matthew chuckled. "No, lass, there haven't. The fact that you can't imagine a society without them is testimony to the success of that innovation."

"So – the Church created the Counselors? But they're not Church men, are they?"

"No – Counselors have a unique status. I've not time to give you a full explanation, but here's the quick version:

"The Church learned from the centuries following the first Collapse – that of the Roman Empire – that it was unwise for her hierarchy to stand too close to the civil authority. Getting the clergy deeply involved in civil government makes for neither good clergy nor good government. But the centuries leading up to the second Collapse taught another lesson: that it was at least as dangerous for the Church to stand too far away from the ordering of society. Without the Church's guidance in matters of faith and morality, laws quickly broke down. The question was, what to do about it?

"The answer the Church has tried is a corps of devout, committed laymen who dedicate themselves to mediate the Church's wisdom and authority into society. Of course, this is the task of all Christian citizens, but the guiding and ordering of it is entrusted to the Order of Counselors. They are so much a part of your life that you take them for granted, but they are relatively new in human history.

"Counselors have no place in the Church hierarchy," Brother Matthew continued. "They do not take Holy Orders – indeed, they could not, given that half of them are women – or religious vows. They do take solemn oaths of fidelity to the Church, and to the communities they serve. They undergo many years of instruction, and must be of the highest character. They must demonstrate wisdom, scholarship, and humility. Despite having no formal authority in the Church, they advise priests and bishops. They hold no political office, yet counsel judges and lawmakers. They are a vital element integrating our society."

Kateri thought of the Counselors who served her town – Lady Patrice and Sir William. Given Father's role as a governor, they called at the house from time to time, and were even guests at their table occasionally. At first Kateri had been awed by them – to think that this pair, who had special seats at town festivities and an honored place at every Mass, were sitting right at their dinner table! But they were both surprisingly ordinary – though they were always polite and dignified, and got along well with everyone. Sir William had an infectious laugh and was an incorrigible tease, while Lady Patrice enjoyed telling stories to the children. Yet even Father looked up to them, and took their counsel very seriously.

"I've always known the Counselors were special types of people," Kateri said. "But how do they help with this integration you speak of?"

"Well, I don't know if I'd call them special types of people," Brother Matthew qualified. "They're the same type of person as the rest of us – sinners saved by grace. Some have very interesting pasts, including exile."

Kateri gasped – that seemed like blasphemy. "Counselors? Exiles? How can that be?"

"Oh, yes," Brother Matthew confirmed with a nod. "Two that I know of. Don't forget the purpose of exile, which is correction and instruction. If the correction is made and the lesson learned, then the person can move on – sometimes much the wiser for the experience.

"What makes the Counselors so special is their sacrifice and determination, helped by their education and understanding. The Church cannot dictate which laws a town or city can pass, but the Counselors can advise the governors when laws might need to be modified to reflect the Church's wisdom. The Church should not be stepping in to resolve disputes between communities, but the Counselors are equipped to mediate, bringing their understanding of their own communities in light of Church teaching. They can supervise cooperative efforts between communities – such as the exile treaties – so that no community can be favored over others.

"So, they are children of the Church, and have a special loyalty to their own communities, but are also responsible to their Order. Balancing all these commitments calls for great wisdom and dedication. This is what sets the Counselors apart, and why we regard them with such honor.

"Much more could be said, but we have said too much already. The court allowed us a very long recess, but I fear we have strained even that, and I hope we have not kept the judges waiting. I will go and see – you remain here until they summon you. If you need to refresh yourself, one of the bailiffs will take you."

With that, Brother Matthew gathered up his papers and took his leave. Kateri sat still, black fear once again descending on her heart as she recalled why she was here. The hour or so of chatting with Brother Matthew had put her back in a school mindset, cheering her and displacing the harsh reality that she was guilty of a crime and was about to be sentenced.

Kateri decided that she'd better heed Brother Matthew's suggestion, and had Mistress Sands escort her outside. When they returned, no word had yet come from the court, so Kateri sat and tried not to dwell on horrible possibilities. If only she could have a book, or some crocheting to keep her hands busy! She tried to pray, and recite some lessons, but her mind would not focus.

Finally, after what seemed like hours, a messenger stuck his head in and nodded to the bailiffs. Kateri stood, her mouth dry, and followed the officers down the hall.

The court seemed to Kateri insufferably hot as she stood before the bench. The prosecutor read the charge against her and the chief judge asked her if she understood what she was being charged with.

"Yes, sir," Kateri answered, trying to keep her voice loud and strong.

The prosecutor spoke again, referencing Kateri's testimony of earlier in the trial, and she glanced quickly around the court. There was Father at the end of the bench, where he'd been before. Just beside him, not behind the bench but seated at the end, was Brother Matthew and, to her surprise, Lady Patrice. She had not been in the court earlier, but now sat beside Brother Matthew.

Kateri refocused her attention on what the prosecutor was saying. It was nothing she didn't know already – she had testified under oath that she had had strong suspicion of a clearly illicit relationship and had not come forward. Finally, the prosecutor ceased speaking and the chief judge asked if she had any additions or corrections to the prosecutor's summary. She didn't, so he then asked if she had anything to say in her defense.

"No, sir," Kateri answered, this time barely managing a whisper. The chief judge, who was Governor Andrews and a good friend of Father's nodded with a sympathetic smile. Then he took up a piece of paper and read it.

"Absent any other testimony, this court finds Kateri Marie Judith Peterson guilty of public negligence. Your sentence is six months common exile, to commence at noon tomorrow. In case of…" He kept talking, but Kateri dropped her head. Part of her was relieved – six months of common exile was the lightest possible sentence, far less than the dark imaginings that her fears had conjured up. But still, it was exile. Tears seeped through her lashes as she thought of the shame it brought to her family to have one of their own an exile. What would Mother say? And her siblings?

Suddenly she was aware that she was being spoken to again. Blinking, she looked up at the chief judge.

"I – I'm sorry, sir?" Kateri gasped.

"I asked, do you understand the sentence?" he said gently.

"Yes – yes, I do, sir," Kateri stammered.

"Do you have any explanations, considerations, or comments pertaining to the court's sentence?"

Kateri was about to shake her head, but suddenly decided that she should say something. She cleared her throat and lifted her chin, not worrying about the tears now streaming down her cheeks. She might not be able to speak eloquently or at length, but for the honor of her family she wouldn't be dragged away howling, as Monica had.

"I understand and accept the court's verdict," Kateri said. "I acknowledge my guilt and repent of the harm I have done to my town, my family and to my friend. I thank the court for its clemency, and…and will do my best—" Her voice started to quaver as tears got the better of her.

The chief judge nodded. "Let the verdict and sentence be recorded. Kateri Peterson, you are released to the custody of your family until details of your sentence are arranged. There being no other business to attend to, this court is adjourned." He banged his gavel.

Suddenly everyone was pushing back chairs, standing up, and starting quiet conversations. Father came around the bench toward her, with Brother Matthew and Lady Patrice following.

"Father," Kateri whispered to him. "I'm so sorry."

Father said nothing, but enfolded her in one of his great hugs. She sobbed into his shirt for a little, then composed herself and stepped back. Father's eyes looked a little damp as well.

"You have a fine daughter, Governor," Lady Patrice said to Father. Kateri turned to her, stunned. Hadn't she been listening?

Kateri had just been exiled! Lady Patrice seemed to read her thoughts, and laid her hand on Kateri's arm with a smile. "I know it's hard now, dear, but the time will pass before you know it, and you'll be home again. We'll be waiting."

Patting Kateri's arm reassuringly, Lady Patrice turned and walked away, Brother Matthew by her side. Kateri remembered what he'd said about knowing Counselors who had been exiles, and wondered if Lady Patrice had been speaking from personal experience. But no, that couldn't be – not Lady Patrice...

"Well, lass," Father said quietly. "Let's go home to your mother."

It was not an easy homecoming, and it was as the family gathered for dinner that the significance of the sentence sank in for everyone. Mother kept turning away and burying her face in her apron. Kateri's older brothers were quiet and more courteous than usual, but her younger siblings sobbed and clung to her, breaking her heart. It was now late October, and counting on her fingers Kateri realized that she would miss Advent, Christmas, Lent, and Easter. All the holidays would be spent in a foreign city with strange customs, separated from her family and friends. She nearly despaired. Now she understood what it had been like for Bridget all those many years ago. Why had Kateri not been more sympathetic and comforting?

The next day Monica was sent away into exile. Given the nature of her offense, all the town maidens had to gather at the North Gate to line the road as she passed. There were other townsfolk there as well, but Kateri was glad that Mother decided to stay away. Mother was not feeling charitable toward Monica at the moment. Monica rode backward on a horse tied to the back of the last trade wagon, her head bowed and the red hood of her exile cast well over her face. The maidens shouted insults at her, with "wanton" being one of the milder ones. At least nobody flung mud – or worse – as she passed. Monica was liked by many, and though her dalliance had ended in shame and disgrace, at least it hadn't been with a town lad, so nobody else's marriage prospects had been damaged. Kateri hadn't the heart to call out anything – she just stood there sobbing for her lost friend, feeling sorry for Monica and sorry for herself.

At noon that same day, Kateri had to don the yellow hood, though she would not be leaving for some days yet. Father had explained this years ago: strict exiles were sent off immediately to the town of their exile with an escort and a record of their sentence. Because every town had facilities to accommodate strict exiles, no prior arrangements were needed. Common exiles took more coordination – messages had to be sent, host families selected, and other details arranged. Sometimes it took a fortnight for everything to be ironed out. So Kateri lived in suspense, not knowing when word would come from the court. Her only small consolation was that these in-between days counted against her sentence.

It was strange for Kateri to wear the yellow hood in her own town. As she went about in the streets, some acquaintances avoided her, embarrassed by her presence. But most friends greeted her, some coming up and expressing their grief and wishing her well. It was reassuring, but also discomfiting, for it reminded her of what she was losing.

But she wasn't out in the streets much, for she spent most of her time at home. Under the shadow of separation, every little thing about her family seemed that much more precious. She helped Mother in the kitchen and the little ones with their lessons. She volunteered for even the smallest chores, relishing every minute with her family.

But the day came when the court messenger knocked on their door and handed Father a sheaf of papers. Father sat down at the table and flipped through them with a somber look on his face, while the little ones gathered around Kateri, clinging to her. At last Father stood with a nod of finality and held the sheaf out to her.

"There, lass," Father said. "I did what I could for you."

Puzzled, Kateri read through the details of her exile. It was to a town she'd heard of, a day's travel on the other side of the Big River. The papers mentioned a few other things, but they didn't hold her attention just then. What mattered was that the arrival of the papers meant her interlude was over. She was going into exile. The foreign town which she knew only by name would be her home for the next six months. She was to depart on the morning barge. She had not even a day remaining with her family.

That evening was quiet and subdued, to the point that Kateri found herself trying to cheer her siblings by pointing out how quickly the time would pass. She got little sleep that night, and was almost grateful to head down to the dock, ready for the ordeal of departure to be over.

There were more hugs and tears at dockside, ending with Mother and Father. Mother just sobbed on Kateri's shoulder for a bit then pulled herself together. Father spoke a few gruff words and hugged her close, then stood her at arm's length. The tears around his eyes almost broke her heart, but she stood straight and cleared her throat.

"I will bring no more disgrace to our family, Father," Kateri said. "I will acquit myself faithfully and return to you honorably."

"I know you will, lass," Father replied, kissing her forehead. "Now go – the bargemen are waiting."

Kateri stepped onto the barge and stood by the gunwale while the bargemen cast off and poled the barge out into the current. She waved at her family until the barge took a curve and they passed out of sight.

Kateri was grieved, but she was a little excited as well. For the first time in her life she was going beyond the Big River! Of course, she was familiar with the Little River, having lived near it her whole life. She'd even traveled the several miles east to the shores of Lake Isaac, that vast expanse of water that stretched to the horizon. She had walked down the rocky beaches, watching the far coast draw closer until the two shores formed the narrows that made the Big River. But that was as close as she'd ever gotten to the other side. Now she was floating down the sluggish, winding Little River to where it joined the Big River, about a mile below the lake. There she'd take a ferry to the port on the other side, where some transport would take her the rest of the way to the town of her exile.

Tears welled in her eyes again, so to distract herself Kateri drew from her wallet the sheaf of papers on which was written her sentence. "Consonant with the nature of the offense..." they read, explaining how she was to live with a young widow who had lost her husband while carrying twins. Sorry as she felt for herself, Kateri could not help but grieve for the mother whom she would be helping, handling newborn twins alone. She could see the need, but was still puzzled by Father's comment about doing what he could.

The long float down the Little River took most of the day, even with the bargemen poling as best they could. They pulled into the small port town at the confluence of the Little River and the Big River in late afternoon. When Kateri handed her papers to the dock master, he directed her to a small hostel run by a brisk, businesslike woman who took her copper and pointed her to a cot in a corner. Kateri was informed that she was free of the city so long as she wore her hood up, but that the hostel door was locked at sunset and did not open again until dawn.

Kateri took advantage of the last hour of daylight to walk the docks and watch great hogsheads and burlap bags being loaded and unloaded. Being harvest time, it was the busy season, and Kateri knew that some of these bags contained grain from her town, to be shipped down the river or up the lake. Her home region was a breadbasket for many far-flung communities, and the trade brought salt fish and leather and wool and iron and many other useful things. The thought of the far exotic ports that were the destinations for some of these goods tugged at Kateri's romantic instincts, but then she thought of how sailing kept men away from their families.

Kateri was back at the hostel well before sunset, where a bowl of porridge and a chunk of cheese was her dinner. She said evening prayers by herself in a corner then curled up on the too-small cot and thought of her family going to bed just up the river. Homesickness overwhelmed her and she sobbed herself to sleep.

Back at Kateri's home, it wasn't quite bedtime, at least for Mother and Father. It had been a difficult day for everyone. Mother had kept dabbing her eyes, Father had been somber and withdrawn, and the children had been restive. But their grief had yielded to amazement when an after-dinner knock at the door had turned out to be Brother Matthew, Lady Patrice, and Sir William. Father was taken aback at the unheard-of honor of having both the town's Counselors and a church scholar pay an informal visit to his home. Mother bustled about quickly tidying and shooing the children upstairs. But when the visitors sat down and explained the reason for their visit, Father and Mother were nearly speechless.

After an hour's intense discussion around the fire, Father and Mother were still shaking their heads in amazement.

"It's so hard to believe," Mother said. "Kateri – our Kateri – a Counselor?"

"A candidate for Counselor Training," Brother Matthew corrected. "There are many steps between candidacy and the Counselor's Rod – the first being ascertaining whether Kateri wishes to undertake the training."

"Still," Father said. "Even to be considered is a signal honor for our family and our community. There has never been a Counselor from our town. Yet it seems so incongruous, having this discussion on the day she begins her exile."

Mother sniffed again, and Lady Patrice patted her arm sympathetically. "Common exile is not a bar to the training – in fact, some maintain that those who have made mistakes and learned from them are wiser than those who stick to the straight and narrow all their days. I have no doubt she will learn from her exile. For her other attributes, we have relied upon Brother Matthew's testimony."

"Kateri's intelligence is unquestionable," Brother Matthew affirmed. "Her devotion to the Lord and His Church is beyond doubt, as is true of the entire Peterson family." Father bowed slightly. "I'd noticed Kateri even as a student, and wondered then if she might be candidate material. But it was my discussion with her on the day of the trial that convinced me. Despite the pressure of the impending sentence, she was engaged and curious. She was as quick as ever to learn, and asked probing questions. That's why I approached Lady Patrice with the question."

"I admired how she accepted her sentence," Lady Patrice added. "Exile is always a blow, but she displayed maturity, character, and strength of will."

"We are always on the lookout for good candidates," Sir William said. "It is hard to find the right combination of devotion, intelligence, character, wisdom, and fortitude in one person. Also, the training is long and rigorous, and many never complete it. It entails five years of University training followed by many more years of apprenticeship and discernment. It takes great sacrifice from the candidates and their families to make a Counselor."

"Of course, it is from the most close-knit and loving families that the best counselors come," Lady Patrice explained. "The very people for whom it is hardest to be separated must embrace the burden of long separation for the good of all."

"Indeed," acknowledged Father. "But still – to have a Counselor in the family!"

"It is a huge step, with grave implications for you all," Lady Patrice said. "You should consider it prayerfully during the months to come. In a way, the timing of Kateri's exile is fortuitous – it will give you time to consider, and then we can speak to Kateri when she returns."

For Kateri's part, waking on a hard cot in a strange house to a breakfast of porridge and cheese was a difficult way to start the day. She was glad to leave the hostel and make her way down to where the ferry docked. It was loaded with goods for the downriver communities, but its first stop would be the port directly across the river. Kateri showed her papers and was boarded with the rest of the passengers.

While the oarsmen took their places and the dock workers bustled about their work, Kateri looked north, seeing where the lake narrowed to form the Big River, which then took a sweeping westward curve before turning to pass by where the Little River flowed into it. In contrast to the sluggish and dingy water of the Little River, the water of the Big River was a deep, startling blue, and seemed to be traveling with amazing speed.

Kateri remembered from school that centuries before, back before the Collapse, the Big River had been a border between two countries. She'd never quite grasped what a country was – the best she could make out, it was something like an alliance of cities and something like a vast super-city that covered an immense amount of land – but the east bank of the Big River had been one country and the west bank had been a different one. There had even been an immense bridge that crossed the river. From the ferry's deck Kateri could look north, near the lake, and see the line of tall columns that marched up on both sides of the river, increasing in height as they approached the banks. The columns were made of the same rocklike stuff which the Old Ones had favored for making roads, bridges, and other things. They were crumbling in spots, but they still marked where the bridge had stood. The other parts of the structure, especially the metal, had long since been stripped away.

There was family lore that in the final days before the Collapse, when the persecution of the Church had grown intense, her ancestors had helped smuggle Christians across the river to safety. She'd always assumed they had taken boats, but looking at the ruins of the bridge, it occurred to her that they might have used that. She wondered in which direction the smuggling had gone, and why it was safer on one side of the river than the other. Perhaps it had had something to do with the countries. There was no way of knowing for certain for most of the records had perished in the Collapse – not that smugglers kept careful records in the first place. It would remain family lore, mysterious and heroic.

There was a bustle by the dockside, and Kateri saw hawsers being cast off and great poles shoving the barge out into the current. Oars were unshipped as the barge cleared the dock, and the sailors began to pull in time to the bosun's call. There was a short mast toward the bow, but there was no sail rigged – Kateri guessed that they wouldn't bother for the short run across the river. She felt the current catch the hull, and the blunt prow pointed east.

The thrill of crossing the Big River for the first time rose again, but with it came the homesickness and the uncertainty about what awaited her. It was exciting to feel the wind in her hair and the surge of the deck beneath her feet, but there was so much she was leaving, and for so long. Yet it seemed impossible for Kateri to stay downcast for long, with so many new things to see!

The trip was over far too soon, and as Kateri disembarked with many of the passengers, part of her longed to stay aboard and sail down the river to see the other ports the barge was visiting. But instead she was presenting her papers to the harbor master, who took her over to where rows of wagons stood waiting to be loaded. The dock master walked among the waggoneers, speaking briefly to them until he found one with whom he spoke for longer. Then he beckoned Kateri over and introduced her. The waggoneer was named Patrick, who was from the town to which she was exiled. He would be taking his wagon there once it was loaded, and was willing to give her a ride.

Patrick tipped his hat to her, but otherwise kept to himself. She sat on the wagon seat and tried to engage him in conversation, but after getting only nods and monosyllables in response, she eventually gave up. It mystified her, for she'd never had trouble getting people to talk to her, especially boys. Only later did it occur to her that she might be experiencing the effect of the exile's hood. This depressed her even more.

Finally, their wagon was called, and Patrick circled it around to the dock where it was loaded swiftly. Then they were off along the rutted trail that led inland. Kateri pulled a blanket out of her luggage to wrap herself against the north wind which was coming off the lake. She huddled beneath it, rosary in hand, and fought the depression that threatened to overwhelm her. This was alien land, and she was an exile. The fields and livestock looked like they did everywhere, but they weren't her fields. She knew that wherever the Church was, there was her family, but every mile that passed beneath the horse's steady hooves took her further from her home and hearth. She was in a land of strangers, with every familiar face on the far side of that river.

As afternoon faded toward twilight, they came within sight of their destination. To Kateri's eyes, the town looked small and dingy and strange. The gateman welcomed them, directing the wagon one way but holding Kateri while a messenger was sent for one of the town officials. When the official arrived, he examined Kateri's papers and wrote something in the gate log.

"Come with me, miss," was all he said, leading her off into the town. Bleakly Kateri trudged behind him with her rucksack over her shoulder, looking at the strange streets and unfamiliar houses and wondering how she would ever bear six months in this place.

At last they came to a cottage where the official knocked on the door, stuck his head in, and announced, "She's here." He then stepped aside so Kateri could go through. In the small room sat a woman rocking one crying baby while nudging a cradle with her foot. Her hair was bound up tight, she was clad in plain widow's black, and her eyes were rimmed by dark circles. Yet there was something vaguely familiar about her. Kateri stepped closer to the firelight as the woman stood with a smile.

"Kateri? My, how you've grown!"

Kateri's eyes grew wide with sudden recognition. "Bridget?"